David Masson, Thomas De Quincey

Select essays, narrative & imaginative

David Masson, Thomas De Quincey

Select essays, narrative & imaginative

ISBN/EAN: 9783337275433

Printed in Europe, USA, Canada, Australia, Japan

Cover: Foto ©Andreas Hilbeck / pixelio.de

More available books at **www.hansebooks.com**

SELECT ESSAYS

OF

THOMAS DE QUINCEY

NARRATIVE & IMAGINATIVE

EDITED AND ANNOTATED

By DAVID MASSON

PROFESSOR OF ENGLISH LITERATURE IN THE UNIVERSITY OF
EDINBURGH

VOL. II

EDINBURGH: ADAM & CHARLES BLACK

MDCCCLXXXVIII

CONTENTS

THE SPANISH MILITARY NUN

VOL. II

B

INTRODUCTION

THE story now entitled THE SPANISH MILITARY NUN appeared first in three instalments, each headed with the words "By Thomas De Quincey," in the numbers of Tait's Edinburgh Magazine for May, June, and July, 1847. It appeared then, however, under the clumsier title of THE NAUTICO-MILITARY NUN OF SPAIN. The change of title was made in 1854, when De Quincey reprinted the paper in Vol. III. of the Collective Edition of his works. There were alterations at the same time in the text of the story, and in some particulars of its form and arrangement. The most important of these latter was the division of the text, which had previously been printed in block, into a succession of short chapters, each topped with a smart descriptive summary of its purport, after the fashion of the Spanish novels of roguish adventure, and of some later English novels. This device for lightening the story and making it brisker for the reader was retained in the later Collective Edition, and is, of course, retained in the present reproduction. As the story professes to be a real one, derived from old Spanish records, something will have to be said, as was the case with the preceding story of THE REVOLT OF THE TARTARS, respecting De Quincey's authorities and his immediate materials. The inquiry, in this case also, will be best postponed till after the story is read. There may be some surprise when its origin and the mode of its manufacture are known; but meanwhile the reader may rest assured that much of what is most amusing and clever in it, and nearly all that will be found in it of higher and more powerful quality, are due to the brain and hand of De Quincey.—D. M.

THE SPANISH MILITARY NUN

Section 1.—*An Extra Nuisance is introduced into Spain.*

ON a night in the year 1592 (but which night is a secret liable to 365 answers), a Spanish "*son of somebody*" (*i.e.*, hidalgo), in the fortified town of St Sebastian,[1] received the disagreeable intelligence from a nurse, that his wife had just presented him with a daughter. No present that the poor misjudging lady could possibly have made him was so entirely useless towards any purpose of his. He had three daughters already ; which happened to be more by $2 + 1$, according to *his* reckoning, than any reasonable allowance of daughters. A supernumerary son might have been stowed away ; but supernumerary daughters were the very nuisance of Spain. He did, therefore, what in such cases every proud and lazy Spanish gentleman endeavoured to do. And surely I need not interrupt myself by any parenthesis to inform the base British reader, who makes it his glory to work hard, that the peculiar point of honour for the Spanish gentleman

[1] *St Sebastian :* a sea-coast town in the north of Spain, in that corner of the Bay of Biscay where Spain begins to be divided from France by the chain of the Pyrenees.—M.

lay precisely in these two qualities of pride and
laziness : for, if he were not proud, or had anything
to do, what could you look for but ruin to the old
Spanish aristocracy ? some of whom boasted that no
member of their house (unless illegitimate, and a
mere *terræ filius*) had done a day's work since the
flood.   In the ark they admitted that Noah kept them
tightly to work ; because, in fact, there was work to
do, that must be done by somebody.   But once
anchored upon Ararat, they insisted upon it most
indignantly that no ancestor of the Spanish *noblesse*
had ever worked, except through his slaves.   And
with a view to new leases of idleness, through new
generations of slaves, it was (as many people think)
that Spain went so heartily into the enterprises of
Cortez and Pizarro.   A sedentary body of Dons,
without needing to uncross their thrice noble legs,
would thus levy eternal tributes of gold and silver
upon eternal mines, through eternal successions of
nations that had been, and were to be, enslaved.
Meantime, until these golden visions should be
realised, aristocratic *daughters*, who constituted the
hereditary torment of the true Castilian Don, were
to be disposed of in the good old way ; viz., by
quartering them for life upon nunneries : a plan
which entailed no sacrifice whatever upon any of
the parties concerned ; except, indeed, the little
insignificant sacrifice of happiness and natural birth-
rights to the daughters.   But this little inevitable
wreck, when placed in the counter scale to the

magnificent purchase of eternal idleness for an
aristocracy so ancient, was surely entitled to little
attention amongst philosophers.   Daughters must
perish by generations, and ought to be proud of
perishing, in order that their papas, being hidalgos,
might luxuriate in laziness.   Accordingly, on this
system, our hidalgo of St Sebastian wrapped the
new little daughter, odious to his paternal eyes, in a
pocket-handkerchief, and then wrapping up his own
throat with a great deal more care, off he bolted to
the neighbouring convent of St Sebastian, meaning
by that term not merely a convent of that city, but
also (amongst several convents) the one dedicated to
that saint.   It is well that in this quarrelsome world
we quarrel furiously about tastes ; since, agreeing
too closely about the objects to be liked, we should
agree too closely about the objects to be appropriated ;
which would breed much more fighting than is bred
by disagreeing.   That little human tadpole, which
the old toad of a father would not suffer to stay ten
minutes in his house, proved as welcome at the
nunnery of St Sebastian as she was odious at home.
The lady superior of the convent was aunt, by the
mother's side, to the new-born stranger.   She therefore kissed and blessed the little lady.   The poor
nuns, who were never to have any babies of their
own, and were languishing for some amusement,
perfectly doated on this prospect of a wee pet.   The
superior thanked the hidalgo for his very splendid
present.   The nuns thanked him each and all ; until

the old crocodile actually began to whimper senti-
mentally at what he now perceived to be excess of munificence in himself.   Munificence, indeed, he remarked,
was his foible, next after parental tenderness.

2.—*Wait a little, Hidalgo!*

What a luxury it is, sometimes, to a cynic that
there go two words to a bargain.   In the convent of
St Sebastian all was gratitude ; gratitude (as afore-
said) to the hidalgo from all the convent for his
present, until at last the hidalgo began to express
gratitude to *them* for their gratitude to *him*.   Then
came a rolling fire of thanks to St Sebastian ; from
the superior, for sending a future saint ; from the nuns,
for sending such a love of a plaything ; and, finally,
from papa, for sending such substantial board and
well-bolted lodgings : "From which," said the malicious old fellow, "my pussy will never find her way
out to a thorny and dangerous world."   Won't she ?
I suspect, son of somebody, that the next time you
see "pussy," which may happen to be also the last,
will not be in a convent of any kind.   At present,
whilst this general rendering of thanks was going on,
one person only took no part in them.   That person
was "pussy," whose little figure lay quietly stretched
out in the arms of a smiling young nun, with eyes
nearly shut, yet peering a little at the candles.   Pussy
said nothing.   It's of no great use to say much, when
all the world is against you.   But if St Sebastian had

enabled her to speak out the whole truth, pussy *would* have said : "So, Mr Hidalgo, you have been engaging lodgings for me ; lodgings for life. Wait a little. We'll try that question, when my claws are grown a little longer."

3.—*Symptoms of Mutiny.*

Disappointment, therefore, was gathering ahead. But for the present there was nothing of the kind. That noble old crocodile, papa, was not in the least disappointed as regarded *his* expectation of having no anxiety to waste, and no money to pay, on account of his youngest daughter. He insisted on his right to forget her ; and in a week *had* forgotten her, never to think of her again but once. The lady superior, as regarded *her* demands, was equally content, and through a course of several years ; for, as often as she asked pussy if she would be a saint, pussy replied that she would, if saints were allowed plenty of sweetmeats. But least of all were the nuns disappointed. Everything that they had fancied possible in a human plaything fell short of what pussy realised in racketing, racing, and eternal plots against the peace of the elder nuns. No fox ever kept a hen-roost in such alarm as pussy kept the dormitory of the senior sisters ; whilst the younger ladies were run off their legs by the eternal wiles, and had their gravity discomposed, even in chapel, by the eternal antics, of this privileged little kitten.

The kitten had long ago received a baptismal name, which was Kitty, or Kate; and *that* in Spanish is Catalina. It was a good name, as it recalled her original name of "pussy." And, by the way, she had also an ancient and honourable surname—viz., *De Erauso*—which is to this day a name rooted in Biscay. Her father, the hidalgo, was a military officer in the Spanish service, and had little care whether his kitten should turn out a wolf or a lamb, having made over the fee simple of his own interest in the little Kate to St Sebastian, "to have and to hold," so long as Kate should keep her hold of this present life. Kate had no apparent intention to let slip that hold; for she was blooming as a rose-bush in June, tall and strong as a young cedar. Yet, not-withstanding this robust health, which forbade one to think of separation from St Sebastian by death, and notwithstanding the strength of the convent walls, which forbade one to think of any other separation, the time was drawing near when St Sebastian's lease in Kate must, in legal phrase, "determine;" and any *chateaux en Espagne* that the saint might have built on the cloistral fidelity of his pet Catalina, must suddenly give way in one hour, like many other vanities in our own days of Spanish growth; such as Spanish constitutions and charters, Spanish financial reforms, Spanish bonds, and other little varieties of Spanish ostentatious mendacity.

4.—*The Symptoms Thicken.*

After reaching her tenth year, Catalina became thoughtful and not very docile. At times she was even headstrong and turbulent, so that the gentle sisterhood of St Sebastian, who had no other pet or plaything in the world, began to weep in secret, fearing that they might have been rearing by mistake some future tigress; for as to infancy, *that*, you know, is playful and innocent even in the cubs of a tigress. But *there* the ladies were going too far. Catalina was impetuous and aspiring, violent sometimes, headstrong and haughty towards those who presumed upon her youth, absolutely rebellious against all open harshness, but still generous and most forgiving, disdainful of petty arts, and emphatically a noble girl. She was gentle, if people would let her be so. But wo to those that took liberties with *her!* A female servant of the convent, in some authority, one day, in passing up the aisle to matins, *wilfully* gave Kate a push; and, in return, Kate, who never left her debts in arrear, gave the servant for a keepsake such a look, as that servant carried with her in fearful remembrance to her grave. It seemed as if Kate had tropic blood in her veins, that continually called her away to the tropics. It was all the fault of that "blue rejoicing sky," of those purple Biscayan mountains, of that glad tumultuous ocean, which she beheld daily from the nunnery gardens. Or, if only half of it was *their* fault, the other half lay in those golden tales, streaming upwards even into the sanctuaries of convents, like morning mists touched by earliest sunlight, of kingdoms overshadowing a new world, which had been founded by her kinsmen with the simple aid of a horse and a lance. The reader is to remember that this is no romance, or at least no fiction, that he is reading ; and it is proper to remind the reader of real romances in Ariosto or our own Spenser, that such martial ladies as the *Marfisa* or *Bradamant* of the first, and *Britomart* of the other, were really not the improbabilities that modern society imagines. Many a stout man, as you will soon see, found that Kate, with a sabre in hand, and well mounted, was no romance at all, but far too serious a fact.

5.—*Good-night, St Sebastian !*

The day is come—the evening is come—when our poor Kate, that had for fifteen years been so tenderly rocked in the arms of St Sebastian and his daughters, and that henceforth shall hardly find a breathing space between eternal storms, must see her peaceful cell, must see the holy chapel, for the last time. It was at vespers, it was during the chanting of the vesper service, that she finally read the secret signal for her departure, which long she had been looking for. It happened that her aunt, the Lady Principal, had forgotten her breviary. As this was in a private 'scrutoire, the prudent lady did not choose to send a

servant for it, but gave the key to her niece.   The
niece, on opening the 'scrutoire, saw, with that
rapidity of eye-glance for the one thing needed in
great emergencies which ever attended her through
life, that *now* was the moment, *now* had the clock
struck, for an opportunity which, if neglected, might
never return.   There lay the total keys, in one
massive *trousseau*, of that monastic fortress, impreg-
nable even to armies from without.   St Sebastian!
do you see what your pet is going to do?   And do
it she will, as sure as your name is St Sebastian.
Kate went back to her aunt with the breviary and
the key; but taking good care to leave that awful
door, on whose hinge revolved her whole future life,
unlocked.   Delivering the two articles to the superior,
she complained of headache—(ah, Kate! what did
you know of headaches?)—upon which her aunt, kissing her forehead, dismissed her to bed.   Now, then,
through three-fourths of an hour Kate will have free
elbow-room for unanchoring her boat, for unshipping
her oars, and for pulling ahead right out of St
Sebastian's cove into the main ocean of life.

Catalina, the reader is to understand, does not
belong to the class of persons in whom pre-eminently
I profess an interest.   But everywhere one loves
energy and indomitable courage.   And always what
is best in its kind one admires, even where the kind
may happen to be not specially attractive.   Kate's
advantages for her *rôle* in this life lay in four things:
viz., in a well-built person, and a particularly strong

wrist; 2d, in a heart that nothing could appal; 3d,
in a sagacious head, never drawn aside from the *hoc
age* (from the instant question of the hour) by any
weakness of imagination; 4th, in a tolerably thick
skin—not literally, for she was fair and blooming,
and eminently handsome, having such a skin, in fact,
as became a young woman of family in northernmost
Spain; but her sensibilities were obtuse as regarded
some modes of delicacy, *some* modes of equity, *some*
modes of the world's opinion, and *all* modes whatever
of personal hardship. Lay a stress on that word
some—for, as to delicacy, she never lost sight of that
kind which peculiarly concerns her sex. Long afterwards she told the Pope himself, when confessing
without disguise to the paternal old man her sad
and infinite wanderings (and I feel convinced of her
veracity), that in this respect—viz., all which concerned her sexual honour—even then she was as
pure as a child. And, as to equity, it was only that
she substituted the rude natural equity of camps for
the specious and conventional equity of courts and
towns. I must add, though at the cost of interrupting the story by two or three more sentences, that
Catalina had also a fifth advantage, which sounds
humbly, but is really of use in a world, where even
to fold and seal a letter adroitly is not the lowest of
accomplishments. She was a *handy* girl. She could
turn her hand to anything; of which I will give you
two memorable instances. Was there ever a girl in
this world but herself that cheated and snapped her

fingers at that awful Inquisition, which brooded over
the convents of Spain? that did this without collusion from outside; trusting to nobody, but to herself,
and what beside? to one needle, two skeins of thread,
and a bad pair of scissors! For that the scissors were
bad, though Kate does not say so in her memoirs,
I know by an *à priori* argument; viz., because *all*
scissors were bad in the year 1607. Now, say all
decent logicians, from a universal to a particular
valet consequentia, the right of inference is good. *All*
scissors were bad, *ergo some* scissors were bad. The
second instance of her handiness will surprise you
even more :—She once stood upon a scaffold, under
sentence of death (but, understand, on the evidence
of false witnesses). Jack Ketch—or, as the present
generation calls him, "*Mr Calcraft*," or "—— *Calcraft,
Esq.*"—was absolutely tying the knot under her ear,
and the shameful man of ropes fumbled so deplorably,
that Kate (who by much nautical experience had
learned from another sort of "Jack" how a knot
should be tied in this world) lost all patience with
the contemptible artist, told him she was ashamed of
him, took the rope out of his hand, and tied the knot
irreproachably herself. The crowd saluted her with
a festal roll, long and loud, of *vivas;* and this word
viva being a word of good augury—but stop; let me
not anticipate.

From this sketch of Catalina's character, the reader
is prepared to understand the decision of her present
proceeding. She had no time to lose : the twilight,

it is true, favoured her ; but in any season twilight is
as short-lived as a farthing rushlight ; and she must
get under hiding before pursuit commenced.   Consequently she lost not one of her forty-five minutes
in picking and choosing.   No *shilly-shally* in Kate.
She saw with the eyeball of an eagle what was indispensable.   Some little money perhaps, in the first
place, to pay the first toll-bar of life : so, out of four
shillings in Aunty's purse, or what amounted to that
English sum in various Spanish coins, she took one.
You can't say *that* was exorbitant.   Which of us
wouldn't subscribe a shilling for poor Kate, to put
into the first trouser-pockets that ever she will wear?
I remember even yet, as a personal experience, that
when first arrayed, at four years old, in nankeen
trousers, though still so far retaining hermaphrodite
relations of dress as to wear a petticoat above my
trousers, all my female friends (because they pitied
me, as one that had suffered from years of ague)
filled my pockets with half-crowns, of which I can
render no account at this day.   But what were my
poor pretensions by the side of Kate's ?   Kate was
a fine blooming girl of fifteen, with no touch of ague ;
and, before the next sun rises, Kate shall draw on
her first trousers, made by her own hand ; and, that
she may do so, of all the valuables in aunty's re-
pository she takes nothing beside, first (for I detest
your ridiculous and most pedantic neologism of *firstly*[1])

----

[1] "Your ridiculous and most pedantic neologism of *firstly*":
characteristic of De Quincey, and worth remembering !—M.

—first, the shilling, for which I have already given a receipt; secondly, two skeins of suitable thread; thirdly, one stout needle, and (as I told you before, if you would please to remember things) one bad pair of scissors. Now she was ready; ready to cast off St Sebastian's towing-rope; ready to cut and run for port anywhere, which port (according to a smart American adage) is to be looked for " at the back of beyond." The finishing touch of her preparations was to pick out the proper keys : even there she showed the same discretion. She did no gratuitous mischief. She did not take the wine-cellar key, which would have irritated the good father confessor; she did not take the key of the closet which held the peppermint-water and other cordials, for *that* would have distressed the elderly nuns. *She* took those keys only that belonged to *her*, if ever keys did; for they were the keys that locked her out from her natural birthright of liberty. Very different views are taken by different parties of this particular act now meditated by Kate. The Court of Rome treats it as the immediate suggestion of Hell, and open to no forgiveness. Another Court, far loftier, ampler, and of larger authority—viz., the Court which holds its dreadful tribunal in the human heart and conscience—pronounces this act an inalienable privilege of man, and the mere reassertion of a birthright that can neither be bought nor sold.

6.—*Kate's First Bivouac and First March.*

Right or wrong, however, in Romish casuistry, Kate was resolved to let herself out; and *did ;* and, for fear any man should creep in while vespers lasted, and steal the kitchen grate, she locked her old friends *in.* Then she sought a shelter. The air was moderately warm. She hurried into a chestnut wood, and upon withered leaves, which furnished to Kate her very first bivouac in a long succession of such experiences, she slept till earliest dawn. Spanish diet and youth leave the digestion undisordered, and the slumbers light. When the lark rose, up rose Catalina. No time to lose; for she was still in the dress of a nun; and therefore, by a law too flagrantly notorious, liable to the peremptory challenge and arrest of any man—the very meanest or poorest—in all Spain. With her *armed* finger (ay, by the way, I forgot the thimble; but Kate did *not*), she set to work upon her amply-embroidered petticoat. She turned it wrong side out; and with the magic that only female hands possess, she had soon sketched and finished a dashing pair of Wellington trousers. All other changes were made according to the materials she possessed, and quite sufficiently to disguise the two main perils—her sex, and her monastic dedication. What was she to do next? Speaking of Wellington trousers anywhere in the north of Spain would remind *us*, but could hardly remind *her*, of Vittoria, where she dimly had heard of some maternal

relative. To Vittoria,[1] therefore, she bent her course;
and, like the Duke of Wellington, but arriving more
than two centuries earlier, she gained a great victory
at that place. She had made a two days' march,
with no provisions but wild berries; she depended,
for anything better, as light-heartedly as the duke,
upon attacking, sword in hand, storming her dear
friend's intrenchments, and effecting a lodgment in
his breakfast-room, should he happen to possess one.
This amiable relative proved to be an elderly man,
who had but one foible, or perhaps it was a virtue,
which had by continual development overshadowed
his whole nature—it was pedantry. On that hint
Catalina spoke : she knew by heart, from the services
of the convent, a good number of Latin phrases.
Latin !—Oh, but *that* was charming; and in one so
young ! The grave Don owned the soft impeach-
ment; relented at once, and clasped the hopeful
young gentleman in the Wellington trousers to his
uncular and rather angular breast. In this house
the yarn of life was of a mingled quality. The table
was good, but that was exactly what Kate cared least
about. On the other hand, the amusement was of
the worst kind. It consisted chiefly in conjugating
Latin verbs, especially such as were obstinately
irregular. To show him a withered frost-bitten verb,

[1] *Vittoria:* a town in the same province of Spain as St Sebastian,
but about fifty miles inland. There Wellington gained one of his
greatest Peninsular War victories over the French on the 21st of
June 1813.—M.

that wanted its preterite, wanted its gerunds, wanted its supines, wanted, in fact, everything in this world, fruits or blossoms, that make a verb desirable, was to earn the Don's gratitude for life. All day long he was, as you may say, marching and counter-marching his favourite brigades of verbs—verbs frequentative, verbs' inceptive, verbs desiderative—horse, foot, and artillery ; changing front, advancing from the rear, throwing out skirmishing parties, until Kate, not given to faint, must have thought of such a resource, as once in her life she had thought so seasonably of a vesper headache. This was really worse than St Sebastian's. It reminds one of a French gaiety in Thiebault, who describes a rustic party, under equal despair, as employing themselves in conjugating the verb *s'ennuyer*—*Je m'ennuie, tu t'ennuies, il s'ennuit ; nous nous ennuyons,* etc. ; thence to the imperfect—*Je m'ennuyois, tu t'ennuyois,* etc. ; thence to the imperative—*Qu'il s'ennuye,* etc. ; and so on, through the whole dolorous conjugation. Now, you know, when the time comes that *nous nous ennuyons,* the best course is, to part. Kate saw *that ;* and she walked off from the Don's (of whose amorous passion for defective verbs one would have wished to know the catastrophe), taking from his mantelpiece rather more silver than she had levied on her aunt. But then, observe, the Don also was a relative ; and really he owed her a small cheque on his banker for turning out on his field-days. A man, if he *is* a kinsman, has no unlimited privilege of boring one :

an uncle has a qualified right to bore his nephews, even when they happen to be nieces ; but he has no right to bore either nephew or niece *gratis.*

7.—*Kate at Court, where she Prescribes Phlebotomy, and is Promoted.*

From Vittoria, Kate was guided by a carrier to Valladolid.[1] Luckily, as it seemed at first, but, in fact, it made little difference in the end, here, at Valladolid, were assembled the King and his Court. Consequently, there was plenty of regiments, and plenty of regimental bands. Attracted by one of these, Catalina was quietly listening to the music, when some street ruffians, in derision of the gay colours and the particular form of her forest-made costume (rascals ! what sort of trousers would *they* have made with no better scissors ?), began to pelt her with stones. Ah, my friends of the genus *black-guard*, you little know who it is that you are selecting for experiments. This is the one creature of fifteen years old in all Spain, be the other male or female, whom nature, and temper, and provocation have qualified for taking the conceit out of you. This she very soon did, laying open with sharp stones more heads than either one or two, and letting out rather too little than too much of bad Valladolid blood. But mark the constant villany of this world. Certain

[1] *Valladolid,* in Old Castille, about 140 miles south-west from Vittoria.—M.

Alguazils[1]—very like some other Alguazils that I know of nearer home—having stood by quietly to see the friendless stranger insulted and assaulted, now felt it their duty to apprehend the poor nun for her most natural retaliation : and had there been such a thing as a treadmill in Valladolid, Kate was booked for a place on it without further inquiry. Luckily, injustice does not *always* prosper. A gallant young cavalier, who had witnessed from his windows the whole affair, had seen the provocation, and admired Catalina's behaviour—equally patient at first, and bold at last—hastened into the street, pursued the officers, forced them to release their prisoner, upon stating the circumstances of the case, and instantly offered to Catalina a situation amongst his retinue. He was a man of birth and fortune ; and the place offered, that of an honorary page, not being at all degrading even to a "daughter of somebody," was cheerfully accepted.

8.—*Too Good to Last !*

Here Catalina spent a happy quarter of a year ! She was now splendidly dressed in dark blue velvet, by a tailor that did not work within the gloom of a chestnut forest. She and the young cavalier, Don Francisco de Cardenas, were mutually pleased, and had mutual confidence. All went well—until one

---

[1] *Alguazils*, police-officers : a Spanish word from the Arabic or Moorish *al* (the) and *wazir* (officer, *vizier*).—M.

evening (but, luckily, not before the sun had been set so long as to make all things indistinct), who should march into the antechamber of the cavalier but that sublime of crocodiles, *papa*, whom we lost sight of fifteen years ago, and shall never see again after this night. He had his crocodile tears all ready for use, in working order, like a good industrious fire-engine. Whom will he speak to first in this lordly mansion? It was absolutely to Catalina herself that he advanced; whom, for many reasons, he could not be supposed to recognise—lapse of years, male attire, twilight, were all against him. Still, she might have the family countenance; and Kate fancied (but it must have been a fancy) that he looked with a suspicious scrutiny into her face, as he inquired for the young Don. To avert her own face, to announce him to Don Francisco, to wish papa on the shores of that ancient river, the Nile, furnished but one moment's work to the active Catalina. She lingered, however, as her place entitled her to do, at the door of the audience-chamber. She guessed already, but in a moment she *heard* from papa's lips, what was the nature of his errand. His daughter Catherine, he informed the Don, had eloped from the convent of St Sebastian, a place rich in delight, radiant with festal pleasure, overflowing with luxury. Then he laid open the unparalleled ingratitude of such a step. Oh, the unseen treasure that had been spent upon that girl! Oh, the untold sums of money, the unknown amounts of cash, that had been sunk in

that unhappy speculation! The nights of sleepless-
ness suffered during her infancy! The fifteen years
of solicitude thrown away in schemes for her improvement! It would have moved the heart of a
stone. The *hidalgo* wept copiously at his own pathos.
And to such a height of grandeur had hê carried his
Spanish sense of the sublime, that he disdained to
mention—yes! positively not even in a parenthesis
would he condescend to notice—that pocket-handkerchief which he had left at St Sebastian's fifteen
years ago, by way of envelope for "pussy," and which,
to the best of pussy's knowledge, was the one sole
memorandum of papa ever heard of at St Sebastian's.
Pussy, however, saw no use in revising and correct-
ing the text of papa's remembrances. She showed
her usual prudence, and her usual incomparable
decision. It did not appear, as yet, that she would
be reclaimed (or was at all suspected for the fugitive)
by her father, or by Don Cardenas. For it is an
instance of that singular fatality which pursued
Catalina through life, that, to her own astonishment
(as she now collected from her father's conference),
nobody had traced her to Valladolid, nor had her
father's visit any connection with any suspicious
traveller in that direction. The case was quite
different. Strangely enough, her street row had
thrown her, by the purest of accidents, into the one
sole household in all Spain that had an official connection with St Sebastian's. That convent had been
founded by the young cavalier's family; and, accord-

ing to the usage of Spain, the young man (as present representative of his house) was the responsible protector and official visitor of the establishment. It was not to the Don as harbourer of his daughter, but to the Don as hereditary patron of the convent, that the hidalgo was appealing. This being so, Kate might have staid safely some time longer. Yet, again, that would but have multiplied the clues for tracing her; and, finally, she would too probably have been discovered; after which, with all his youthful generosity, the poor Don could not have protected her. Too terrific was the vengeance that awaited an abettor of any fugitive nun; but, above all, if such a crime were perpetrated by an official mandatory of the church. Yet, again, so far it was the more hazardous course to abscond, that it almost revealed her to the young Don as the missing daughter. Still, if it really *had* that effect, nothing at present obliged him to pursue her, as might have been the case a few weeks later. Kate argued (I daresay) rightly, as she always did. Her prudence whispered eternally, that safety there was none for her, until she had laid the Atlantic between herself and St Sebastian's. Life was to be for *her* a Bay of Biscay; and it was odds but she had first embarked upon this billowy life from the literal Bay of Biscay. Chance ordered otherwise. Or, as a Frenchman says, with eloquent ingenuity, in connection with this very story, " Chance is but the *pseudonyme* of God for those particular cases which he does not

choose to subscribe openly with his own sign manual."
She crept up-stairs to her bedroom. Simple are the
travelling preparations of those that, possessing
nothing, have no imperials to pack. She had
Juvenal's qualification for carolling gaily through a
forest full of robbers [1]; for she had nothing to lose
but a change of linen, that rode easily enough under
her left arm, leaving the right free for answering
the questions of impertinent customers. As she crept
down-stairs, she heard the crocodile still weeping
forth his sorrows to the pensive ear of twilight, and
to the sympathetic Don Francisco. Ah! what a
beautiful idea occurs to me at this point ! Once, on
the hustings at Liverpool, I saw a mob orator, whose
brawling mouth, open to its widest expansion, suddenly some larking sailor, by the most dexterous of
shots, plugged up with a paving-stone. Here, now,
at Valladolid was another mouth that equally required
plugging. What a pity, then, that some gay brother
page of Kate's had not been there to turn aside into
the room, armed with a roasted potato, and, taking
a sportsman's aim, to have lodged it in the crocodile's
abominable mouth ! Yet, what an anachronism !
There *were* no roasted potatoes in Spain at that date
(1608), which can be apodeictically proved, because
in Spain there were no potatoes at all, and very few

---

[1] An allusion to the line in Juvenal's Tenth Satire :—

"Cantabit vacuus coram latrone viator ;"

which may be translated :—

"The empty-pocketed tramp will sing in the face of a robber."—M.

in England. But anger drives a man to say anything.

9.—*How to Choose Lodgings.*

Catalina had seen her last of friends and enemies
in Valladolid. Short was her time there ; but she
had improved it so far as to make a few of both.
There was an eye or two in Valladolid that would
have glared with malice upon her, had she been seen
by *all* eyes in that city, as she tripped through the
streets in the dusk ; and eyes there were that would
have softened into tears, had they seen the desolate
condition of the child, or in vision had seen the
struggles that were before her. But what's the use
of wasting tears upon our Kate ? Wait till to-morrow
morning at sunrise, and see if she is particularly in
need of pity. What, now, should a young lady do—
I propose it as a subject for a prize essay—that finds
herself in Valladolid at nightfall, having no letters of
introduction, and not aware of any reason, great or
small, for preferring this or that street in general,
except so far as she knows of some reason for avoid-
ing one street in particular ?, The great problem I
have stated, Kate investigated as she went along ;
and she solved it with the accuracy which she ever
applied to *practical* exigencies. Her conclusion was
—that the best door to knock at, in such a case,
was the door where there was no need to knock at
all, as being deliberately left open to all comers.
For she argued, that within such a door there would

be nothing to steal, so that, at least, you could not
be mistaken in the dark for a thief. Then, as to
stealing from *her*, they might do that if they could.

Upon these principles, which hostile critics will in
vain endeavour to undermine, she laid her hand upon
what seemed a rude stable-door. Such it proved;
and the stable was not absolutely empty: for there
was a cart inside—a four-wheeled cart. True, there
was so; but you couldn't take *that* away in your
pocket; and there were also five loads of straw—
but then of those a lady could take no more than her
reticule would carry, which perhaps was allowed by
the courtesy of Spain. So Kate was right as to the
difficulty of being challenged for a thief. Closing
the door as gently as she had opened it, she dropped
her person, handsomely dressed as she was, upon the
nearest heap of straw. Some ten feet further were
lying two muleteers, honest and happy enough, as
compared with the lords of the bedchamber then in
Valladolid: but still gross men, carnally deaf from
eating garlic and onions, and other horrible substances. Accordingly, they never heard her; nor
were aware, until dawn, that such a blooming person
existed. But she was aware of *them*, and of their
conversation. In the intervals of their sleep, they
talked much of an expedition to America, on the
point of sailing under Don Ferdinand de Cordova.
It was to sail from some Andalusian port. That was
the thing for *her*. At daylight she woke, and jumped
up, needing little more toilet than the birds that

already were singing in the gardens, or than the two muleteers, who, good, honest fellows, saluted the handsome boy kindly—thinking no ill at his making free with *their* straw, though no leave had been asked.

With these philo-garlic men Kate took her departure. The morning was divine: and, leaving Valladolid with the transports that befitted such a golden dawn, feeling also already, in the very obscurity of her exit, the pledge of her final escape, she cared no longer for the crocodile, nor for St Sebastian, nor (in the way of fear) for the protector of St Sebastian, though of *him* she thought with some tenderness; so deep is the remembrance of kindness mixed with justice. Andalusia she reached rather slowly; many weeks the journey cost her; but, after all, what are weeks? She reached Seville many months before she was sixteen years old, and quite in time for the expedition.[1]

10.—*An Ugly Dilemma, where Right and Wrong is reduced to a Question of Right or Left.*

Ugly indeed is that dilemma where shipwreck and the sea are on one side of you, and famine on the other; or, if a chance of escape is offered, apparently

[1] Arrived at Seville in Andalusia after her long journey, Kate, the reader will understand, was now in the south of Spain, at the extreme opposite point of the map from her native St Sebastian, having traversed the entire diagonal distance of more than 450 miles between the two places.—M.

it depends upon taking the right road where there
is no guide-post.

St Lucar being the port of rendezvous for the
Peruvian expedition, thither she went.[1]   All comers
were welcome on board the fleet ; much more a fine
young fellow like Kate.   She was at once engaged
as a mate ; and *her* ship, in particular, after doubling
Cape Horn without loss, made the coast of Peru.
Paita was the port of her destination.[2]   Very near
to this port they were, when a storm threw them
upon a coral reef.   There was little hope of the ship
from the first, for she was unmanageable, and was
not expected to hold together for twenty-four hours.
In this condition, with death before their faces, mark
what Kate did ; and please to remember it for her
benefit, when she does any other little thing that
angers you.   The crew lowered the long-boat.
Vainly the captain protested against this disloyal de-
sertion of a king's ship, which might yet, perhaps,
be run on shore, so as to save the stores.   All the
crew, to a man, deserted the captain.   You may say

[1] *St Lucar:* a seaport of Andalusia, at the mouth of the
Guadalquivir, somewhat north of Cadiz.—M.

[2] The reader who would follow Kate's adventures geographically
must not neglect these two short and hasty sentences.   They carry
her away from Spain and Europe altogether, across the Atlantic to
South America,—nay, not only across the Atlantic to South
America, but round Cape Horn, to the *west* or *Pacific* coast of
South America, and to a point far north on that coast.   Paita or
Payta is a seaport of the Pacific in the extreme north of Peru,
about five degrees below the Equator.   All the long voyage of
thousands of miles is suppressed.—M.

that literally ; for the single exception was *not* a man, being our bold-hearted Kate. She was the only sailor that refused to leave her captain, or the King of Spain's ship. The rest pulled away for the shore, and with fair hopes of reaching it. But one half-hour told another tale : just about that time came a broad sheet of lightning, which, through the darkness of evening, revealed the boat in the very act of mounting like a horse upon an inner reef, instantly filling, and throwing out the crew, every man of whom disappeared amongst the breakers. The night which succeeded was gloomy for both the representatives of his Catholic Majesty. It cannot be denied by the underwriters at Lloyd's, that the muleteer's stable at Valladolid was worth twenty such ships, though the stable was *not* insured against fire, and the ship *was* insured against the sea and the wind by some fellow that thought very little of his engagements. But what's the use of sitting down to cry ? That was never any trick of Catalina's. By daybreak, she was at work with an axe in her hand. I knew it, before ever I came to this place in her memoirs. I felt, as sure as if I had read it, that when day broke we should find Kate at work. Thimble or axe, trousers or raft, all one to *her*.

The captain, though true to his duty, faithful to his king, and on his king's account even hopeful, seems from the first to have desponded on his own. He gave no help towards the raft. Signs were speaking, however, pretty loudly that he must do

something; for notice to quit was now served pretty
liberally. Kate's raft was ready; and she encouraged
the captain to think that it would give both of them
something to hold by in swimming, if not even carry
double. At this moment, when all was waiting for
a start and the ship herself was waiting only for a
final lurch to say *Good-by* to the King of Spain, Kate
went and did a thing which some erring people will
misconstrue. She knew of a box laden with gold
coins, reputed to be the King of Spain's, and meant
for contingencies on the voyage out. This she
smashed open with her axe, and took out a sum in
ducats and pistoles equal to one hundred guineas
English; which, having well secured in a pillow-case,
she then lashed firmly to the raft. Now this, you
know, though not "*flotsom*," because it would not float,
was certainly, by maritime law, "*jetsom*." It would be
the idlest of scruples to fancy that the sea or a shark
had a better right to it than a philosopher, or a
splendid girl who showed herself capable of writing
a very fair 8vo, to say nothing of her decapitating in
battle, as you will find, more than one of the king's
enemies, and recovering the king's banner. No sane
moralist would hesitate to do the same thing under
the same circumstances, even on board an English
vessel, and though the First Lord of the Admiralty,
and the Secretary, that pokes his nose into everything
nautical, should be looking on. The raft was now
thrown into the sea. Kate jumped after it, and then
entreated the captain to follow her. He attempted

it; but, wanting her youthful agility, he struck his
head against a spar, and sank like lead, giving notice
below that his ship was coming after him as fast as
she could make ready. Kate's luck was better : she
mounted the raft, and by the rising tide was gradually
washed ashore, but so exhausted, as to have lost all
recollection. She lay for hours, until the warmth of
the sun revived her. On sitting up, she saw a desolate
shore stretching both ways—nothing to eat, nothing
to drink, but fortunately the raft and the money had
been thrown near her ; none of the lashings having
given way—only what is the use of a gold ducat,
though worth nine shillings in silver, or even of a
hundred, amongst tangle and sea-gulls ? The money
she distributed amongst her pockets, and soon found
strength to rise and march forward. But which *was*
forward ? and which backward ? She knew by the
conversation of the sailors that Paita must be in the
neighbourhood ; and Paita, being a port, could not
be in the inside of Peru, but, of course, somewhere
on its outside—and the outside of a maritime land
must be the shore ; so that, if she kept the shore, and
went far enough, she could not fail of hitting her
foot against Paita at last, in the very darkest of nights,
provided only she could first find out which was
up and which was *down;* else she might walk her
shoes off, and find herself, after all, a thousand miles
in the wrong. Here was an awkward case, and all
for want of a guide-post. Still, when one thinks of
Kate's prosperous horoscope ; that, after so long a

voyage, *she* only, out of the total crew, was thrown on the American shore, with one hundred and five pounds in her purse of clear gain on the voyage, a conviction arises that she *could* not guess wrongly. She might have tossed up, having coins in her pocket, *heads or tails !* but this kind of sortilege was then coming to be thought irreligious in Christendom, as a Jewish and a heathen mode of questioning the dark future. She simply guessed, therefore ; and very soon a thing happened which, though adding nothing to strengthen her guess as a true one, did much to sweeten it, if it should prove a false one. On turning a point of the shore, she came upon a barrel of biscuit washed ashore from the ship. Biscuit is one of the best things I know, even if not made by Mrs Bobo[1]; but it is the soonest spoiled ; and one would like to hear counsel on one puzzling point,

---

[1] Who is Mrs Bobo ? The reader will say, " I know not Bobo." Possibly ; but, for all *that*, Bobo is known to senates. From the American Senate (Friday, March 10, 1854) Bobo received the amplest testimonials of merits, that have not yet been matched.   In the debate on William Nevins' claim for the extension of his patent for a machine that rolls and cuts crackers and biscuits, thus spoke Mr Adams, a most distinguished senator, against Mr Badger— " It is said this is a discovery of the patentee for making the best biscuits.   Now, if it be so, he must have got his invention from Mrs Bobo of Alabama ; for she certainly makes better biscuit than anybody in the world.   I can prove by my friend from Alabama (Mr Clay), who sits beside me, and by any man who ever staid at Mrs Bobo's house, that she makes better biscuit than anybody else in the world ; and if this man has the best plan for making biscuit, he must have got it from *her*."   Henceforward I hope we know where to apply for biscuit.

why it is that a touch of water utterly ruins it, taking its life, and leaving behind a *caput mortuum.* Upon this *caput,* in default of anything better, Kate breakfasted. And, breakfast being over, she rang the bell for the waiter to take away, and to —— Stop! what nonsense! There could be no bell; besides which, there could be no waiter. Well, then, without asking the waiter's aid, she that was always prudent packed up some of the Catholic king's biscuit, as she had previously packed up far too little of his gold. But in such cases a most delicate question occurs, pressing equally on dietetics and algebra. It is this: if you pack up too much, then, by this extra burden of salt provisions, you may retard for days your arrival at fresh provisions; on the other hand, if you pack up too little, you may famish, and never arrive at all. Catalina hit the *juste milieu;* and, about twilight on the third day, she found herself entering Paita, without having had to swim any *very* broad river in her walk.

11.—*From the Malice of the Sea, to the Malice of Man and Woman.*

The first thing, in such a case of distress, which a young lady does, even if she happens to be a young gentleman, is to beautify her dress. Kate always attended to *that.* The man she sent for was not properly a tailor, but one who employed tailors, he himself furnishing the materials. His name was

Urquiza, a fact of very little importance to us in
1854,[1] if it had stood only at the head and foot of
Kate's little account.   But, unhappily for Kate's *début*
on this vast American stage, the case was otherwise.
Mr Urquiza had the misfortune (equally common in
the Old World and the New) of being a knave;
and also a showy, specious knave.   Kate, who had
prospered under sea allowances of biscuit and hardship, was now expanding in proportions.   With very
little vanity or consciousness on that head, she now
displayed a really magnificent person; and, when
dressed anew in the way that became a young officer
in the Spanish service, she looked [2] the representative
picture of a Spanish *caballador*.   It is strange that
such an appearance, and such a rank, should have
suggested to Urquiza the presumptuous idea of

[1] This date is substituted by De Quincey in the reprint in the
Collective Edition of his works for the original "1847" in Tait's
Magazine.—M.

[2] "*She looked*," etc. :—If ever the reader should visit Aix-la-
Chapelle, he will probably feel interest enough in the poor, wild,
impassioned girl to look out for a picture of her in that city,
and the only one known *certainly* to be authentic.   It is in the
collection of Mr Sempeller.   For some time it was supposed that
the best (if not the only) portrait of her lurked somewhere in Italy.
Since the discovery of the picture at Aix-la-Chapelle, that notion
has been abandoned.   But there is great reason to believe that,
both in Madrid and Rome, many portraits of her must have been
painted to meet the intense interest which arose in her history
subsequently amongst all men of rank, military or ecclesiastical,
whether in Italy or Spain.   The date of these would range between
sixteen and twenty-two years from the period which we have
now reached (1608).

wishing that Kate might become his clerk.   He *did*,
however, wish it; for Kate wrote a beautiful hand;
and a stranger thing is, that Kate accepted his pro-
posal.   This might arise from the difficulty of moving
in those days to any distance in Peru.   The ship
which threw Kate ashore had been merely bringing
stores to the station of Paita; and no corps of the
royal armies was readily to be reached, whilst something must be done at once for a livelihood.   Urquiza
had two mercantile establishments—one at Trujillo,
to which he repaired in person, on Kate's agreeing to
undertake the management of the other in Paita.[1]
Like the sensible girl that we have always found her,
she demanded specific instructions for her guidance
in duties so new.   Certainly she was in a fair way
for seeing life.   Telling her beads at St Sebastian's,
manœuvring irregular verbs at Vittoria, acting as
gentleman-usher at Valladolid, serving his Spanish
Majesty round Cape Horn, fighting with storms and
sharks off the coast of Peru, and now commencing as
book-keeper or *commis* to a draper at Paita—does she
not justify the character that I myself gave her, just
before dismissing her from St Sebastian's, of being a
" handy " girl ?   Mr Urquiza's instructions were
short, easy to be understood, but rather comic; and
yet (which is odd) they led to tragic results.   There
were two debtors of the shop (*many*, it is to be hoped,
but two meriting his affectionate notice), with respect

[1] *Trujillo* or *Truxillo* is a coast-town of Peru, about 250 miles
south from Paita.—M.

to whom he left the most opposite directions. The one was a very handsome lady; and the rule as to *her* was, that she was to have credit unlimited; strictly unlimited. That seemed plain. The other customer, favoured by Mr Urquiza's valedictory thoughts, was a young man, cousin to the handsome lady, and bearing the name of Reyes. This youth occupied in Mr Urquiza's estimate the same hyperbolical rank as the handsome lady, but on the opposite side of the equation. The rule as to *him* was, that he was to have *no* credit; strictly none. In this case, also, Kate saw no difficulty; and when she came to know Mr Reyes a little, she found the path of pleasure coinciding with the path of duty. Mr Urquiza could not be more precise in laying down the rule, than Kate was in enforcing it. But in the other case a scruple arose. *Unlimited* might be a word, not of Spanish law, but of Spanish rhetoric; such as, "*Live a thousand years*," which even annuity offices utter without a pang. Kate therefore wrote to Trujillo, expressing her honest fears, and desiring to have more definite instructions. These were positive. If the lady chose to send for the entire shop, her account was to be debited instantly with *that*. She had, however, as yet, not sent for the shop, but she began to manifest strong signs of sending for the shop*man*. Upon the blooming young Biscayan had her roving eye settled; and she was in the course of making up her mind to take Kate for a sweetheart. Poor Kate saw this with a heavy heart. And, at the same time that she had a prospect of a tender friend more than she wanted, she had become certain of an extra enemy that she wanted quite as little. What she had done to offend Mr Reyes, Kate could not guess, except as to the matter of the credit ; but then, in that she only followed her instructions. Still, Mr Reyes was of opinion that there were two ways of executing orders : but the main offence was unintentional on Kate's part. Reyes (though as yet she did not know it) had himself been a candidate for the situation of clerk ; and intended probably to keep the equation precisely as it was with respect to the allowance of credit, only to change places with the handsome lady—keeping *her* on the negative side, himself on the affirmative ; an arrangement, you know, that in the final result could have made no sort of pecuniary difference to Urquiza.

Thus stood matters, when a party of vagrant comedians strolled into Paita. Kate, being a native Spaniard, ranked as one of the Paita aristocracy, and was expected to attend. She did so ; and there also was the malignant Reyes. He came and seated himself purposely so as to shut out Kate from all view of the stage. She, who had nothing of the bully in her nature, and was a gentle creature, when her wild Biscayan blood had not been kindled by insult, courteously requested him to move a little ; upon which Reyes replied, that it was not in his power to oblige the clerk as to that, but that he *could* oblige him by cutting his throat. The tiger that slept in

Catalina wakened at once. She seized him, and
would have executed vengeance on the spot, but that
a party of young men interposed, for the present, to
part them. The next day, when Kate (always ready
to forget and forgive) was thinking no more of the
row, Reyes passed; by spitting at the window, and
other gestures insulting to Kate, again he roused her
Spanish blood. Out she rushed, sword in hand; a
duel began in the street; and very soon Kate's sword
had passed into the heart of Reyes. Now that the
mischief was done, the police were, as usual, all alive
for the pleasure of avenging it. Kate found herself
suddenly in a strong prison, and with small hopes of
leaving it, except for execution.

12.—*From the Steps leading up to the Scaffold, to the Steps leading down to Assassination.*

The relatives of the dead man were potent in
Paita, and clamorous for justice; so that the *corrégidor*, in a case where he saw a very poor chance of
being corrupted by bribes, felt it his duty to be sub-
limely incorruptible. The reader knows, however,
that amongst the connections of the deceased bully
was that handsome lady, who differed as much from
her cousin in her sentiments as to Kate, as she did
in the extent of her credit with Mr Urquiza. To
her Kate wrote a note; and, using one of the Spanish
King's gold coins for bribing the jailer, got it safely
delivered. That, perhaps, was unnecessary; for the

lady had been already on the alert, and had summoned
Urquiza from Trujillo. By some means not very
luminously stated, and by paying proper fees in
proper quarters, Kate was smuggled out of the
prison at nightfall, and smuggled into a pretty house
in the suburbs. Had she known exactly the footing
she stood on as to the law, she would have been
decided. As it was, she was uneasy, and jealous of
mischief abroad ; and, before supper, she understood
it all. Urquiza briefly informed his clerk that it
would be requisite for him (the clerk) to marry the
handsome lady. But why? Because, said Urquiza,
after talking for hours with the *corrégidor*, who was
infamous for obstinacy, he had found it impossible to
make him "hear reason," and release the prisoner,
until this compromise of marriage was suggested.
But how could public justice be pacified for the
clerk's unfortunate homicide of Reyes, by a female
cousin of the deceased man engaging to love, honour,
and obey the clerk for life? Kate could not see her
way through this logic. "Nonsense, my friend,"
said Urquiza, " you don't comprehend. As it stands,
the affair is a murder, and hanging the penalty. But,
if you marry into the murdered man's house, then it
becomes a little family murder—all quiet and com-
fortable amongst ourselves. What has the *corrégidor*
to do with that? or the public either? Now, let
me introduce the bride." Supper entered at that
moment, and the bride immediately after. The
thoughtfulness of Kate was narrowly observed, and

even alluded to, but politely ascribed to the natural
anxieties of a prisoner, and the very imperfect state
of his liberation even yet from prison *surveillance.*
Kate had, indeed, never been in so trying a situation
before.   The anxieties of the farewell night at St
Sebastian were nothing to this ; because, even if she
had failed *then*, a failure might not have been always
irreparable.   It was but to watch and wait.   But
now, at this supper table, she was not more alive to
the nature of the peril than she was to the fact,
that if, before the night closed, she did not by
some means escape from it, she never *would* escape
with life.   The deception as to her sex, though resting on no motive that pointed to these people, or at
all concerned them, would be resented as if it had.
The lady would regard the case as a mockery ; and
Urquiza would lose his opportunity of delivering
himself from an imperious mistress.   According to
the usages of the times and country, Kate knew that
within twelve hours she would be assassinated.

People of infirmer resolution would have lingered
at the supper table, for the sake of putting off the
evil moment of final crisis.   Not so Kate.   She had
revolved the case on all its sides in a few minutes,
and had formed her resolution.   This done, she was
as ready for the trial at one moment as another ;
and, when the lady suggested that the hardships of
a prison must have made repose desirable, Kate
assented, and instantly rose.   A sort of procession
formed, for the purpose of doing honour to the

interesting guest, and escorting him in pomp to his bedroom. Kate viewed it much in the same light as that procession to which for some days she had been expecting an invitation from the *corrégidor*. Far ahead ran the servant-woman, as a sort of outrider; then came Urquiza, like a pacha of two tails, who granted two sorts of credit—viz., unlimited and none at all—bearing two wax-lights, one in each hand, and wanting only cymbals and kettle-drums to express emphatically the pathos of his Castilian strut; next came the bride, a little in advance of the clerk, but still turning obliquely towards him, and smiling graciously into his face; lastly, bringing up the rear, came the prisoner—our poor ensnared Kate —the nun, the page, the mate, the clerk, the homicide, the convict; and for this night only, by particular desire, the bridegroom elect.

It was Kate's fixed opinion, that, if for a moment she entered any bedroom having obviously no outlet, her fate would be that of an ox once driven within the shambles. Outside, the bullock might make some defence with his horns; but once in, with no space for turning, he is muffled and gagged. She carried her eye, therefore, like a hawk's, steady, though restless, for vigilant examination of every angle she turned. Before she entered any bedroom, she was resolved to reconnoitre it from the doorway, and, in case of necessity, show fight at once before entering, as the best chance in a crisis where all chances were bad. Everything ends; and at last

the procession reached the bedroom-door, the outrider
having filed off to the rear.   One glance sufficed to
satisfy Kate that windows there were none, and
therefore no outlet for escape.   Treachery appeared
even in *that;* and Kate, though unfortunately without
arms, was now fixed for resistance.   Mr Urquiza
entered first, with a strut more than usually grandiose,
and inexpressibly sublime—"Sound the trumpets!
Beat the drums!"   There were, as we know already,
no windows; but a slight interruption to Mr Urquiza's pompous tread showed that there were steps
downwards into the room.   Those, thought Kate,
will suit me even better.   She had watched the
unlocking of the bedroom-door—she had lost nothing
—she had marked that the key was left in the lock.
At this moment, the beautiful lady, as one acquainted
with the details of the house, turning with the air of
a gracious monitress, held out her fair hand to guide
Kate in careful descent of the steps.   This had the
air of taking out Kate to dance; and Kate, at that
same moment, answering to it by the gesture of a
modern waltzer, threw her arm behind the lady's
waist; hurled her headlong down the steps right
against Mr Urquiza, draper and haberdasher; and
then, with the speed of lightning, throwing the door
home within its architrave, doubly locked the creditor
and unlimited debtor into the rat-trap which they
had prepared for herself.

     The affrighted outrider fled with horror; she
knew that the clerk had already committed one

homicide ; a second would cost him still less thought ;
and thus it happened that egress was left easy.

13.—*From Human Malice, back again to the Malice of Winds and Waves.*

But, when abroad, and free once more in the
bright starry night, which way should Kate turn?
The whole city would prove but one vast rat-trap
for her, as bad as Mr Urquiza's, if she was not off
before morning. At a glance she comprehended
that the sea was her only chance. To the port she
fled. All was silent. Watchmen there were none ;
and she jumped into a boat. To use the oars was
dangerous, for she had no means of muffling them.
But she contrived to hoist a sail, pushed off with a
boat-hook, and was soon stretching across the water
for the mouth of the harbour, before a breeze light
but favourable. Having cleared the difficulties of
exit, she lay down, and unintentionally fell asleep.
When she awoke, the sun had been up three or four
hours ; all was right otherwise ; but, had she not
served as a sailor, Kate would have trembled upon
finding that, during her long sleep of perhaps seven
or eight hours, she had lost sight of land ; by what
distance she could only guess ; and in what direction,
was to some degree doubtful. All this, however,
seemed a great advantage to the bold girl, throwing
her thoughts back on the enemies she had left behind.
The disadvantage was—having no breakfast, not

even damaged biscuit; and some anxiety naturally
arose as to ulterior prospects a little beyond the
horizon of breakfast. But who's afraid? As sailors
whistle for a wind, Catalina really had but to whistle
for anything with energy, and it was sure to come.
Like Cæsar to the pilot of Dyrrhachium, she might
have said, for the comfort of her poor timorous boat
(though a boat that in fact was destined soon to
perish), "*Catalinam vehis, et fortunas ejus.*" [1] Meantime, being very doubtful as to the best course for
sailing, and content if her course did but lie off
shore, she "carried on," as sailors say, under easy
sail, going, in fact, just whither and just how the
Pacific breezes suggested in the gentlest of whispers.
All right behind, was Kate's opinion; and, what was
better, very soon she might say, *all right ahead;* for,
some hour or two before sunset, when dinner was
for once becoming, even to Kate, the most interesting
of subjects for meditation, suddenly a large ship
began to swell upon the brilliant atmosphere. In
those latitudes, and in those years, any ship was pretty
sure to be Spanish: sixty years later, the odds were
in favour of its being an English buccaneer; which
would have given a new direction to Kate's energy.
Kate continued to make signals with a handkerchief
whiter than the crocodile's of Ann. Dom. 1592, else
it would hardly have been noticed. Perhaps, after
all, it would not, but that the ship's course carried
her very nearly across Kate's. The stranger lay to

[1] " You carry Catalina, and her fortunes."—M.

for her. It was dark by the time Kate steered herself under the ship's quarter; and *then* was seen an instance of this girl's eternal wakefulness. Something was painted on the stern of her boat, she could not see *what ;* but she judged that, whatever this might be, it would express some connection with the port that she had just quitted. Now, it was her wish to break the chain of traces connecting her with such a scamp as Urquiza; since else, through his commercial correspondence, he might disperse over Peru a portrait of herself by no means flattering. How should she accomplish this? It was dark; and she stood, as you may see an Etonian do at times, rocking her little boat from side to side, until it had taken in water as much as might be agreeable. Too much it proved for the boat's constitution, and the ¡boat perished of dropsy—Kate declining to tap it. She got a ducking herself; but what cared she? Up the ship's side she went, as gaily as ever, in those years when she was called pussy, she had raced after the nuns of St Sebastian; jumped upon deck, and told the first lieutenant, when he questioned her about her adventures, quite as much truth as any man, under the rank of admiral, had a right to expect.

14.—*Bright Gleams of Sunshine.*

This ship was full of recruits for the Spanish army, and bound to Conception.[1] Even in that

---

[1] *Concepcion :* on the coast of Chili, some 2400 miles south from Paita, on the shore of the Pacific.—M.

destiny was an iteration, or repeating memorial of
the significance that ran through Catalina's most
casual adventures.   She had enlisted amongst the
soldiers ; and, on reaching port, the very first person
who came off from shore was a dashing young
military officer, whom at once, by his name and rank
(though she had never consciously seen him), she
identified as her own brother.   He was splendidly
situated in the service, being the Governor-General's
secretary, besides his rank as a cavalry officer ; and
his errand on board being to inspect the recruits,
naturally, on reading in the roll one of them described as a Biscayan, the ardent young man came
up with high-bred courtesy to Catalina, took the
young recruit's hand with kindness, feeling that to
be a compatriot at so great a distance was to be a
sort of relative, and asked with emotion after old
boyish remembrances.   There was a scriptural pathos
in what followed, as if it were some scene of domestic
re-union opening itself from patriarchal ages.   The
young officer was the eldest son of the house, and
had left Spain when Catalina was only three years
old.   But, singularly enough, Catalina it was, the
little wild cat that he yet remembered seeing at St
Sebastian's, upon whom his earliest inquiries settled.
" Did the recruit know his family, the De Erausos ? "
Oh yes ; everybody knew *them*.   " Did the recruit
know little Catalina ? "   Catalina smiled, as she replied
that she did ; and gave such an animated description
of the little fiery wretch, as made the officer's eye

flash with gratified tenderness, and with certainty
that the recruit was no counterfeit Biscayan. Indeed,
you know, if Kate couldn't give a good description
of "pussy," who could ?   The issue of the interview
was, that the officer insisted on Kate's making a
home of his quarters.   He did other services for his
unknown sister.   He placed her as a trooper in his
own regiment, and favoured her in many a way that
is open to one having authority.   But the person,
after all, that did most to serve our Kate, was Kate.
War was then raging with Indians, both from Chili
and Peru.   Kate had always done her duty in action;
but at length, in the decisive battle of Puren,[1] there
was an opening for doing something more.   Havoc
had been made of her own squadron; most of the
officers were killed, and the standard was carried off.
Kate gathered around her a small party—galloped
after the Indian column that was carrying away the
trophy—charged—saw all her own party killed—
but, in spite of wounds on her face and shoulder,
succeeded in bearing away the recovered standard.
She rode up to the general and his staff; she dismounted; she rendered up her prize; and fainted
away, much less from the blinding blood, than from
the tears of joy which dimmed her eyes, as the
general, waving his sword in admiration over her
head, pronounced our Kate on the spot an *Alférez*,[2]

[1] I cannot identify the battle ; but this may be gross ignorance, and some reader may hit the thing at once.—M.

[2] "*Alférez:*"—This rank in the Spanish army is, or was, on a
level with the modern *sous-lieutenant* of France.

or standard-bearer, with a commission from the King of Spain and the Indies.   Bonny Kate ! noble Kate ! I would there were not two centuries laid between us, so that I might have the pleasure of kissing thy fair hand.

15.—*The Sunshine is Overcast.*

Kate had the good sense to see the danger of revealing her sex, or her relationship, even to her own brother.   The grasp of the church never relaxed, never "prescribed," unless freely and by choice.   The nun, if discovered, would have been taken out of the horse-barracks or the dragoon-saddle.   She had the firmness, therefore, for many years, to resist the sisterly impulses that sometimes suggested such a confidence.   For years, and those years the most important of her life—the years that developed her character—she lived undetected as a brilliant cavalry officer, under her brother's patronage.   And the bitterest grief in poor Kate's whole life, was the tragical (and, were it not fully attested, one might say the ultra-scenical) event that dissolved their long connection.   Let me spend a word of apology on poor Kate's errors.   We all commit many ; both you and I, reader.   No, stop ; that's not civil.   You, reader, I know, are a saint ; I am *not*, though very near it. I *do* err at long intervals ; and then I think with indulgence of the many circumstances that plead for this poor girl.   The Spanish armies of that day

inherited, from the days of Cortez and Pizarro, shin-
ing remembrances of martial prowess, and the very
worst of ethics. To think little of bloodshed, to
quarrel, to fight, to gamble, to plunder, belonged to
the very atmosphere of a camp, to its indolence, to
its ancient traditions. In your own defence, you
were obliged to do such things. Besides all these
grounds of evil, the Spanish army had just then an
extra demoralisation from a war with savages—faith-
less and bloody. Do not think too much, reader, of
killing a man—do not, I beseech you! That word
"*kill*" is sprinkled over every page of Kate's own
autobiography. It ought not to be read by the light
of these days. Yet, how if a man that she killed
were ——? Hush! It was sad; but is better
hurried over in a few words. Years after this period,
a young officer, one day dining with Kate, entreated
her to become his second in a duel. Such things
were every-day affairs. However, Kate had reasons
for declining the service, and did so. But the officer,
as he was sullenly departing, said, that if he were
killed (as he thought he *should* be), his death would
lie at Kate's door. I do not take *his* view of the
case, and am not moved by his rhetoric or his logic.
Kate *was*, and relented. The duel was fixed for
eleven at night, under the walls of a monastery.
Unhappily, the night proved unusually dark, so that
the two principals had to tie white handkerchiefs
round their elbows, in order to descry each other.
In the confusion they wounded each other mortally.

Upon that, according to a usage not peculiar to Spaniards, but extending (as doubtless the reader knows) for a century longer to our own countrymen, the two seconds were obliged in honour to do something towards avenging their principals. Kate had her usual fatal luck. Her sword passed sheer through the body of her opponent : this unknown opponent falling dead, had just breath left to cry out, "Ah, villain ! you have killed me !" in a voice of horrific reproach; and the voice was the voice of her brother!

The monks of the monastery under whose silent shadows this murderous duel had taken place, roused by the clashing of swords and the angry shouts of combatants, issued out with torches, to find one only of the four officers surviving. Every convent and altar had the right of asylum for a short period. According to the custom, the monks carried Kate, insensible with anguish of mind, to the sanctuary of their chapel. There for some days they detained her ; but then, having furnished her with a horse and some provisions, they turned her adrift. Which way should the unhappy fugitive turn ? In blindness of heart, she turned towards the sea. It was the sea that had brought her to Peru ; it was the sea that would perhaps carry her away. It was the sea that had first showed her this land and its golden hopes ; it was the sea that ought to hide from her its fearful remembrances.[1] The sea it was that had twice

---

[1] De Quincey seems to have forgotten that Kate was not now in Peru, but in Chili. Although the fightings with the Indians in

spared her life in extremities; the sea it was that might now, if it chose, take back the bauble that it had spared in vain.

16.—*Kate's Ascent of the Andes.*

Three days our poor heroine followed the coast.[1] Her horse was then almost unable to move ; and on which she had been engaged during the years that had elapsed since her arrival at the Chilian town of Conception may have carried her far enough north in Chili from that town, they could hardly have taken her back into Peru. So one fancies at least; for all has been left to fancy. The geography of the last few pages, telling the story of Kate's years of military service as a cavalry-officer under her brother, has been singularly vague. We have certainly been in the Spanish Indies all the while, but whether in Chili or Peru, or in both, we have not known, and have not inquired. The chronology is as vague as the geography ; but Kate must have been ten or twelve years in South America by this time, and has to be imagined as about thirty years of age, more or less, at this point of her story.—M.

[1] It becomes necessary here to have some more definite conception of that matter of Kate's whereabouts at this time which has been mooted in the last note. Kate was about to commence her great feat of the ascent of the Andes ; but the Andes are a mountain - chain, 4500 miles long, running parallel with the Pacific through the whole extent of the South American Continent from Panama to Patagonia. At what point in this vast range was Kate about to make the ascent? De Quincey is at his ease on the subject, and gives us no information. From evidence which will appear in the sequel, however, we have to assume that it was over the northern portion of the Chilian Andes that Kate's ascent was to be made. Accordingly, if any reader should think it worth his while to follow the poor girl's adventures on the map, he must imagine the piece of sea-shore along which she is now wandering, before her ascent begins, to be the northern coast of Chili.—M.

his account she turned inland to a thicket, for grass
and shelter. As she drew near to it, a voice
challenged, "*Who goes there?*"—Kate answered,
"*Spain.*"—"*What people?*"—"*A friend.*" It was
two soldiers, deserters, and almost starving. Kate
shared her provisions with these men; and, on hearing
their plan, which was to go over the Cordilleras,[1] she
agreed to join the party. *Their* object was the wild
one of seeking the river *Dorado*, whose waters rolled
along golden sands, and whose pebbles were emeralds.
Hers was to throw herself upon a line the least liable
to pursuit, and the readiest for a new chapter of life,
in which oblivion might be found for the past.
After a few days of incessant climbing and fatigue,
they found themselves in the regions of perpetual
snow. Summer came even hither; but came as
vainly to this kingdom of frost as to the grave of
her brother. No fire, but the fire of human blood
in youthful veins, could ever be kept burning in
these aerial solitudes. Fuel was rarely to be found,
and kindling a fire by interfriction of dry sticks was
a secret almost exclusively Indian. However, our
Kate can do everything; and she's the girl, if ever
girl *did* such a thing, that I back at any odds for
crossing the Cordilleras. I would bet you something
now, reader, if I thought you would deposit your
stakes by return of post (as they play at chess,
through the post-office), that Kate does the trick;

---

[1] *Cordilleras:* a general word for any mountain chain in
Spanish America ; applied here specifically to the Andes.—M.

that she gets down to the other side; that the soldiers do *not;* and that the horse, if preserved at all, is preserved in a way that will leave him very little to boast of.

The party had gathered wild berries and esculent roots at the foot of the mountains, and the horse was of very great use in carrying them. But this larder was soon emptied. There was nothing then to carry; so that the horse's value, as a beast of burden, fell cent. per cent. In fact, very soon he could not carry himself, and it became easy to calculate when he would reach the bottom on the wrong side the Cordilleras. He took three steps back for one upwards. A council of war being held, the small army resolved to slaughter their horse. He, though a member of the expedition, had no vote; and, if he had, the votes would have stood three to one—majority, two against him. He was cut into quarters—a difficult fraction to distribute amongst a triad of claimants. No saltpetre or sugar could be had; but the frost was antiseptic. And the horse was preserved in as useful a sense as ever apricots were preserved or strawberries; and *that* was the kind of preservation which one page ago I promised to the horse.

On a fire, painfully devised out of broom and withered leaves, a horse-steak was dressed; for drink, snow was allowed *à discretion.* This ought to have revived the party : and Kate, perhaps, it *did.* But the poor deserters were thinly clad, and they had not the boiling heart of Catalina. More and more they drooped. Kate did her best to cheer them. But the march was nearly at an end for *them ;* and they were going, in one half-hour, to receive their last billet. Yet, before this consummation, they have a strange spectacle to see—such as few places could show but the upper chambers of the Cordilleras. They had reached a billowy scene of rocky masses, large and small, looking shockingly black on their perpendicular sides as they rose out of the vast snowy expanse. Upon the highest of these that was accessible, Kate mounted to look around her, and she saw—oh, rapture at such an hour !—a man sitting on a shelf of rock, with a gun by his side. Joyously she shouted to her comrades, and ran down to communicate the good news. Here was a sportsman, watching, perhaps, for an eagle ; and now they would have relief. One man's cheek kindled with the hectic of sudden joy, and he rose eagerly to march. The other was fast sinking under the fatal sleep that frost sends before herself as her merciful minister of death ; but hearing in his dream the tidings of relief, and assisted by his friends, he also staggeringly arose. It could not be three minutes' walk, Kate thought, to the station of the sportsman. That thought supported them all. Under Kate's guidance, who had taken a sailor's glance at the bearings, they soon unthreaded the labyrinth of rocks so far as to bring the man within view. He had not left his resting-place ; their steps on the soundless snow, naturally, he could not hear; and, as their road brought them upon him from the rear, still less could he see them. Kate hailed him; but so keenly was he absorbed in some speculation, or in the object of his watching, that he took no notice of them, not even moving his head. Coming close behind him, Kate touched his shoulder, and said, "My friend, are you sleeping?" Yes, he *was* sleeping—sleeping the sleep from which there is no awaking; and the slight touch of Kate having disturbed the equilibrium of the corpse, down it rolled on the snow: the frozen body rang like a hollow iron cylinder; the face uppermost, and blue with mould, mouth open, teeth ghastly and bleaching in the frost, and a frightful grin upon the lips. This dreadful spectacle finished the struggles of the weaker man, who sank and died at once. The other made an effort with so much spirit, that, in Kate's opinion, horror had acted upon him beneficially as a stimulant. But it was not really so. It was simply a spasm of morbid strength. A collapse succeeded; his blood began to freeze; he sat down in spite of Kate, and *he* also died without further struggle. Yes, gone are the poor suffering deserters; stretched out and bleaching upon the snow; and insulted discipline is avenged. Great kings have long arms; and sycophants are ever at hand for the errand of the potent. What had frost and snow to do with the quarrel? Yet *they* made themselves sycophantic servants to the King of Spain; and *they* it was that dogged his deserters up to the summit of the Cordilleras, more surely than any Spanish bloodhound, or any Spanish tirailleur's bullet.

17.—*Kate stands alone on the Summit of the Andes.*

Now is our Kate standing alone on the summits of the Andes ; and in solitude that is frightful, for she is alone with her own afflicted conscience. Twice before she had stood in solitude as deep upon the wild, wild waters of the Pacific ; but her conscience had been then untroubled. Now is there nobody left that can help ; her horse is dead—the soldiers are dead. There is nobody that she can speak to, except God ; and very soon you will find that she *does* speak to Him ; for already on these vast aerial deserts He has been whispering to *her*. The condition of Kate in some respects resembled that of Coleridge's "Ancient Mariner." But possibly, reader, you may be amongst the many careless readers that have never fully understood what that condition was. Suffer me to enlighten you ; else you ruin the story of the mariner ; and by losing all its pathos, lose half its beauty.

There are three readers of the "Ancient Mariner." The first is gross enough to fancy all the imagery of the mariner's visions delivered by the poet for actual facts of experience ; which being impossible, the whole pulverises, for that reader, into a baseless fairy tale. The second reader is wiser than *that ;* he knows that the imagery is the imagery of febrile delirium; really seen, but not seen as an external reality. The mariner had caught the pestilential fever, which carried off all his mates; he only had survived—the delirium had vanished; but the visions that had haunted the delirium remained. "Yes," says the third reader, "they remained; naturally they did, being scorched by fever into his brain; but how did they happen to remain on his belief as gospel truths? The delirium had vanished: why had not the painted scenery of the delirium vanished, except as visionary memorials of a sorrow that was cancelled? Why was it that craziness settled upon this mariner's brain, driving him, as if he were a Cain, or another Wandering Jew, to 'pass like night from land to land;' and, at certain intervals, wrenching him until he made rehearsal of his errors, even at the difficult cost of 'holding children from their play, and old men from the chimney corner?'"[1] That craziness, as the *third* reader deciphers, rose out of a deeper soil than any bodily affection. It had its root in penitential sorrow. Oh, bitter is the sorrow to a conscientious heart, when, too late, it discovers the depth of a love that has been trampled under foot! This mariner had slain the creature that, on all the earth, loved him best. In the darkness of his cruel superstition he had done it, to save his human

---

[1] The beautiful words of Sir Philip Sydney [more correctly Sidney], in his "Defense of Poesie" [more correctly "Apologie for Poetrie"].

brothers from a fancied inconvenience ; and yet, by that very act of cruelty, he had himself called destruction upon their heads. The Nemesis that followed punished *him* through *them*—him that wronged through those that wrongfully he sought to benefit. That spirit who watches over the sanctities of love is a strong angel—is a jealous angel; and this angel it was

> "That loved the bird, that loved the man
> That shot him with his bow."

He it was that followed the cruel archer into silent and slumbering seas :—

> " Nine fathom deep he had follow'd him,
> Through the realms of mist and snow."

This jealous angel it was that pursued the man into noonday darkness, and the vision of dying oceans, into delirium, and finally (when recovered from disease), into an unsettled mind.

Not altogether unlike, though free from the criminal intention of the mariner, had been the offence of Kate; not unlike, also, was the punishment that now is dogging her steps. She, like the mariner, had slain the one sole creature that loved her upon the whole wide earth ; she, like the mariner, for this offence, had been hunted into frost and snow —very soon will be hunted into delirium ; and from *that* (if she escapes with life), will be hunted into the trouble of a heart that cannot rest. There was the excuse of one darkness, physical darkness, for *her ;* there was the excuse of another darkness, the darkness of superstition, for the mariner. But, with all the excuses that earth, and the darkness of earth, can furnish, bitter it would be for any of us, reader, through every hour of life, waking or dreaming, to look back upon one fatal moment when we had pierced the heart that would have died for *us*. In this only the darkness had been merciful to Kate—that it had hidden for ever from her victim the hand that slew him. But now, in such utter solitude, her thoughts ran back to their earliest interview. She remembered with anguish, how, on touching the shores of America, almost the first word that met her ear had been from *him*, the brother whom she had killed, about the "pussy" of times long past; how the gallant young man had hung upon her words, as in her native Basque she described her own mischievous little self, of twelve years back; how his colour went and came, whilst his loving memory of the little sister was revived by her own descriptive traits, giving back, as in a mirror, the fawn-like grace, the squirrel-like restlessness, that once had kindled his own delighted laughter; how he would take no denial, but showed on the spot, that simply to have touched—to have kissed—to have played with the little wild thing, that glorified, by her innocence, the gloom of St Sebastian's cloisters, gave a *right* to his hospitality; how, through *him* only, she had found a welcome in camps; how, through *him*, she had found the avenue to honour and distinction. And yet this brother, so loving

and generous, who, without knowing, had cherished
and protected her, and all from pure holy love for
herself as the innocent plaything of St Sebastian's,
him in a moment she had dismissed from life. She
paused; she turned round, as if looking back for his
grave; she saw the dreadful wildernesses of snow
which already she had traversed. Silent they were
at this season, even as in the panting heats of noon
the Saharas of the torrid zone are oftentimes silent.
Dreadful was the silence; it was the nearest thing to
the silence of the grave. Graves were at the foot of
the Andes, *that* she knew too well; graves were at
the summit of the Andes, *that* she saw too well. And,
as she gazed, a sudden thought flashed upon her,
when her eyes settled upon the corpses of the poor
deserters—Could she, like *them*, have been all this
while unconsciously executing judgment upon herself?
Running from a wrath that was doubtful, into the
very jaws of a wrath that was inexorable? Flying
in panic—and behold! there was no man that pursued? For the first time in her life, Kate trembled.
Not for the first time, Kate wept. Far less for the
first time was it, that Kate bent her knee—that Kate
clasped her hands—that Kate prayed. But it *was*
the first time that she prayed as *they* pray, for whom
no more hope is left but in prayer.

Here let me pause a moment, for the sake of
making somebody angry. A Frenchman, who sadly
misjudges Kate, looking at her through a Parisian
opera-glass, gives it as *his* opinion—that, because Kate

first *records* her prayer on this occasion, therefore, now first of all she prayed.[1]   *I* think not so.   *I* love this Kate, bloodstained as she is ; and I could not love a woman that never bent her knee in thankfulness or in supplication.   However, we have all a right to our own little opinion ; and it is not *you* "*mon cher*," you Frenchman, that I am angry with, but somebody else that stands behind you.   You, Frenchman, and your compatriots, I love oftentimes for your festal gaiety of heart ; and I quarrel only with your levity, and that eternal worldliness that freezes too fiercely—that absolutely blisters with its frost, like the upper air of the Andes.   *You* speak of Kate only as too readily you speak of all women ; the instinct of a natural scepticism being to scoff at all hidden depths of truth. Else you are civil enough to Kate ; and your "*homage*" (such as it may happen to be) is always at the service of a woman on the shortest notice.   But behind *you* I see a worse fellow—a gloomy fanatic, a religious sycophant, that seeks to propitiate his circle by bitterness against the offences that are most unlike his own.   And against him, I must say one word for Kate to the too hasty reader.   This villain opens his fire on our Kate under shelter of a lie.   For there is a standing lie in the very constitution of civil society —a *necessity* of error, misleading us as to the propor-tions of crime.   Mere necessity obliges man to create

---

[1] Who this Frenchman was will appear from the Appended Note, *Original of De Quincey's Story of the Spanish Military Nun.*—M.

many acts into felonies, and to punish them as the heaviest offences, which his better sense teaches him secretly to regard as perhaps among the lightest. Those poor mutineers or deserters, for instance, were they necessarily without excuse? They might have been oppressively used ; but, in critical times of war, no matter for the individual palliations, the mutineer *must* be shot : there is no help for it : as, in extremities of general famine, we shoot the man (alas! we are *obliged* to shoot him) that is found robbing the common stores, in order to feed his own perishing children, though the offence is hardly visible in the sight of God. Only blockheads adjust their scale of guilt to the scale of human punishments. Now, our wicked friend the fanatic, who calumniates Kate, abuses the advantage which, for such a purpose, he derives from the exaggerated social estimate of all violence. Personal security being so main an object of social union, we are obliged to frown upon all modes of violence, as hostile as the central principle of that union. We are *obliged* to rate it, according to the universal results towards which it tends, and scarcely at all according to the special condition of circumstances in which it may originate. Hence a horror arises for that class of offences, which is (philosophically speaking) exaggerated ; and by daily use, the ethics of a police-office translate themselves, insensibly, into the ethics even of religious people. But I tell that sycophantish fanatic—not this only, viz., that he abuses unfairly, against Kate, the advantage which he has from the *inevitably* distorted bias of society—but also I tell him this second little thing, that, upon turning away the glass from that one obvious aspect of Kate's character, her too fiery disposition to vindicate all rights by violence, and viewing her in relation to *general* religious capacities, she was a thousand times more promisingly endowed than himself. It is impossible to be noble in many things, without having many points of contact with true religion. If you deny *that*, you it is that calumniate religion. Kate *was* noble in many things. Her worst errors never took a shape of self-interest or deceit. She was brave, she was generous, she was forgiving, she bore no malice, she was full of truth— qualities that God loves either in man or woman. She hated sycophants and dissemblers. *I* hate them; and more than ever at this moment on her behalf. I wish she were but here, to give a punch on the head to that fellow who traduces her. And, coming round again to the occasion from which this short digression has started—viz., the question raised by the Frenchman, whether Kate were a person likely to *pray* under other circumstances than those of extreme danger—I offer it as *my* opinion, that she was. Violent people are not alway such from choice, but perhaps from situation. And, though the circumstances of Kate's position allowed her little means for realising her own wishes, it is certain that those wishes pointed continually to peace and an unworldly happiness, if *that* were possible. The stormy clouds that enveloped her in camps, opened overhead at intervals, showing her a far-distant blue serene. She yearned, at many times, for the rest which is not in camps or armies; and it is certain that she ever combined with any plans or day-dreams of tranquillity, as their most essential ally, some aid derived from that dove-like religion which, at St Sebastian's, from her infant days she had been taught so profoundly to adore.

18.—*Kate begins to Descend the Mighty Staircase.*

Now, let us rise from this discussion of Kate against libellers, as Kate herself is rising from prayer, and consider, in conjunction with *her*, the character and promise of that dreadful ground which lies immediately before her. What is to be thought of it? I could wish we had a theodolite here, and a spirit-level, and other instruments, for settling some important questions. Yet, no; on consideration, if one *had* a wish allowed by that kind fairy, without whose assistance it would be quite impossible to send even for the spirit-level, nobody would throw away the wish upon things so paltry. I would not put the fairy upon such an errand: I would order the good creature to bring no spirit-level, but a stiff glass of spirits for Kate; also, next after which, I would request a palanquin, and relays of fifty stout bearers —all drunk, in order that they might not feel the cold. The main interest at this moment, and the main difficulty—indeed, the "open question" of the case—was, to ascertain whether the ascent were yet accomplished or not; and when would the descent commence? or had it, perhaps, long commenced? The character of the ground, in those immediate successions that could be connected by the eye, decided nothing; for the undulations of the level had been so continual for miles, as to perplex any eye, even an engineer's, in attempting to judge whether, upon the whole, the tendency were upwards or downwards. Possibly it was yet neither way; it is indeed probable that Kate had been for some time travelling along a series of terraces that traversed the whole breadth of the topmost area at that point of crossing the Cordilleras; and this area, perhaps, but not certainly, might compensate any casual tendencies downwards by corresponding reascents. Then came the question, how long would these terraces yet continue? and had the ascending parts *really* balanced the descending? Upon *that* seemed to rest the final chance for Kate. Because, unless she very soon reached a lower level and a warmer atmosphere, mere weariness would oblige her to lie down, under a fierceness of cold that would not suffer her to rise after once losing the warmth of motion; or, inversely, if she even continued in motion, continued extremity of cold would, of itself, speedily absorb the little surplus energy for moving which yet remained unexhausted by weariness—that is, in short, the excessive weariness would give a murderous advantage to the cold, or the excessive cold would give a corresponding advantage to the weariness.

At this stage of her progress, and whilst the agonising question seemed yet as indeterminate as ever, Kate's struggle with despair, which had been greatly soothed by the fervour of her prayer, revolved upon her in deadlier blackness. All turned, she saw, upon a race against time, and the arrears of the road ; and she, poor thing ! how little qualified could *she* be, in such a condition, for a race of any kind—and against two such obstinate brutes as Time and Space ! This hour of the progress, this noontide of Kate's struggle, must have been the very crisis of the whole. Despair was rapidly tending to ratify itself. Hope, in any degree, would be a cordial for sustaining her efforts. But to flounder along a dreadful chaos of snow-drifts, or snow-chasms, towards a point of rock which, being turned, should expose only another interminable succession of the same character— might *that* be endured by ebbing spirits, by stiffening limbs, by the ghastly darkness that was now beginning to gather upon the inner eye ? And, if once despair became triumphant, all the little arrear of physical strength would collapse at once.

Oh ! verdure of human fields, cottages of men and women (that now suddenly, in the eyes of Kate, seemed all brothers and sisters), cottages with children around them at play, that are so far below—oh! spring and summer, blossoms and flowers, to which, as to *his* symbols, God has given the gorgeous privilege of rehearsing for ever upon earth his most mysterious perfection—Life, and the resurrections of Life—is it indeed true that poor Kate must never see you more? Mutteringly she put that question to herself. But strange are the caprices of ebb and flow in the deep fountains of human sensibilities. At this very moment, when the utter incapacitation of despair was gathering fast at Kate's heart, a sudden lightening, as it were, or flashing inspiration of hope, shot far into her spirit, a reflux almost supernatural, from the earliest effects of her prayer. Dimmed and confused had been the accuracy of her sensations for hours; but all at once a strong conviction came over her—that more and more was the sense of descent becoming steady and continuous. Turning round to measure backwards with her eye the ground traversed through the last half-hour, she identified, by a remarkable point of rock, the spot near which the three corpses were lying. The silence seemed deeper than ever. Neither was there any phantom memorial of life for the eye or for the ear, nor wing of bird, nor echo, nor green leaf, nor creeping thing that moved or stirred, upon the soundless waste. Oh, what a relief to this burden of silence would be a human groan! Here seemed a motive for still darker despair. And yet, at that very moment, a pulse of joy began to thaw the ice at her heart. It struck her, as she reviewed the ground, from that point where the corpses lay, that undoubtedly it had been for some time slowly descending. Her senses were much dulled by suffering;

but this thought it was, suggested by a sudden apprehension of a continued descending movement, which had caused her to turn round. Sight had confirmed the suggestion first derived from her own steps. The distance attained was now sufficient to establish the tendency. Oh yes, yes; to a certainty she *was* descending—she *had* been descending for some time. Frightful was the spasm of joy which whispered that the worst was over. It was as when the shadow of midnight, that murderers had relied on, is passing away from your beleaguered shelter, and dawn will soon be manifest. It was as when a flood, that all day long has raved against the walls of your house, ceases (you suddenly think) to rise; yes! measured by a golden plummet, it *is* sinking beyond a doubt, and the darlings of your household are saved. Kate faced round in agitation to her proper direction. She saw, what previously, in her stunning confusion, she had *not* seen, that hardly two stone-throws in advance lay a mass of rock, split as into a gateway. Through that opening it now became certain that the road was lying. Hurrying forward, she passed within these natural gates. Gates of paradise they were. Ah, what a vista did that gateway expose before her dazzled eye! what a revelation of heavenly promise! Full two miles long, stretched a long narrow glen, everywhere descending, and in many parts rapidly. All was now placed beyond a doubt. She *was* descending; for hours, perhaps, *had* been descending insensibly, the mighty staircase.

Yes, Kate is leaving behind her the kingdom of frost and the victories of death. Two miles farther, there may be rest, if there is not shelter. And very soon, as the crest of her new-born happiness, she distinguished at the other end of that rocky vista a pavilion-shaped mass of dark green foliage—a belt of trees, such as we see in the lovely parks of England, but islanded by a screen of thick bushy undergrowth! Oh! verdure of dark olive foliage, offered suddenly to fainting eyes, as if by some winged patriarchal herald of wrath relenting—solitary Arab's tent, rising with saintly signals of peace in the dreadful desert— must Kate indeed die even yet, whilst she sees but cannot reach you? Outpost on the frontier of man's dominions, standing within life, but looking out upon everlasting death, wilt thou hold up the anguish of thy mocking invitation only to betray? Never, perhaps, in this world was the line so exquisitely grazed that parts salvation and ruin. As the dove to her dovecot from the swooping hawk—as the Christian pinnace to the shelter of Christian batteries, from the bloody Mahometan corsair—so flew, so tried to fly, towards the anchoring thickets, that, alas! could not weigh their anchors, and make sail to meet her, the poor exhausted Kate from the vengeance of pursuing frost.

And she reached them; staggering, fainting, reeling, she entered beneath the canopy of umbrageous trees. But as oftentimes the Hebrew fugitive to a city of refuge, flying for his life before the avenger of blood, was pressed so hotly, that on entering the

archway of what seemed to *him* the heavenly city
gate, as he kneeled in deep thankfulness to kiss its
holy merciful shadow, he could not rise again, but
sank instantly with infant weakness into sleep—sometimes to wake no more; so sank, so collapsed upon
the ground, without power to choose her couch, and
with little prospect of ever rising again to her feet,
the martial nun. She lay as luck had ordered it,
with her head screened by the undergrowth of bushes
from any gales that might arise; she lay exactly as
she sank, with her eyes up to heaven; and thus it
was that the nun saw, before falling asleep, the two
sights that upon earth are fittest for the closing eyes
of a nun, whether destined to open again, or to close
for ever. She saw the interlacing of boughs overhead forming a dome, that seemed like the dome of
a cathedral. She saw, through the fretwork of the
foliage, another dome, far beyond the dome of an
evening sky, the dome of some heavenly cathedral,
not built with hands. She saw upon this upper dome
the vesper lights, all alive with pathetic grandeur
of colouring from a sunset that had just been rolling
down like a chorus. She had not, till now, consciously observed the time of day; whether it were
morning, or whether it were afternoon, in the confusion of her misery, she had not distinctly known.
But now she whispered to herself, "*It is evening:*"
and what lurked half unconsciously in these words
might be, "The sun, that rejoices, has finished his
daily toil; man, that labours, has finished *his;* I,

that suffer, have finished mine." That might be what she thought, but what she *said* was, "It is evening; and the hour is come when the *Angelus* is sounding through St Sebastian." What made her think of St Sebastian, so far away in depths of space and time? Her brain was wandering, now that her feet were *not ;* and, because her eyes had descended from the heavenly to the earthly dome, *that* made her think of earthly cathedrals, and of cathedral choirs, and of St Sebastian's chapel, with its silvery bells that carried the echoing *Angelus* far into mountain recesses. Perhaps, as her wanderings increased, she thought herself back into childhood; became "pussy" once again; fancied that all since then was a frightful dream; that she was not upon the dreadful Andes, but still kneeling in the holy chapel at vespers; still innocent as then; loved as then she had been loved; and that all men were liars, who said her hand was ever stained with blood. Little is mentioned of the delusions which possessed her; but that little gives a key to the impulse which her palpitating heart obeyed, and which her rambling brain for ever reproduced in multiplying mirrors. Restlessness kept her in waking dreams for a brief half-hour. But then fever and delirium would wait no longer; the killing exhaustion would no longer be refused; the fever, the delirium, and the exhaustion, swept in together with power like an army with banners; and the nun ceased through the gathering twilight any more to watch the cathedrals of earth, or the more solemn cathedrals that rose in the heavens above.

19.—*Kate's Bedroom is Invaded by Horsemen.*

All night long she slept in her verdurous St Bernard's hospice without awaking ; and whether she would *ever* awake seemed to depend upon accident. The slumber that towered above her brain was like that fluctuating silvery column which stands in scientific tubes, sinking, rising, deepening, lightening, contracting, expanding ; or like the mist that sits, through sultry afternoons, upon the river of the American St Peter, sometimes rarefying for minutes into sunny gauze, sometimes condensing for hours into palls of funeral darkness.   You fancy that, after twelve hours of *any* sleep, she must have been refreshed ; better, at least, than she was last night. Ah ! but sleep is not always sent upon missions of refreshment.   Sleep is sometimes the secret chamber in which death arranges his machinery, and stations his artillery.   Sleep is sometimes that deep mysterious atmosphere, in which the human spirit is slowly unsettling its wings for flight from earthly tenements. It is now eight o'clock in the morning ; and, to all appearance, if Kate should receive no aid before noon, when next the sun is departing to his rest, then, alas ! Kate will be departing to hers : when next the sun is holding out his golden Christian signal to man, that the hour is come for letting his anger go down, Kate will be sleeping away for ever into the arms of brotherly forgiveness.

What is wanted just now for Kate, supposing Kate herself to be wanted by this world, is, that this world would be kind enough to send her a little brandy before it is too late. The simple truth was, and a truth which I have known to take place in more ladies than Kate, who died or did *not* die, accordingly as they had or had not an adviser like myself, capable of giving an opinion equal to Captain Bunsby's,[1] on this point—viz., whether the jewelly star of life had descended too far down the arch towards setting, for any chance of reascending by *spontaneous* effort. The fire was still burning in secret, but needed, perhaps, to be rekindled by potent artificial breath. It lingered, and *might* linger, but apparently would never culminate again, without some stimulus from earthly vineyards.[2] Kate was

[1] The sage Captain Bunsby in Dickens's *Dombey & Son.*—M.

[2] Though not exactly in the same circumstances as Kate, or sleeping, *à la belle étoile*, on a declivity of the Andes, I have known (or heard circumstantially reported) the cases of many ladies, besides Kate, who were in precisely the same critical danger of perishing for want of a little brandy. A dessert-spoonful or two would have saved them. Avaunt! you wicked "Temperance" medalist! repent as fast as ever you can, or, perhaps, the next time we hear of you, *anasarca* and *hydro-thorax* will be running after you, to punish your shocking excesses in water. Seriously, the case is one of constant recurrence, and constantly ending fatally from *unseasonable* and pedantic rigour of temperance. Dr. Darwin, the famous author of "Zoonomia," "The Botanic Garden," etc., sacrificed his life to the very pedantry and superstition of temperance, by refusing a glass of brandy in obedience to a system, at a

ever lucky, though ever unfortunate ; and the world, being of my opinion that Kate was worth saving, made up its mind about half-past eight o'clock in the

moment when (according to the opinion of all around him) one single glass would have saved his life. The fact is, that the medical profession composes the most generous and liberal body of men amongst us ; taken generally, by much the most enlightened ; but, professionally, the most timid. Want of boldness in the administration of opium, etc., though they can be bold enough with mercury, is their besetting infirmity. And from this infirmity females suffer most. One instance I need hardly mention, the fatal case of an august lady, mourned by nations [the Princess Charlotte, who died in child-birth 6th Nov. 1817], with respect to whom it was, and is, the belief of multitudes to this hour (well able to judge), that she would have been saved by a glass of brandy ; and her chief medical attendant, Sir R. C. [Sir Richard Croft], who shot himself, came to think so too late—too late for *her*, and too late for himself. Amongst many cases of the same nature, which personally I have been acquainted with, thirty years ago, a man illustrious for his intellectual accomplishments[1] mentioned to me that his own wife, during her first or second confinement, was suddenly reported to him, by one of her female attendants (who slipped away unobserved by the medical people), as undoubtedly sinking fast. He hurried to her chamber, and *saw* that it was so. On this, he suggested earnestly some stimulant—laudanum or alcohol. The presiding medical authority, however, was inexorable. "Oh, by no means," shaking his ambrosial wig ; "any stimulant at this crisis would be fatal." But no authority could overrule the concurrent testimony of all symptoms, and of all unprofessional opinions. By some pious falsehood, my friend smuggled the doctor out of the room, and immediately smuggled a glass of brandy into the poor lady's lips. She recovered as if under the immediate afflatus of magic ; so sudden was her recovery, and so complete. The doctor is now dead, and went to his grave

[1] On second thoughts, I see no reason for scrupling to mention that this man was Robert Southey.

morning to save her. Just at that time, when the night was over, and its sufferings were hidden—in one of those intermitting gleams that for a moment or two lightened the clouds of her slumber—Kate's dull ear caught a sound that for years had spoken a familiar language to *her*. What was it? It was the sound, though muffled and deadened, like the ear that heard it, of horsemen advancing. Interpreted by the tumultuous dreams of Kate, was it the cavalry of Spain, at whose head so often she had charged the bloody Indian scalpers? Was it, according to the legend of ancient days, cavalry that had been sown by her brother's blood—cavalry that rose from the ground on an inquest of retribution, and were racing up the Andes to seize her? Her dreams, that had opened sullenly to the sound, waited for no answer, but closed again into pompous darkness. Happily, the horsemen had caught the glimpse of some bright

under the delusive persuasion—that not any vile glass of brandy, but the stern refusal of all brandy, was the thing that saved his collapsing patient. The patient herself, who might naturally know something of the matter, was of a different opinion. She sided with the factious body around her bed (comprehending all, beside the doctor), who felt sure that death was rapidly approaching, *barring* that brandy. The same result, in the same appalling crisis, I have known repeatedly produced by twenty-five drops of laudanum. Many will say, "Oh, never listen to a non-medical man like this writer. Consult in such a case your medical adviser." You will, will you? Then let me tell you, that you are missing the very logic of all I have been saying for the improvement of blockheads, which is—that you should consult any man *but* a medical man, since no other man has any obstinate prejudice of professional timidity.

ornament, clasp, or aiguillette, on Kate's dress. They were hunters and foresters from below—servants in the household of a beneficent lady; and, in pursuit of some flying game, had wandered far beyond their ordinary limits. Struck by the sudden scintillation from Kate's dress played upon by the morning sun, they rode up to the thicket. Great was their surprise, great their pity, to see a young officer in uniform stretched within the bushes upon the ground, and apparently dying. Borderers from childhood on this dreadful frontier, sacred to winter and death, they understood the case at once. They dismounted, and, with the tenderness of women, raising the poor frozen cornet in their arms, washed her temples with brandy, whilst one, at intervals, suffered a few drops to trickle within her lips. As the restoration of a warm bed was now most likely to be the one thing needed, they lifted the helpless stranger upon a horse, walking on each side with supporting arms. Once again our Kate is in the saddle, once again a Spanish caballero. But Kate's bridle-hand is deadly cold. And her spurs, that she had never unfastened since leaving the monastic asylum, hung as idle as the flapping sail that fills unsteadily with the breeze upon a stranded ship.

This procession had many miles to go, and over difficult ground; but at length it reached the forest-like park and the chateau of the wealthy proprietress. Kate was still half-frozen and speechless, except at intervals. Heavens! can this corpse-like, languishing

young woman be the Kate that once, in her radiant
girlhood, rode with a handful of comrades into a
column of two thousand enemies, that saw her
comrades die, that persisted when all were dead, that
tore from the heart of all resistance the banner of
her native Spain? Chance and change have "written
strange defeatures in her face." Much is changed;
but some things are not changed, either in herself or in
those about her: there is still kindness that over-
flows with pity: there is still helplessness that asks
for this pity without a voice: she is now received by a
senora, not less kind than that maternal aunt who,
on the night of her birth, first welcomed her to a
loving home; and she, the heroine of Spain, is herself
as helpless now as that little lady, who, then at ten
minutes of age, was kissed and blessed by all the
household of St Sebastian.[1]

---

[1] At this point De Quincey had reached the close of the *second
part* of the story as it originally appeared in Tait's Edinburgh
Magazine. As the *first part* (May 1847) had closed with the
intimation "*To be concluded in the next Number*," he thought it
necessary to apologise for the non-fulfilment of that promise and
the protraction of the story into a *third part*. This he did in the
following paragraph, inserted at this point in the Magazine, but
omitted, of course, in the reprint:—"Last month, reader, I promised,
" or some one promised *for* me, that I should drive through to the
" end of the journey in the next stage. But, oh, dear reader!
" these Andes, in Jonathan's phrase, are a 'severe' range of hills.
" It takes 'the kick' out of any horse, or, indeed, out of any cornet
" of horse, to climb up this cruel side of the range. Rest I really
" must, whilst Kate is resting. But next month I will carry you
" down the other side at such a flying gallop, that you shall suspect
" me (though most unjustly) of a plot against your neck. Now,

20.—*A Second Lull in Kate's Stormy Life.*

Let us suppose Kate placed in a warm bed.   Let us suppose her in a few hours recovering steady consciousness ; in a few days recovering some power of self-support ; in a fortnight able to seek the gay saloon, where the senora was sitting alone, and able to render thanks, with that deep sincerity which ever characterised our wild-hearted Kate, for the critical services received from that lady and her establishment.

This lady, a widow, was what the French call a *mélisse*, the Spaniards a *mestizza*—that is, the daughter of a genuine Spaniard, and an Indian mother.   I will call her simply a *Creole*,[2] which will indicate her want of pure Spanish blood sufficiently to explain her deference for those who had it.   She was a kind, liberal women ; rich rather more than needed where

"let me throw down the reins ; and then, in our brother Jonathan's "sweet sentimental expression, 'let's liquor.' "—There is some pathos now in this careless piece of slang, scribbled by De Quincey as a stop-gap for his magazine readers in 1847.   "Rest I really must," "Let me throw down the reins," "Let's liquor,"—in these phrases, and with real fun in the last, one sees De Quincey yet, pen in hand more than forty years ago, in some fatigued moment in his Edinburgh or Glasgow lodging.—M.

[1] "*Creole :*"—At that time the infusion of negro or African blood was small.   Consequently, none of the negro hideousness was diffused. After those intercomplexities had arisen between all complications and interweavings of descent from three original strands—European, American, African—the distinctions of social consideration founded on them bred names so many, that a court calendar was necessary to keep you from blundering.   As yet (*i.e.*, in Kate's time), the varieties were few.   Meantime, the word *Creole* has always been

there were no opera-boxes to rent; a widow about fifty years old in the wicked world's account, some forty-two in her own; and happy, above all, in the possession of a most lovely daughter, whom even the wicked world did not accuse of more than sixteen years. This daughter Juana, was —— But stop— let her open the door of the saloon in which the senora and the cornet are conversing, and speak for herself. She did so, after an hour had passed; which length of time, to *her* that never had any business whatever in her innocent life, seemed sufficient to settle the business of the Old World and the New. Had Pietro Diaz (as Catalina now called herself) been really a Peter, and not a sham Peter, what a vision of loveliness would have rushed upon his sensibilities as the door opened. Do not expect me to describe her, for which, however, there are materials extant, sleeping in archives, where they have slept for two hundred and twenty-eight years. It is enough that she is reported to have united the stately tread of Andalusian women with the innocent voluptuousness of Peruvian eyes. As to her complexion and figure, be it known that Juana's father was a gentleman

misapplied in our English colonies to a person (though of strictly European blood), simply if *born* in the West Indies. In this English use, the word *Creole* expresses exactly the same difference as the Romans indicated by *Hispanus* and *Hispanicus*. The first meant a person of Spanish blood, a native of Spain; the second, a Roman born in Spain. So of *Germanus* and *Germanicus*, *Italus* and *Italicus*, *Anglus* and *Anglicus*, etc.; an important distinction, on which see Isaac Casaubon *apud Scriptores Hist. Augustan.*

from Grenada, having in his veins the grandest blood
of all this earth—blood of Goths and Vandals,
tainted (for which Heaven be thanked!) twice over
with blood of Arabs—once through Moors, once
through Jews;[1] whilst from her grandmother Juana
drew the deep subtle melancholy, and the beautiful
contours of limb, which belonged to the Indian race—
a race destined (ah, wherefore?) silently and slowly
to fade away from the earth.   No awkwardness was
or could be in this antelope, when gliding with forest
grace into the room ; no town-bred shame ; nothing
but the unaffected pleasure of one who wishes to
speak a fervent welcome, but knows not if she ought ;
the astonishment of a Miranda, bred in utter solitude,
when first beholding a princely Ferdinand, and just
so much reserve as to remind you, that, if Catalina
thought fit to dissemble her sex, she did *not*.   And
consider, reader, if you look back, and are a great
arithmetician, that whilst the senora had only fifty
per cent. of Spanish blood, Juana had seventy-five ;
so that her Indian melancholy, after all, was swallowed

---

[1] It is well known, that the very reason why the Spanish beyond
all nations became so gloomily jealous of a Jewish cross in the
pedigree, was because, until the vigilance of the church rose into
ferocity, in no nation was such a cross so common.   The hatred of
fear is ever the deepest.   And men hated the Jewish taint, as once in
Jerusalem they hated the leprosy, because, even whilst they raved
against it, the secret proofs of it might be detected amongst their
own kindred ; even as in the Temple, whilst once a Hebrew king
rose in mutiny against the priesthood (2 Chron. xxvi. 16-20),
suddenly the leprosy that dethroned him, blazed out upon his
forehead.

up for the present by her Visigothic, by her Vandal, by her Arab, by her Spanish fire.

Catalina, seared as she was by the world, has left it evident in her memoirs that she was touched more than she wished to be by this innocent child. Juana formed a brief lull for Catalina in her too stormy existence. And if for *her* in this life the sweet reality of a sister had been possible, here was the sister she would have chosen. On the other hand, what might Juana think of the cornet? To have been thrown upon the kind hospitalities of her native home, to have been rescued by her mother's servants from that fearful death which, lying but a few miles off, had filled her nursery with traditionary tragedies—*that* was sufficient to create an interest in the stranger. Such things it had been that wooed the heavenly Desdemona. But his bold martial demeanour, his yet youthful style of beauty, his frank manners, his animated conversation, that reported a hundred contests with suffering and peril, wakened for the first time her admiration. Men she had never seen before, except menial servants, or a casual priest. But here was a gentleman, young like herself, a splendid cavalier, that rode in the cavalry of Spain ; that carried the banner of the only potentate whom Peruvians knew of—the King of the Spains and the Indies ; that had doubled Cape Horn ; that had crossed the Andes ; that had suffered shipwreck ; that had rocked upon fifty storms ; and had wrestled for life through fifty battles.

The reader already guesses all that followed. The sisterly love which Catalina did really feel for this young mountaineer was inevitably misconstrued. Embarrassed, but not able, from sincere affection, or almost in bare propriety, to refuse such expressions of feeling as corresponded to the artless and involuntary kindnesses of the ingenuous Juana, one day the cornet was surprised by mamma in the act of encircling her daughter's waist with his martial arm, although waltzing was premature by at least two centuries in Peru.[1] She taxed him instantly with dishonourably abusing her confidence. The cornet made but a bad defence. He muttered something about "*fraternal affection*," about "esteem," and a great deal of metaphysical words that are destined to remain untranslated in their original Spanish. The good senora, though she could boast only of forty-two years' experience, or say forty-four, was not altogether to be "*had*" in that fashion : she was as learned as if she had been fifty, and she brought matters to a speedy crisis. "You are a Spaniard," she said, "a gentleman, therefore ; *remember* that you are a gentle-

---

[1] On the supposition that Catalina had crossed the Andes from some point in the north of Chili, she must now,—after having descended "the mighty staircase" on the other side, and found refuge in the house of the kind senora,—been in the part of Spanish South America known as La Plata. But there have been many changes in the territorial divisions of South America since the beginning of the seventeenth century ; and *Peru* or *Peruvia* was then a name for a much larger extent of Spanish South America than at present. —M.

man. This very night, if your intentions are not serious, quit my house. Go to Tucuman; you shall command my horses and servants; but stay no longer to increase the sorrow that already you will have left behind you. My daughter loves you. That is sorrow enough, if you are trifling with us. But, if not, and you also love *her*, and can be happy in our solitary mode of life, stay with us—stay for ever. Marry Juana with my free consent. I ask not for wealth. Mine is sufficient for you both." The cornet protested that the honour was one never contemplated by *him*—that it was too great—that ——. But, of course, reader, you know that "gammon" flourishes in Peru, amongst the silver mines, as well as in some more boreal lands, that produce little better than copper and tin. "Tin," however, has its uses. The delighted senora overruled all objections, great and small; and she confirmed Juana's notion that the business of two worlds could be transacted in an hour, by settling her daughter's future happiness in exactly twenty minutes. The poor, weak Catalina, not acting now in any spirit of recklessness, grieving sincerely for the gulf that was opening before her, and yet shrinking effeminately from the momentary shock that would be inflicted by a firm adherence to her duty, clinging to the anodyne of a short delay, allowed herself to be installed as the lover of Juana. Considerations of convenience, however, postponed the marriage. It was requisite to make various purchases; and for this, it was requisite to visit Tucuman, where also the marriage ceremony could be performed with more circumstantial splendour. To Tucuman, therefore, after some weeks' interval, the whole party repaired.[1] And at Tucuman it was that the tragical events arose, which, whilst interrupting such a mockery for ever, left the poor Juana still happily deceived, and never believing for a moment that hers was a rejected or a deluded heart.

One reporter of Mr De Ferrer's narrative forgets his usual generosity when he says, that the senora's gift of her daughter to the Alférez was not quite so disinterested as it seemed to be.[2] Certainly it was not so disinterested as European ignorance might fancy it : but it was quite as much so as it ought to have been, in balancing the interests of a child.

---

[1] It is this mention of Tucuman that throws light at last on the question, mooted in notes at p. 53 and p. 84, as to the point at which Catalina had crossed the Andes and the part of Spanish America in which she had found herself after that feat. Tucuman is the name of one of the provinces of the present Republic of La Plata, in the interior of South America ; and the town Tucuman, which gives it the name, and which has a present population of about 11,000, is between 250 and 300 miles east from the Andes frontier of North Chili. Therefore, unless Catalina had crossed the Andes from northern Chili, one can hardly see how Tucuman could be the nearest town to that residence of the Creole lady in which Catalina had been a guest after having crossed them. But a large part of what is now La Plata was then included in the viceroyalty of Peru.—M.

[2] This "reporter" is the same person as the Frenchman attacked previously in p. 62-63. Who he was is explained in the Appended Note, *Original of De Quincey's Story of the Spanish Military Nun.* —M.

Very true it is, that, being a genuine Spaniard, who
was still a rare creature in so vast a world as Peru—
being a Spartan amongst Helots—a Spanish Alférez
would, in those days, and in that region, have been
a natural noble. His alliance created honour for his
wife and for his descendants. Something, therefore,
the cornet would add to the family consideration.
But, instead of selfishness, it argued just regard for
her daughter's interest to build upon this, as some
sort of equipoise to the wealth which her daughter
would bring.

Spaniard, however, as she was, our Alférez, on
reaching Tucuman, found no Spaniards to mix with,
but instead, twelve Portuguese.[1]

21.—*Kate once more in Storms.*

Catalina remembered the Spanish proverb, "Pump
out of a Spaniard all his good qualities, and the re-
mainder makes a pretty fair Portuguese ;" but as
there was nobody else to gamble with, she entered
freely into their society. Soon she suspected that
there was foul play : for all modes of doctoring dice
had been made familiar to *her* by the experience of
camps. She watched ; and, by the time she had lost
her final coin, she was satisfied that she had been

---

[1] The interior parts of South America were then a meeting
ground, and their native inhabitants a common prey, for the Spanish
colonists of Peru, Chili, etc., in the west of South America, and
the Portuguese colonists of Brazil in the east of the same continent.—M.

plundered. In her first anger, she would have been
glad to switch the whole dozen across the eyes; but
as twelve to one were too great odds, she determined
on limiting her vengeance to the immediate culprit.
Him she followed into the street; and coming near
enough to distinguish his profile reflected on a wall,
she continued to keep him in view from a short
distance. The lighthearted young cavalier whistled,
as he went, an old Portuguese ballad of romance, and
in a quarter-of-an-hour came up to a house, the front-
door of which he began to open with a pass-key.
This operation was the signal for Catalina that the
hour of vengeance had struck; and stepping up
hastily, she tapped the Portuguese on the shoulder,
saying, " Senor, you are a robber !" The Portuguese
turned coolly round, and seeing his gaming antagonist,
replied, " Possibly, sir ; but I have no particular fancy
for being told so," at the same time drawing his sword.
Catalina had not designed to take any advantage ;
and the touching him on the shoulder, with the
interchange of speeches, and the known character of
Kate, sufficiently imply it. But it is too probable,
in such cases, that the party whose intention had
been regularly settled from the first, will, and must,
have an advantage unconsciously over a man so
abruptly thrown on his defence. However this
might be, they had not fought a minute before
Catalina passed her sword through her opponent's
body ; and, without a groan or a sigh, the Portuguese
cavalier fell dead at his own door. Kate searched

the street with her ears, and (as far as the indistinct-
ness of night allowed) with her eyes. All was profoundly silent; and she was satisfied that no human
figure was in motion. What should be done with the
body? A glance at the door of the house settled
that: Fernando had himself opened it at the very
moment when he received the summons to turn round.
She dragged the corpse in, therefore, to the foot of
the staircase, put the key by the dead man's side,
and then issuing softly into the street, drew the door
close with as little noise as possible. Catalina again
paused to listen and to watch, went home to the
hospitable senora's house, retired to bed, fell asleep,
and early the next morning was awakened by the
corrégidor and four alguazils.

The lawlessness of all that followed strikingly
exposes the frightful state of criminal justice at that
time, wherever Spanish law prevailed. No evidence
appeared to connect Catalina in any way with the
death of Fernando Acosta. The Portuguese gam-
blers, besides that perhaps they thought lightly of
such an accident, might have reasons of their own
for drawing off public attention from their pursuits
in Tucuman. Not one of these men came forward
openly, else the circumstances at the gaming-table,
and the departure of Catalina so closely on the heels
of her opponent, would have suggested reasonable
grounds for detaining her until some further light
should be obtained. As it was, her imprisonment
rested upon no colourable ground whatever, unless

the magistrate had received some anonymous information, which, however, he never alleged.   One comfort
there was, meantime, in Spanish injustice : it did
not loiter.   Full gallop it went over the ground :
one week often sufficed for informations—for trial—
for execution ; and the only bad consequence was,
that a second or a third week sometimes exposed
the disagreeable fact that everything had been "premature ;" a solemn sacrifice had been made to offended
justice, in which all was right except as to the victim ;
it was the wrong man ; and *that* gave extra trouble ;
for then all was to do over again—another man to
be executed, and, possibly, still to be caught.

Justice moved at her usual Spanish rate in the
present case.   Kate was obliged to rise instantly ;
not suffered to speak to anybody in the house, though,
in going out, a door opened, and she saw the young
Juana looking out with her saddest Indian expression.
In one day the trial was finished.   Catalina said
(which was true) that she hardly knew Acosta ; and
that people of her rank were used to attack their
enemies face to face, not by murderous surprises.
The magistrates were impressed with Catalina's
answers (yet answers to *what,* or to *whom,* in a case
where there was no distinct charge, and no avowed
accuser ?)   Things were beginning to look well, when
all was suddenly upset by two witnesses, whom the
reader (who is a sort of accomplice after the fact,
having been privately let into the truths of the case,
and having concealed his knowledge) will know at

once to be false witnesses, but whom the old Spanish buzwigs doated on as models of all that could be looked for in the best. Both were ill-looking fellows, as it was their duty to be. And the first deposed as follows :—That through *his* quarter of Tucuman, the fact was notorious of Acosta's wife being the object of a criminal pursuit on the part of the Alférez (Catalina) ; that, doubtless, the injured husband had surprised the prisoner, which, of course, had led to the murder—to the staircase—to the key—to everything, in short, that could be wished. No—stop ! what am I saying ?—to everything that ought to be abominated. Finally—for he had now settled the main question—that he had a friend who would take up the case where he himself, from shortsightedness, was obliged to lay it down. This friend—the Pythias of this shortsighted Damon—started up in a frenzy of virtue at this summons, and, rushing to the front of the alguazils, said, "That since his friend had proved sufficiently the fact of the Alférez having been lurking in the house, and having murdered a man, all that rested upon *him* to show was, how that murderer got out of that house ; which he could do satisfactorily ; for there was a balcony running along the windows on the second floor, one of which windows he himself, lurking in a corner of the street, saw the Alférez throw up, and from the said balcony take a flying leap into the said street." Evidence like this was conclusive ; no defence was listened to, nor indeed had the prisoner any to produce. The

Alférez could deny neither the staircase nor the
balcony : the street is there to this day, like the
bricks in Jack Cade's chimney, testifying all that
may be required ; and as to our friend who saw the
leap, there he was—nobody could deny *him*.   The
prisoner might indeed have suggested that she never
heard of Acosta's wife, nor had the existence of such
a wife been proved, or even ripened into a suspicion.
But the bench were satisfied ; chopping logic in
defence was henceforward impertinence ; and sentence
was pronounced—that, on the eighth day from the
day of arrest, the Alférez should be executed in the
public square.

It was not amongst the weaknesses of Catalina—
who had so often inflicted death, and, by her own
journal, thought so lightly of inflicting- it (unless
under cowardly advantages)—to shrink from facing
death in her own person.   Many incidents in her
career show the coolness and even gaiety with which,
in any case where death was apparently inevitable,
she would have gone forward to meet it.   But in
this case she *had* a temptation for escaping it, which
was certainly in her power.   She had only to reveal
the secret of her sex, and the ridiculous witnesses,
beyond whose testimony there was nothing at all
against her, must at once be covered with derision.
Catalina had some liking for fun ; and a main induce-
ment to this course was, that it would enable her to
say to the judges, " Now you see what old fools
you've made of yourselves ; every woman and child

in Peru will soon be laughing at you." I must acknowledge my own weakness; this last temptation I could *not* have withstood; flesh is weak, and fun is strong. But Catalina *did*. On consideration, she fancied that, although the particular motive for murdering Acosta would be dismissed with laughter, still this might not clear her of the murder, which, on some *other* motive, she might be supposed to have committed. But, allowing that she were cleared altogether, what most of all she feared was, that the publication of her sex would throw a reflex light upon many past transactions in her life; would instantly find its way to Spain; and would probably soon bring her within the tender attentions of the Inquisition. She kept firm, therefore, to the resolution of not saving her life by this discovery. And so far as her fate lay in her own hands, she would to a certainty have perished—which to me seems a most fantastic caprice; it was to court a certain death and a present death, in order to evade a remote contingency of death. But even at this point how strange a case! A woman *falsely* accused (because accused by lying witnesses) of an act which she really *did* commit! And falsely accused of a true offence upon a motive that was impossible!

As the sun was setting upon the seventh day, when the hours were numbered for the prisoner, there filed into her cell four persons in religious habits. They came on the charitable mission of preparing the poor convict for death. Catalina, however, watching all things narrowly, remarked something earnest and significant in the eye of the leader, as of one who had some secret communication to make. She contrived, therefore, to clasp this man's hands, as if in the energy of internal struggles, and *he* contrived to slip into hers the very smallest of billets from poor Juana. It contained, for indeed it *could* contain, only these three words—"Do not confess.—J." This one caution, so simple and so brief, proved a talisman. It did not refer to any confession of the crime; *that* would have been assuming what Juana was neither entitled nor disposed to assume; but it referred, in the technical sense of the church, to the act of devotional confession. Catalina found a single moment for a glance at it; understood the whole; resolutely refused to confess, as a person unsettled in her religious opinions, that needed spiritual instructions; and the four monks withdrew to make their report. The principal judge, upon hearing of the prisoner's impenitence, granted another day. At the end of *that*, no change having occurred either in the prisoner's mind or in the circumstances, he issued his warrant for the execution. Accordingly, as the sun went down, the sad procession formed within the prison. Into the great square of Tucuman it moved, where the scaffold had been built, and the whole city had assembled for the spectacle. Catalina steadily ascended the ladder of the scaffold; even then she resolved not to benefit by revealing her sex; even then it was that she expressed her scorn for the lubberly executioner's mode of tying a knot; did it herself in a "ship-shape," orthodox manner; received in return the enthusiastic plaudits of the crowd, and so far ran the risk of precipitating her fate; for the timid magistrates, fearing a rescue from the fiery clamours of the impetuous mob, angrily ordered the executioner to finish the scene. The clatter of a galloping horse, however, at this instant forced them to pause. The crowd opened a road for the agitated horseman, who was the bearer of an order from the President of La Plata to suspend the execution until two prisoners could be examined. The whole was the work of the senora and her daughter. The elder lady, having gathered informations against the witnesses, had pursued them to La Plata. There, by her influence with the governor, they were arrested, recognised as old malefactors, and in their terror had partly confessed their perjury. Catalina was removed to La Plata; solemnly acquitted; and, by the advice of the president, for the present the connection with the senora's family was indefinitely postponed.[1]

[1] The story thinks nothing of shifting Catalina some hundreds of miles in a mere sentence or two and without any intimation of difficulty. The town once called *Plata* or *La Plata*, but now known as *Chuquisaca*, the capital of Bolivia, is about 600 miles due north of Tucuman. What is now Bolivia was then Upper Peru; and at Plata, even more than in Tucuman, Kate was among Peruvian Spaniards.—M.

22.—*Kate's Penultimate Adventure.*

Now was the last-but-one adventure at hand that
ever Catalina should see in the New World.   Some
fine sights she may yet see in Europe, but nothing
after this (*which she has recorded*) in America.   Europe,
if it had ever heard of her name (as very shortly it
shall hear), Kings, Pope, Cardinals, if they were but
aware of her existence (which in six months they *shall*
be), would thirst for an introduction to our Catalina.
You hardly thought now, reader, that she was such
a great person, or anybody's pet but yours and mine.
Bless you, sir, she would scorn to look at *us*.   I tell
you, that Eminences, Excellencies, Highnesses—nay,
even Royalties and Holinesses—are languishing to
see her, or soon *will* be.   But how can this come to
pass, if she is to continue in her present obscurity?
Certainly it cannot without some great *peripetteia*, or
vertiginous whirl of fortune; which, therefore, you
shall now behold taking place in one turn of her
next adventure.   *That* shall let in a light, *that* shall
throw back a Claude Lorraine gleam over all the past,
able to make kings, that would have cared not for her
under Peruvian daylight, come to glorify her setting
beams.

The senora—and, observe, whatever kindness she
does to Catalina speaks secretly from two hearts, her
own and Juana's—had, by the advice of Mr President
Mendonia, given sufficient money for Catalina's
travelling expenses.   So far well.   But Mr M. chose

to add a little codicil to this bequest of the senora's, never suggested by her or by her daughter. "Pray," said this inquisitive president, who surely might have found business enough within his own neighbourhood —"pray, Senor Pietro Diaz, did you ever live at Conception? And were you ever acquainted there with Signor Miguel de Erauso? That man, sir, was my friend." What a pity that on this occasion Catalina could not venture to be candid! What a capital speech it would have made to say, "*Friend* were you? I think you could hardly be *that*, with seven hundred miles between you. But that man was *my* friend also; and, secondly, my brother. True it is I killed him. But if you happen to know that this was by pure mistake in the dark, what an old rogue you must be to throw *that* in my teeth, which is the affliction of my life!" Again, however, as so often in the same circumstances, Catalina thought that it would cause more ruin than it could heal to be candid; and, indeed, if she were really *P. Diaz, Esq.*, how came she to be brother to the late Mr Erauso? On consideration, also, if she could not tell *all*, merely to have professed a fraternal connection which never was avowed by either whilst living together, would not have brightened the reputation of Catalina. Still, from a kindness for poor Kate, I feel uncharitably towards the president for advising Senor Pietro "to travel for his health." What had *he* to do with people's health? However, Mr Peter, as he had pocketed the senora's money, thought it right to pocket also the advice that accompanied its payment. That he might be in a condition to do so, he went off to buy a horse. On that errand, in all lands, for some reason only half explained, you must be in luck if you do not fall in, and eventually fall out, with a knave. But on this particular day Kate *was* in luck. For, beside money and advice, she obtained at a low rate a horse both beautiful and serviceable for a journey. To Paz it was, a city of prosperous name, that the cornet first moved.[1] But Paz did not fulfil the promise of its name. For it laid the grounds of a feud that drove our Kate out of America.

Her first adventure was a bagatelle, and fitter for a jest-book than for a serious history; yet it proved no jest either, since it led to the tragedy that followed. Riding into Paz, our gallant standard-bearer and her bonny black horse drew all eyes, *comme de raison*, upon their separate charms. This was inevitable amongst the indolent population of a Spanish town; and Kate was used to it. But, having recently had a little too much of the public attention, she felt nervous on re-marking two soldiers eyeing the handsome horse and the handsome rider, with an attention that seemed too earnest for mere *æsthetics*. However, Kate was not the kind of person to let anything dwell on her spirits, especially if it took the shape of impudence; and,

---

[1] Another quiet locomotive leap ! Paz, or La Paz, the capital of the department of that name in the present Bolivia, is about 300 miles north-west from Plata or Chuquisaca.—M.

whistling gaily, she was riding forward, when—who
should cross her path but the Alcalde of Paz! Ah!
alcalde, you see a person now that has a mission against
you and all that you inherit; though a mission known
to herself as little as to you. Good were it for you,
had you never crossed the path of this Biscayan
Alférez. The alcalde looked so sternly, that Kate
asked if his worship had any commands. "Yes. These
men," said the alcalde, "these two soldiers, say that this
horse is stolen." To one who had so narrowly and
so lately escaped the balcony witness and his friend,
it was really no laughing matter to hear of new
affidavits in preparation. Kate was nervous, but
never disconcerted. In a moment she had twitched
off a saddle-cloth on which she sat; and throwing it
over the horse's head, so as to cover up all between
the ears and the mouth, she replied, "That she had
bought and paid for the horse at La Plata. But
now, your worship, if this horse has really been
stolen from these men, they must know well of which
eye it is blind; for it *can* be only in the right eye or
the left." One of the soldiers cried out instantly
that it was the left eye; but the other said, "No,
no; you forget, it's the right." Kate maliciously
called attention to this little schism. But the men
said, "Ah, *that* was nothing—they were hurried; but
now, on recollecting themselves, they were agreed
that it was the left eye."—"Did they stand to that?"
—"Oh yes, positive they were—left eye—left."

Upon which our Kate, twitching off the horse-

cloth, said gaily to the magistrate, "Now, sir, please
to observe that this horse has nothing the matter
with either eye." And, in fact, it *was* so. Upon *that*,
his worship ordered his alguazils to apprehend the
two witnesses, who posted off to bread and water,
with other reversionary advantages; whilst Kate rode
in quest of the best dinner that Paz could furnish.

23.—*Preparation for Kate's Final Adventure in Peru.*

This alcalde's acquaintance, however, was not
destined to drop here. Something had appeared in
the young caballero's bearing which made it painful
to have addressed him with harshness, or for a
moment to have entertained such a charge against
such a person. He despatched his cousin, therefore,
Don Antonio Calderon, to offer his apologies; and
at the same time to request that the stranger, whose
rank and quality he regretted not to have known,
would do him the honour to come and dine with him.
This explanation, and the fact that Don Antonio had
already proclaimed his own position as cousin to the
magistrate, and nephew to the Bishop of Cuzco,
obliged Catalina to say, after thanking the gentlemen
for their obliging attentions, "I myself hold the rank
of Alférez in the service of his Catholic Majesty. I
am a native of Biscay, and I am now repairing to
Cuzco on private business."[1]—"To Cuzco!" exclaimed
Antonio; "and you from dear lovely Biscay! How

[1] Cuzco is about 300 miles north-west from La Paz. It was the

very fortunate! My cousin is a Basque like you; and, like you, he starts for Cuzco to-morrow morning; so that, if it is agreeable to you, Senor Alférez, we will travel together." It was settled that they should. To travel—amongst "balcony witnesses," and anglers for "blind horses"—not merely with a just man, but with the very abstract idea and riding allegory of justice, was too delightful to the storm-wearied cornet; and he cheerfully accompanied Don Antonio to the house of the magistrate, called Don Pedro de Chavarria. Distinguished was his reception; the alcalde personally renewed his regrets for the ridiculous scene of the two scampish oculists, and presented Kate to his wife—a most splendid Andalusian beauty, to whom he had been married about a year.

This lady there is a reason for describing; and the French reporter of Catalina's memoirs dwells upon the theme. She united, he says, the sweetness of the German lady with the energy of the Arabian —a combination hard to judge of. As to her feet, he adds, I say nothing, for she had scarcely any at all. "*Je ne parle point de ses pieds, elle n'en avait presque pas.*" "Poor lady!" says a compassionate rustic: "no feet! What a shocking thing that so fine a woman should have been so sadly mutilated!" Oh, my dear rustic, you're quite in the wrong box. The Frenchman means this as the very highest com-

capital of the native Peruvian Empire of the Incas, and is one of the most important cities, and the capital of one of the provinces, of the present and much restricted Peru.—M.

pliment. Beautiful, however, she must have been; and a Cinderella, I hope, but still not a Cinderellula, considering that she had the inimitable walk and step of Andalusian women, which cannot be accomplished without something of a proportionate basis to stand upon.

The reason which there is (as I have said) for describing this lady, arises out of her relation to the tragic events which followed. She, by her criminal levity, was the cause of all. And I must here warn the moralising blunderer of two errors that he is likely to make: 1st, that he is invited to read some extract from a licentious amour, as if for its own interest; 2dly, or on account of Donna Catalina's memoirs, with a view to relieve their too martial character. I have the pleasure to assure him of his being so utterly in the darkness of error, that any possible change he can make in his opinions, right or left, must be for the better: he cannot stir, but he will mend, which is a delightful thought for the moral and blundering mind. As to the first point, what little glimpse he obtains of a licentious amour is, as a court of justice will sometimes show him such a glimpse, simply to make intelligible the subsequent facts which depend upon it. Secondly, as to the conceit that Catalina wished to embellish her memoirs, understand that no such practice then existed—certainly not in Spanish literature. Her memoirs are electrifying by their facts; else, in the manner of telling these facts, they are systematically dry.

But let us resume. Don Antonio Calderon was a handsome, accomplished cavalier. And in the course of dinner Catalina was led to judge, from the behaviour to each other of this gentleman and the lady, the alcalde's beautiful wife, that they had an improper understanding. This also she inferred from the furtive language of their eyes. Her wonder was, that the alcalde should be so blind; though upon that point she saw reason in a day or two to change her opinion. Some people see everything by affecting to see nothing. The whole affair, however, was nothing at all to *her ;* and she would have dismissed it altogether from her thoughts, but for the dreadful events on the journey.

This went on but slowly, however steadily. Owing to the miserable roads, eight hours a-day of travelling was found quite enough for man and beast; the product of which eight hours was from ten to twelve leagues, taking the league at $2\frac{1}{4}$ miles. On the last day but one of the journey, the travelling party, which was precisely the original dinner party, reached a little town ten leagues short of Cuzco. The corrégidor of this place was a friend of the alcalde; and through *his* influence the party obtained better accommodations than those which they had usually commanded in a hovel calling itself a *venta*, or in a sheltered corner of a barn. The alcalde was to sleep at the corrégidor's house; the two young cavaliers, Calderon and our Kate, had sleeping-rooms at the public *locanda ;* but for the lady was reserved a little pleasure-house in an enclosed garden. This was a mere toy of a house; but the season being summer, and the house surrounded with tropical flowers, the lady preferred it (in spite of its loneliness) to the damp mansion of the official grandee, who, in her humble opinion, was quite as fusty as his mansion, and his mansion not much less so than himself.

After dining gaily together at the *locanda*, and possibly taking a "rise" out of his worship the corrégidor, as a repeating echo of Don Quixote (then growing popular in Spanish America), the young man Don Antonio, who was no young officer, and the young officer Catalina, who was no young man, lounged down together to the little pavilion in the flower-garden, with the purpose of paying their respects to the presiding belle. They were graciously received, and had the honour of meeting there his mustiness the alcalde, and his fustiness the corrégidor; whose conversation ought surely to have been edifying, since it was anything but brilliant. How they got on under the weight of two such muffs, has been a mystery for two centuries. But they *did* to a certainty, for the party did not break up till eleven. *Tea and turn out* you could not call it; for there was the *turn-out* in rigour, but not the *tea*. One thing, however, Catalina by mere accident had an opportunity of observing, and observed with pain. The two official gentlemen, on taking leave, had gone down the steps into the garden. Catalina, having forgot her hat, went back into the little vestibule to look for it. There stood the lady and Don Antonio, exchanging a few final words (they *were* final) and a few final signs. Amongst the last Kate observed distinctly this, and distinctly she understood it. First of all, by raising her forefinger, the lady drew Calderon's attention to the act which followed as one of significant pantomime; which done, she snuffed out one of the candles. The young man answered it by a look of intelligence; and then all three passed down the steps together. The lady was disposed to take the cool air, and accompanied them to the garden-gate; but, in passing down the walk, Catalina noticed a second ill-omened sign that all was not right. Two glaring eyes she distinguished amongst the shrubs for a moment, and a rustling immediately after. "What's that?" said the lady; and Don Antonio answered, carelessly, "A bird flying out of the bushes." But birds do not amuse themselves by staying up to midnight; and birds do not wear rapiers.

Catalina, as usual, had read everything. Not a wrinkle or a rustle was lost upon *her*. And, therefore, when she reached the *locanda*, knowing to an iota all that was coming, she did not retire to bed, but paced before the house. She had not long to wait: in fifteen minutes the door opened softly, and out stepped Calderon. Kate walked forward, and faced him immediately; telling him laughingly that it was not good for his health to go abroad on this night. The young man showed some impatience; upon which, very seriously, Kate acquainted him with her suspicions, and with the certainty that the alcalde was not so blind as he had seemed. Calderon thanked her for the information; would be upon his guard, but, to prevent further expostulation, he wheeled round instantly into the darkness. Catalina was too well convinced, however, of the mischief on foot to leave him thus. She followed rapidly, and passed silently into the garden, almost at the same time with Calderon. Both took their stations behind trees; Calderon watching nothing but the burning candles, Catalina watching circumstances to direct her movements. The candles burned brightly in the little pavilion. Presently one was extinguished. Upon this, Calderon pressed forward to the steps, hastily ascended them, and passed into the vestibule. Catalina followed on his traces. What succeeded was all one scene of continued, dreadful dumb show; different passions of panic, or deadly struggle, or hellish malice, absolutely suffocated all articulate utterances.

In the first moments a gurgling sound was heard, as of a wild beast attempting vainly to yell over some creature that it was strangling. Next came a tumbling out at the door of one black mass, which heaved and parted at intervals into two figures, which closed, which parted again, which at last fell down the steps together. Then appeared a figure in white. It was the unhappy Andalusian; and she, seeing the outline of Catalina's person, ran up to her, unable to utter one syllable. Pitying the agony of her horror, Catalina took her within her own cloak, and carried her out at the garden gate. Calderon had by this time died ; and the maniacal alcalde had risen up to pursue his wife. But Kate, foreseeing what he would do, had stepped silently within the shadow of the garden wall. Looking down the road to the town, and seeing nobody moving, the maniac, for some purpose, went back to the house. This moment Kate used to recover the *locanda*, with the lady still panting in horror. What was to be done ? To think of concealment in this little place was out of the question. The alcalde was a man of local power, and it was certain that he would kill his wife on the spot. Kate's generosity would not allow her to have any collusion with this murderous purpose. At Cuzco, the principal convent was ruled by a near relative of the Andalusian ; and there she would find shelter. Kate therefore saddled her horse rapidly, placed the lady behind, and rode off in the darkness.

24.—*A Steeple Chase.*

About five miles out of the town their road was crossed by a torrent, over which they could not hit the bridge. "Forward !" cried the lady; "Oh, heavens ! forward !" and Kate repeating the word to the horse, the docile creature leaped down into the water. They were all sinking at first; but, having its head free, the horse swam clear of all obstacles through the midnight darkness, and scrambled out on the opposite bank. The two riders were dripping from the shoulders downward. But, seeing a light twinkling from a cottage window, Kate rode up; obtaining a little refreshment, and the benefit of a fire, from a poor labouring man. From this man she also bought a warm mantle for the lady, who, besides her torrent bath, was dressed in a light evening robe, so that but for the horseman's cloak of Kate she would have perished. But there was no time to lose. They had already lost two hours from the consequences of their cold bath. Cuzco was still eighteen miles distant; and the alcalde's shrewdness would at once divine this to be his wife's mark. They remounted: very soon the silent night echoed the hoofs of a pursuing rider; and now commenced the most frantic race, in which each party rode as if the whole game of life were staked upon the issue. The pace was killing: and Kate has delivered it as her opinion, in the memoirs which she wrote, that the alcalde was the better mounted. This may be doubted. And certainly Kate had ridden too many years in the Spanish cavalry, to have any fear of his worship's horsemanship; but it was a prodigious disadvantage that *her* horse had to carry double; while the horse ridden by her opponent was one of those belonging to the murdered Don Antonio, and known to Kate as a powerful animal. At length they had come within three miles of Cuzco. The road after this descended the whole way to the city, and in some places rapidly, so as to require a cool rider. Suddenly a deep trench appeared traversing the whole extent of a broad heath. It was useless to evade it. To have hesitated, was to be lost. Kate saw the necessity of clearing it; but she doubted much whether her poor exhausted horse, after twenty-one miles of work so severe, had strength for the effort. However, the race was nearly finished; a score of dreadful miles had been accomplished; and Kate's maxim, which never yet had failed, both figuratively for life, and literally for the saddle, was— to ride at everything that showed a front of resistance. She did so now. Having come upon the trench rather too suddenly, she wheeled round for the advantage of coming down upon it with more impetus, rode resolutely at it, cleared it, and gained the opposite bank. The hind feet of her horse were sinking back from the rottenness of the ground; but the strong supporting bridle-hand of Kate carried him forward; and in ten minutes more they would be in Cuzco. This being seen by the vengeful alcalde, who had built great hopes on the trench, he unslung his carbine, pulled up, and fired after the bonny black horse and its two bonny riders. But this vicious manœuvre would have lost his worship any bet that he might have had depending on this admirable steeple-chase. For the bullets, says Kate in her memoirs, whistled round the poor clinging lady *en croupe*—luckily none struck *her;* but one wounded

the horse. And that settled the odds. Kate now
planted herself well in her stirrups to enter Cuzco,
almost dangerously a winner; for the horse was so
maddened by the wound, and the road so steep, that
he went like blazes; and it really became difficult for
Kate to guide him with any precision through narrow
episcopal[1] paths. Henceforwards the wounded horse
required unintermitting attention; and yet, in the
mere luxury of strife, it was impossible for Kate to
avoid turning a little in her saddle to see the alcalde's
performance on this tight-rope of the trench. His
worship's horsemanship being, perhaps, rather rusty,
and he not perfectly acquainted with his horse, it
would have been agreeable for *him* to compromise
the case by riding round, or dismounting. But all
that was impossible. The job must be done. And
I am happy to report, for the reader's satisfaction,
the sequel—so far as Kate could attend the performance. Gathering himself up for mischief, the alcalde
took a mighty sweep, as if ploughing out the line of
some vast encampment, or tracing the *pomœrium* for
some future Rome; then, like thunder and lightning,
with arms flying aloft in the air, down he came upon
the trembling trench. But the horse refused the
leap; to take the leap was impossible; absolutely to
refuse it, the horse felt, was immoral; and therefore,
as the only compromise that *his* unlearned brain
could suggest, he threw his worship right over his

[1] "*Episcopal:*"—The roads around Cuzco were made, and
maintained, under the patronage and control of the bishop.

ears, lodging him safely in a sand-heap, that rose
with clouds of dust and screams of birds into the
morning air.   Kate had now no time to send back
her compliments in a musical halloo.   The alcalde
missed breaking his neck on this occasion very
narrowly; but his neck was of no use to him in
twenty minutes more, as the reader will find.   Kate
rode right onwards; and, coming in with a lady
behind her, horse bloody, and pace such as no hounds
could have lived with, she ought to have made a
great sensation in Cuzco.   But, unhappily, the people
of Cuzco, the spectators that *should* have been, were
fast asleep in bed.[1]

The steeple-chase into Cuzco had been a fine

[1] As the ride from Paz to Cuzco has been described with excep-
tional spirit and minuteness, so that our attention has been bespoken
more strongly for Cuzco than for any other of the towns in the
circuit of Kate's South American wanderings since she left Paita
(except perhaps Conception and Tucuman), the following account
of Cuzco from the description of Peru given in Heylyn's *Cosmo-
graphy* may not be unwelcome :—" Cusco, in the latitude of 13
" degrees and 30 minutes, about 130 leagues to the east of Lima,
" and situate in a rugged and uneven soil, begirt with mountains,
" but on both sides of a pleasant and commodious river.   Once the
" Seat-Royal of the Ingas or Peruvian Kings; who, the more to
" beautifie this city, commanded every one of the nobility to build
" here a palace for their continual abode.   Still of most credit in
" this country, both for beauty and bigness and the multitudes of
" inhabitants ; here being thought to dwell 3000 Spaniards and
" 10,000 of the natives, besides women and children.   The Palace
" of the King, advanced on a lofty mountain, was held to be a work
" of so great magnificence, built of such huge and massive stones, that
" the Spaniards thought it to have been the work rather of devils
" than of men.   Now miserably defaced, most of the stones being

headlong thing, considering the torrent, the trench, the wounded horse, the lovely Andalusian lady, with her agonising fears, mounted behind Kate, together with the meek dove-like dawn: but the finale crowded together the quickest succession of changes that out of a melodrama ever *can* have been witnessed. Kate reached the convent in safety; carried into the cloisters, and delivered like a parcel, the fair Andalusian.   But to rouse the servants and obtain admission to the convent caused a long delay; and on returning to the street through the broad gateway of the convent, whom should she face but the alcalde! How he had escaped the trench, who can tell?   He had no time to write memoirs; his horse was too illiterate.   But he *had* escaped; temper not at all improved by that adventure, and now raised to a hell of malignity by seeing that he had lost his prey. The morning light showed him how to use his sword, and whom he had before him, and he attacked Kate with fury.   Both were exhausted; and Kate, besides

"tumbled down to build private houses in the city: some of the "churches raised also by the ruins of it; and amongst them per- "haps both the Bishop's Palace and Cathedral, whose annual "rents are estimated at 20,000 ducats.   Yet did not this vast "building yield more lustre to the City of Cusco than a spacious "Market-place, the centre in which those highways did meet "together which the Ingas had caused to be made cross the king- "dom, both for length and breadth, with most incredible charge "and pains, for the use of their subjects."—This description of Cuzco by Heylyn in the middle of the seventeenth century may serve for Cuzco as Kate came into it and saw it some twenty-five years earlier.—M.

that she had no personal quarrel with the alcalde, having now accomplished her sole object in saving the lady, would have been glad of a truce. She could with difficulty wield her sword : and the alcalde had so far the advantage, that he wounded Kate severely. That roused her ancient Biscayan blood ; and she turned on him now with deadly determination. At that moment in rode two servants of the alcalde, who took part with their master. These odds strengthened Kate's resolution, but weakened her chances. Just then, however, rode in and ranged himself on Kate's side, the servant of the murdered Don Calderon. In an instant Kate had pushed her sword through the alcalde, who died upon the spot. In an instant the servant of Calderon had fled. In an instant the alguazils had come up. They and the servants of the alcalde pressed furiously on Kate, who was again fighting for her life with persons not even known to her by sight. Against such odds, she was rapidly losing ground ; when, in an instant, on the opposite side of the street, the great gates of the Episcopal Palace rolled open. Thither it was that Calderon's servant had fled. ·The bishop and his attendants hurried across. "Senor Caballero," said the bishop, "in the name of the Virgin, I enjoin you to surrender your sword."—"My lord," said Kate, "I dare not do it with so many enemies about me."—"But I," replied the bishop, "become answerable to the law for your safe keeping." Upon which, with filial reverence, all parties dropped their swords. Kate being severely

wounded, the bishop led her into his palace.   In
another instant came the catastrophe: Kate's discovery
could no longer be delayed; the blood flowed too
rapidly; and the wound was in her bosom.   She
requested a private interview with the bishop; all
was known in a moment; surgeons and attendants
were summoned hastily; and Kate had fainted.
The good bishop pitied her, and had her attended in
his palace; then removed to a convent; then to a
second convent at Lima; and, after many months
had passed, his report of the whole extraordinary case
in all its details to the supreme government at
Madrid, drew from the king, Philip IV., and from
the papal legate, an order that the nun should be
transferred to Spain.[1]

[1] Lima, the capital of Peru, is on the Pacific coast about 300
miles north-west from Cuzco, and about 600 miles south from the
Peruvian town of Paita where Kate's South American adventures
had begun sixteen years before.   The geography of her transatlantic
wanderings during these sixteen years may therefore be now
reviewed thus :—(1) By sea from Paita in Peru to Conception in
Chili, a distance of 2400 miles.   (2) In Chili and Peru, or backwards and forwards between them, in military service in the
Spanish armies, for an indefinite number of years.   (3) Across the
Andes, presumably somewhere from the north of Chili, and so to
her residence with the Creole Senora somewhere at the eastern foot
of the Andes in what is now La Plata, but was then part of Peru.
(4) At Tucuman in that part of Peru; thence to La Plata or
Chuquisaca; thence to La Paz; thence to Cuzco, where her sex
was discovered and her game was at an end; and so finally to
Lima, where she was nearer her original starting-point of Paita
than she had been yet in all her long previous circuit from it, and
whence she was to be shipped back to Spain.—M.

25.—*St Sebastian is finally Checkmated.*

Yes, at length the warrior lady, the blooming cornet—this nun that is so martial, this dragoon that is so lovely—must visit again the home of her childhood, which now for seventeen years she has not seen.[1] All Spain, Portugal, Italy, rang with her adventures. Spain, from north to south, was frantic with desire to behold her fiery child, whose girlish romance, whose patriotic heroism, electrified the national imagination. The King of Spain must kiss his *faithful* daughter, that would not suffer his banner to see dishonour. The Pope must kiss his *wandering* daughter, that henceforwards will be a lamb travelling back into the Christian fold. Potentates so great as these, when *they* speak words of love, do not speak in vain. All was forgiven; the sacrilege, the bloodshed, the flight, and the scorn of St Sebastian's (consequently of St Peter's) keys; the pardons were made out, were signed, were sealed; and the chanceries of earth were satisfied.

Ah! what a day of sorrow and of joy was *that* one day, in the first week of November, 1624, when the returning Kate drew near to the shore of Andalusia; when descending into the ship's barge, she was rowed to the piers of Cadiz by bargemen in the

[1] These seventeen years had brought her, if the data are correct, from 1608, when she landed in South America at Paita a girl of seventeen, to 1624, when she embarked on her return voyage to Spain from Lima, at the age of thirty-three.—M.

royal liveries ; when she saw every ship, street, house, convent, church, crowded, as if on some mighty day of judgment, with human faces, with men, with women, with children, all bending the lights of their flashing eyes upon herself !   Forty myriads of people had gathered in Cadiz alone.   All Andalusia had turned out to receive her.[1]   Ah ! what joy for *her*, if she had not looked back to the Andes, to their dreadful summits, and their more dreadful feet.   Ah ! what sorrow, if she had not been forced by music, and endless banners, and the triumphant jubilations of her countrymen, to turn away from the Andes, and to fix her thoughts for the moment upon that glad tumultuous shore which she approached.

Upon this shore stood, ready to receive her, in front of all this mighty crowd, the Prime Minister of Spain, that same Condé Olivarez,[2] who but one year before had been so haughty and so defying to our haughty and defying Duke of Buckingham.   But a year ago the Prince of Wales had been in Spain, seeking a Spanish bride, and he also was welcomed with triumph and great joy ;[3] but not with the

---

[1] The precise day of this reception of Catalina at Cadiz on her return from the New World is given as 1st November 1624 in other documents. —M.

[2] Olivarez was Prime Minister in Spain from 1621 to 1643. —M.

[3] It was in February 1622-3 that James I. of England despatched his heir-apparent, Prince Charles, afterwards Charles I., to Spain, under the escort of the splendid royal favourite, George Villiers, Marquis of Buckingham, on the famous business of the Spanish match, — *i.e.*, for the conclusion of the long pending

hundredth part of that enthusiasm which now met the returning nun. And Olivarez, that had spoken so roughly to the English duke, to *her* "was sweet as summer."[1] Through endless crowds of welcoming compatriots he conducted her to the king. The king folded her in his arms, and could never be satisfied with listening to her. He sent for her continually to his presence; he delighted in her conversation, so new, so natural, so spirited; he settled a pension upon her (at that time of unprecedented amount); and by *his* desire, because the year 1625 was a year of jubilee,[2] she departed in a few months from

negotiations for a marriage between the Prince and the Spanish Infanta, daughter of the late Philip III. of Spain, and sister of Philip IV. The Prince and Buckingham remained at the Spanish Court some months,—the Prince eager for the match, but Buckingham's attitude in the matter becoming that of obstruction and of open quarrel with the Spanish officials. In September 1623 the two were back in England, reporting that they had been duped; and, greatly to the delight of the English people, the Spanish match business, and all friendly relations with Roman Catholic Spain were at an end. Buckingham had been raised to the dignity of Duke during his absence.—M.

[1] Griffith in Shakspere, when vindicating, in that immortal scene with Queen Catherine, Cardinal Wolsey.

[2] "*A year of jubilee:*"—This is an institution of the Roman Catholic Church, dating from 1300, when, by a bull of Pope Boniface VIII., a plenary indulgence was granted to all pilgrims who visited Rome in that year, and complied with certain other conditions. It was then intended that the festival should be repeated every hundredth year; but the interval was afterwards abridged to fifty years, and latterly, with changed conditions, to twenty-five years. The jubilee of 1625 was the seventh on the twenty-five years' system.—M.

Madrid to Rome. She went through Barcelona;
there and everywhere welcomed as the lady whom
the king delighted to honour. She travelled to
Rome, and all doors flew open to receive her. She
was presented to his Holiness, with letters from his
most Catholic majesty. But letters there needed
none. The Pope admired her as much as all before
had done. He caused her to recite all her adventures; and what he loved most in her account was
the sincere and sorrowing spirit in which she described herself as neither better nor worse than she
had been. Neither proud was Kate, nor sycophant-
ishly and falsely humble. Urban VIII. it was then
that filled the chair of St Peter.[1] He did not
neglect to raise his daughter's thoughts from earthly
things: he pointed her eyes to the clouds that
were floating in mighty volumes above the dome of
St Peter's Cathedral; he told her what the cathedral
had told her amongst the gorgeous clouds of the
Andes and the solemn vesper lights—how sweet a
thing, how divine a thing, it was for Christ's sake to
forgive all injuries; and how he trusted that no
more she would think of bloodshed; but that, if
again she should suffer wrongs, she would resign all
vindictive retaliation for them into the hands of God,
the final Avenger. I must also find time to mention,
although the press and the compositors are in a fury
at my delays, that the Pope, in his farewell audience
to his dear daughter, whom he was to see no more,

[1] Urban VIII. was Pope from 1623 to 1644.—M.

gave her a general license to wear henceforth in all countries—even in *partibus Infidelium*—a cavalry officer's dress—boots, spurs, sabre ; in fact, anything that she and the Horse Guards might agree upon. Consequently, reader, say not one word, nor suffer any tailor to say one word, or the ninth part of a word, against those Wellington trousers made in the chestnut forest ; for, understanding that the papal indulgence as to this point runs backwards as well as forwards, it sanctions equally those trousers in the forgotten rear, and all possible trousers yet to come.

From Rome, Kate returned to Spain. She even went to St Sebastian's—to the city, but—whether it was that her heart failed her or not—never to the convent. She roamed up and down ; everywhere she was welcome—everywhere an honoured guest ; but everywhere restless. The poor and humble never ceased from their admiration of her ; and amongst the rich and aristocratic of Spain, with the king at their head, Kate found especial love from two classes of men. The cardinals and bishops all doated upon her—as their daughter that was returning. The military men all doated upon her—as their sister that was retiring.

26.—*Farewell to the Daughter of St Sebastian !*

Now, at this moment, it has become necessary for me to close, but I allow to the reader one question

before laying down my pen.   Come now, reader, be
quick ; "look sharp ;" and ask what you *have* to ask ;
for in one minute and a-half I am going to write in
capitals the word FINIS ; after which, you know, I
am not at liberty to add a syllable.   It would be
shameful to 'do so ; since that word *Finis* enters
into a secret covenant with the reader that he shall
be molested no more with words, small or great.
Twenty to one, I guess what your question will be.
You desire to ask me, What became of Kate ?
What was her end ?

Ah, reader ! but, if I answer that question, you
will say I have *not* answered it.   If I tell you that
secret, you will say that the secret is still hidden.
Yet, because I have promised, and because you will
be angry if I do not, let me do my best.   After ten
years of restlessness in Spain, with thoughts always
turning back to the dreadful Andes, Kate heard of
an expedition on the point of sailing to Spanish
America.[1]   All soldiers knew *her*, so that she had
information of everything which stirred in camps.
Men of the highest military rank were going out
with the expedition ; but Kate was a sister everywhere privileged ; she was as much cherished and as
sacred, in the eyes of every brigade or *tertia*, as their
own regimental colours ; and every member of the

[1] This brings us to the year 1635, when Kate, after her ten
years or so of attempted rest and quasi-respectability in Spain or
elsewhere in Europe, had attained the forty-third year of her
age. —M.

staff, from the highest to the lowest, rejoiced to hear
that she would join their mess on board ship.   This
ship, with others, sailed; whither finally bound, I
really forget.   But, on reaching America, all the
expedition touched at *Vera Cruz*.[1]   Thither a great
crowd of the military went on shore.   The leading
officers made a separate party for the same purpose.
Their intention was, to have a gay, happy dinner,
after their long confinement to a ship, at the chief
hotel; and happy in perfection the dinner could not
be, unless Kate would consent to join it.   She, that
was ever kind to brother soldiers, agreed to do so.
She descended into the boat along with them, and in
twenty minutes the boat touched the shore.   All the
bevy of gay laughing officers, junior and senior, like
so many schoolboys let loose from school, jumped on
shore, and walked hastily, as their time was limited,
up to the hotel.   Arriving there, all turned round
in eagerness, saying, "Where is our dear Kate?"
Ah, yes, my dear Kate, at that solemn moment,
where, indeed, were *you*?   She had, beyond all doubt,
taken her seat in the boat: that was certain, though

---

[1] If De Quincey had not been here huddling up the conclusion
of his story for *Tait's Magazine* on pressure from the printers,
he would certainly have explained that Vera Cruz is not on that
western or Pacific shore of South America with which Kate had
already been familiar by her previous adventures, nor in any part
of South America at all, but is on the East or Atlantic side of
Spanish North America,—being, in fact, the chief port of Mexico,
and situated far within the Gulf of Mexico, about 190 miles from
the inland city of Mexico itself.—M.

nobody, in the general confusion, was certain of having seen her actually step ashore. The sea was searched for her—the forests were ransacked. But the sea did not give up its dead, if *there* indeed she lay ; and the forests made no answer to the sorrowing hearts which sought her amongst *them.* Have I never formed a conjecture of my own upon the mysterious fate which thus suddenly enveloped her, and hid her in darkness for ever ? Yes, I have. But it is a conjecture too dim and unsteady to be worth repeating. Her brother soldiers, that should naturally have had more materials for guessing than myself, were all lost in sorrowing perplexity, and could never arrive even at a plausible conjecture.[1]

That happened two hundred and twenty-one years ago ! And here is the brief upshot of all :—This nun sailed from Spain to Peru, and she found no rest for the sole of her foot. This nun sailed back from Peru to Spain, and she found no rest for the agitations of her heart. This nun sailed again from Spain to America, and she found—the rest which all of us find. But where it was, could never be made known to the father of Spanish camps, that sat in Madrid ; nor to Kate's spiritual father, that sat in Rome. Known it is to the great Father of all, that once whispered to Kate on the Andes ; but else it has been a secret for more than two centuries ; and to man it remains a secret for ever and ever !

[1] See Appended Note, *Original of De Quincey's Story of the Spanish Military Nun.*

POSTSCRIPT

THERE are some narratives, which, though pure fictions from first to last, counterfeit so vividly the air of grave realities, that, if deliberately offered for such, they would for a time impose upon everybody. In the opposite scale there are other narratives, which, whilst rigorously true, move amongst characters and scenes so remote from our ordinary experience, and through a state of society so favourable to an adventurous cast of incidents, that they would everywhere pass for romances, if severed from the documents which attest their fidelity to facts. In the former class stand the admirable novels of Defoe; and, on a lower range within the same category, the inimitable "Vicar of Wakefield;" upon which last novel, without at all designing it, I once became the author of the following instructive experiment. I had given a copy of this little novel to a beautiful girl of seventeen, the daughter of a 'statesman in Westmoreland, not designing any deception (nor so much as any concealment) with respect to the fictitious character of the incidents and of the actors in that famous tale. Mere accident it was that had intercepted those explanations as to the extent of fiction in these points which in this case it would have been so natural to make. Indeed, considering the exquisite verisimilitude of the work, meeting with such absolute inexperience in the reader, it was almost a duty to have made them. This duty, however, something had caused me to forget; and when next I saw the young mountaineer, I forgot that I *had* forgotten it. Consequently, at first I was perplexed by the unfaltering gravity with which my fair young friend spoke of Dr Primrose, of Sophia and her sister, of Squire Thornhill, etc., as real and probably living personages, who could sue and be sued. It appeared that this artless young rustic, who had never heard of novels and romances as a bare possibility amongst all the shameless devices of London swindlers, had read with religious fidelity every word of this tale, so thoroughly life-like, surrendering her perfect faith and loving sympathy to the different persons in the tale and the natural distresses in which they are involved, without suspecting for a moment that, by so much as a breathing of exaggeration or of embellishment, the pure gospel truth of the narrative could have been sullied. She listened in a kind of breathless stupor to my frank explanation—that not part only, but the whole, of this natural tale was a pure invention. Scorn and indignation flashed from her eyes. She regarded herself as one who had been hoaxed and swindled; begged me to take back the book; and never again, to the end of her life, could endure to look into the book, or to be reminded of that criminal imposture which Dr Oliver Goldsmith had practised upon her youthful credulity.

In that case, a book altogether fabulous, and not meaning to offer itself for anything else, had been read as genuine history. Here, on the other hand, the adventures of the Spanish Nun, which, in every detail of time and place have since been sifted and authenticated, stood a good chance at one period of being classed as the most lawless of romances. It is, indeed, undeniable—and this arises as a natural result from the bold adventurous character of the heroine, and from the unsettled state of society at that period in Spanish America—that a reader, the most credulous, would at times be startled with doubts upon what seems so unvarying a tenor of danger and lawless violence. But, on the other hand, it is also undeniable that a reader, the most obstinately sceptical, would be equally startled in the very opposite direction, on remarking that the incidents are far from being such as a romance-writer would have been likely to invent; since, if striking, tragic, and even appalling, they are at times repulsive. And it seems evident, that, once putting himself to the cost of a wholesale fiction, the writer would have used his privilege more freely for his own advantage. Whereas the author of these memoirs clearly writes under the coercion and restraint of a notorious reality, that would not suffer him to ignore or to modify the leading facts. Then, as to the objection that few people or none have an experience presenting such

uniformity of perilous adventure, a little closer attention shows that the experience in this case is *not*
uniform; and so far otherwise, that a period of
several years in Kate's South American life is confessedly suppressed; and on no other ground whatever, than that this long parenthesis is *not* adventurous, not essentially differing from the monotonous
character of ordinary Spanish life.

Suppose the case, therefore, that Kate's memoirs
had been thrown upon the world with no vouchers
for their authenticity beyond such internal presump-
tions as would have occurred to thoughtful readers,
when reviewing the entire succession of incidents, I
am of opinion that the person best qualified by legal
experience to judge of evidence would finally have
pronounced a favourable award; since it is easy to
understand, that in a world so vast as the Peru, the
Mexico, the Chili, of Spaniards during the first quarter
of the seventeenth century, and under the slender modification of Indian manners as yet effected by the papal
Christianisation of these countries, and in the neighbourhood of a river-system so awful—of a mountain-
system so unheard-of in Europe,—there would probably,
by blind, unconscious sympathy, grow up a tendency
to lawless and gigantesque ideals of adventurous life;
under which, united with the duelling code of Europe,
many things would become trivial and commonplace
experiences that to us home-bred English ("*qui musas
colimus severiores*") seem monstrous and revolting.

Left, therefore, to itself, *my* belief is, that the

story of the Military Nun would have prevailed
finally against the demurs of the sceptics.   However,
in the meantime, all such demurs were suddenly and
officially silenced for ever.   Soon after the publication
of Kate's memoirs, in what you may call an early
stage of her *literary* career, though two centuries after
her *personal* career had closed, a regular controversy
arose upon the degree of credit due to these extraordinary confessions (such they may be called) of the
poor conscience-haunted nun.   Whether these in
Kate's original MS. were entitled "Autobiographic
Sketches," or "Selections Grave and Gay," from the
military experiences of a Nun, or possibly "The Confessions of a Biscayan Fire-Eater," is more than I
know.   No matter : confessions they were ; and confessions that, when at length published, were absolutely mobbed and hustled by a gang of misbelieving
(*i.e., miscreant*) critics.   And this fact is most remarkable, that the person who originally headed the
incredulous party—viz., Senor De Ferrer, a learned
Castilian—was the very same who finally authenticated, by *documentary* evidence, the extraordinary
narrative in those parts which had most of all invited
scepticism.   The progress of the dispute threw the
decision at length upon the archives of the Spanish
Marine.   Those for the southern ports of Spain had
been transferred, I believe, from Cadiz and St Lucar
to Seville ; chiefly, perhaps, through the confusions
incident to the two French invasions of Spain in our
own day (1st, that under Napoleon ; 2dly, that under

the Duc d'Angoulême.)   Amongst these archives, subsequently amongst those of Cuzco in South America; 3dly, amongst the records of some royal courts in Madrid; 4thly, by collateral proof from the Papal Chancery; 5thly, from Barcelona—have been drawn together ample attestations of all the incidents recorded by Kate.   The elopement from St Sebastian's, the doubling of Cape Horn, the shipwreck on the coast of Peru, the rescue of the royal banner from the Indians of Chili, the fatal duel in the dark, the astonishing passage of the Andes, the tragical scenes at Tucuman and Cuzco, the return to Spain in obedience to a royal and a papal summons, the visit to Rome and the interview with the pope; finally, the return to South America, and the mysterious disappearance at Vera Cruz, upon which no light was ever thrown—all these capital heads of the narrative have been established beyond the reach of scepticism : and, in consequence, the story was soon after adopted as historically established, and was reported at length by journals of the highest credit in Spain and Germany, and by a Parisian journal so cautious and so distinguished for its ability as the "Revue des Deux Mondes."   I must not leave the impression upon my readers, that this complex body of documentary evidences has been searched and appraised by myself. Frankly I acknowledge that, on the sole occasion when any opportunity offered itself for such a labour, I shrank from it as too fatiguing—and also as superfluous; since, if the proofs had satisfied the compatriots of Catalina, who came to the investigation with hostile feelings of partisanship, and not dissembling their incredulity, armed also (and in Mr De Ferrer's case conspicuously armed) with the appropriate learning for giving effect to this incredulity—it could not become a stranger to suppose himself qualified for disturbing a judgment that had been so deliberately delivered. Such a tribunal of native Spaniards being satisfied, there was no further opening for demur. The ratification of poor Kate's memoirs is now therefore to be understood as absolute, and without reserve.[1]

This being stated—viz., such an attestation from competent authorities to the truth of Kate's narrative, as may save all readers from my fair Westmoreland friend's disaster—it remains to give such an answer, as without further research *can* be given, to a question pretty sure of arising in all reflective readers' thoughts—viz., Does there anywhere survive a portrait of Kate? I answer—and it would be both mortifying and perplexing if I could *not*—*Yes.* One such portrait there is confessedly; and seven years ago this was to be found at Aix-la-Chapelle, in the collection of Herr Sempeller. The name of the artist I am not able to report; neither can I say whether Herr Sempeller's collection still remains intact, and remains at Aix-la-Chapelle.

But inevitably to most readers, who review the circumstances of a case so extraordinary, it will occur,

---

[1] See Appended Note, *Original of De Quincey's Story of the Spanish Military Nun.*—M.

that beyond a doubt *many* portraits of the adventurous nun must have been executed.   To have
affronted the wrath of the Inquisition, and to have
survived such an audacity, would of itself be enough
to found a title for the martial nun to a national interest.   It is true that Kate had not taken the veil ;
she had stopped short of the deadliest crime known
to the Inquisition ; but still her transgressions were
such as to require a special indulgence ; and this indulgence was granted by a pope to the intercession
of a king—the greatest then reigning.   It was a
favour that could not have been asked by any greater
man in this world, nor granted by any less.   Had no
other distinction settled upon Kate, this would have
been enough to fix the gaze of her own nation.   But
her whole life constituted Kate's supreme distinction.
There can be no doubt, therefore, that, from the year
1624 (*i.e.*, the last year of our James I.), she became
the object of an admiration in her own country that
was almost idolatrous.   And this admiration was not
of a kind that rested upon any partisan-schism
amongst her countrymen.   So long as it was kept
alive by her bodily presence amongst them, it was an
admiration equally aristocratic and popular, shared
alike by the rich and the poor—by the lofty and the
humble.   Great, therefore, would be the demand for
her portrait.   There is a tradition that Velasquez,
who had in 1623 executed a portrait of Charles I.
(then Prince of Wales), was amongst those who in
the three or four following years ministered to this

demand.[1] It is believed also, that in travelling from Genoa and Florence to Rome, she sat to various artists, in order to meet the interest about herself already rising amongst the cardinals and other dignitaries of the Romish Church. It is probable, therefore, that numerous pictures of Kate are yet lurking both in Spain and Italy, but not known as such. For, as the public consideration granted to her had grown out of merits and qualities purely personal, and were kept alive by no local or family memorials rooted in the land, or surviving herself, it was inevitable that, as soon as she herself died, all identification of her portraits would perish : and the portraits would thenceforwards be confounded with the similar memorials, past all numbering, which every year accumulates as the wrecks from household remembrances of generations that are passing or passed, that are fading or faded, that are dying or buried. It is well, therefore, amongst so many irrecoverable ruins, that, in the portrait at Aix-la-Chapelle, we still possess one undoubted representation (and therefore in some degree a means for identifying *other* representations) of a female so memorably adorned by nature ; gifted with capacities so unparalleled both of doing and suffering ; who lived a life so stormy, and perished by a fate so unsearchably mysterious.

[1] Velasquez, b. 1599, d. 1660. His great celebrity may be said to date from 1623, when, on his second visit to Madrid at the age of twenty-four, he painted portraits of Philip IV., Olivarez, and other Spanish magnates, besides that of the English Prince Charles mentioned in the text,—which last, unfortunately, has been lost.—M.

APPENDED NOTE

ORIGINAL OF DE QUINCEY'S STORY OF THE SPANISH MILITARY NUN

IT was a bad habit of De Quincey to be secretive when there was little need for being so ; and he would have saved himself trouble if, instead of mystifying his readers with the elaborate explanations in his Postscript, he had simply informed them that his story of the Spanish Military Nun was a cooked, and spiced, and De Quinceyfied (which means electrified and glorified) translation from the French.

Such, at all events, is the fact.   In the *Revue des Deux Mondes* of 15th February 1847, or two months and a half before the publication of the first instalment of De Quincey's story in *Tait's Edinburgh Magazine,* there appeared, under the title "Catalina de Erauso," an article of forty-nine pages, signed "Alexis de Valon," and containing the same tissue of adventures which De Quincey thought it worth his while to turn into English.   The writer of that article announced, near the beginning of it, that he took his facts from autobiographic notes in the old Castilian tongue left by the heroine herself, and bearing the title *Historia de la Monja Alferez, Donna Catalina de Erauso, escrita por ella misma* ("History of the Nun-Lieutenant, Donna Catalina de Erauso, written by herself") ; and the last section of the article was devoted to a farther account of what the author called "the history of this history" ("*l'histoire de cette histoire*").   According to this account, a certain M. de Ferrer at one time a Spanish political refugee in France, having, in his readings in Spanish records, come upon some glowing mention of the exploits of the Nun of St. Sebastian, and feeling the more interested because he was himself a native of the province to which the Nun belonged, remembered that he had heard of her original manuscript memoirs as one of the preserved curiosities in the Royal Library of Seville, and of a copy of them as existing among the archives of the Office of Marine at Madrid. Having made inquiries and obtained a copy for his own use, he was sceptical at first as to the authenticity of the memoirs, the copyist having written *Araujo* for *Erauso*, and M. de Ferrer not recognising *Araujo* as ever having been the name of any family in his province. When the error was rectified, however, all became plain. On writing to St. Sebastian, M. de Ferrer obtained the most definite testimony, from parish registers, the convent registers, etc., as to the existence of a Catalina de Erauso in that town at the time alleged, and as to the accuracy of the particulars in the earlier part of her reputed autobiography. Research among the Government records at Seville, especially those relating to the Spanish American Colonies in the seventeenth century, having proved the substantial accuracy of all the rest, and traces having been found of a portrait of the Nun as having once existed in Rome, and an actual portrait of her having been discovered at Aix-la-Chapelle, M. de Ferrer no longer hesitated. "He published, " for himself and his friends, the manuscript of Catalina. This " was just before the Revolution of July [1830], and it was an " ill-chosen time. The political excitement whirled away the " unfortunate book, which disappeared as mysteriously as the " heroine whose history it related. It can hardly have been " seen by more than a few rare amateurs, and it has passed now " into the state of a bibliographical curiosity." M. Alexis de Valon, the writer in the *Revue des Deux Mondes* for February 1847, we are to assume, had a copy then before him, and founded his article upon it. The article, indeed, contains a description of the literary style of Catalina's memoirs of herself, and a criticism of M. de Ferrer's attached editorial comments.

Of the memoirs themselves M. Alexis de Valon gives no very

favourable opinion. "The original memoirs of Catalina," he writes, "are, it is my duty to say, clumsily written. They are " less a narrative than matter for a narrative; they are a dry " and short summary, without animation and without life. " One feels that the hand which held the pen had been " hardened by holding a sword; and I find in the very inex- " perience of the narrator the best guarantee of her veracity. " If a fiction, these memoirs would have been wholly different; " a writer of fiction would have done better or otherwise. The " style of Catalina is rude, coarse, often obscure, and sometimes " of an untranslateable frankness, verging on impudence. On " the whole, the narrative, though Spanish, is far from being " orthodox. If a scrupulous reader should find it even deplorable " from the point of view of morality, I should be noway sur- " prised; plenty of rogues have been hanged who were infinitely " more respectable characters, I fancy, than the Nun-Lieutenant. " Her faults, however, great as they may have been, do not " inspire disgust. Hers is a savage, self-abandoned nature, " which has a conscience neither for good nor for evil. Bred " up to the age of fifteen by ignorant *religieuses*, abandoned " from that time to all the hazards of a wandering life, all the " instincts of a vulgar nature, Catalina could learn no other " morality than that of the highways, camps, and life on board " ship. She evidently did not know what she did; she herself " tells, without malice, without bragging, without even think- " ing of excusing herself, of actions of hers such as now-a-days " would come before an assize-court. She robs with candour, " worthy woman, and she kills with *naïveté*. For her a man's " death is a very small thing." So much for the criticism of the memoirs themselves and their author by the writer in the *Revue des Deux Mondes*. His criticism on their editor, M. de Ferrer, is good-natured on the whole, but rather sarcastic in parts. M. de Ferrer's painstaking research is praised; but he is quizzed for his over-enthusiasm for his subject, and for having written about a person who, at the best, was but a man-woman adventuress of the seventeenth century, entitled to the same kind of interest as that which attached to the famous Chevalier d'Éon of the eighteenth, as if there had been the makings in her of a Saint Theresa, an Aspasia, or a Madame de Stael.—One passage quoted from M. de Ferrer, purporting to be a description of Catalina's personal appearance in her more advanced life by a contemporary Spanish historian, may be worth re-quotation here :—"She is of large size for a woman," reports this authority, "without, however, having the stature of a fine man. She " has no throat or bust to speak of. Her figure is neither good " nor bad. Her eyes are black, brilliant, and well-opened ; " and her features have been changed more by the fatigues she " has undergone than by age. She has black hair, short like " that of a man, and pommaded in the fashion. She is dressed " like a Spaniard. Her gait is elegant and light, and she " carries a sword well. She has a martial air. Her hands " alone have a something feminine about them, and this more " in their *pose* than in their shape. Finally, her upper lip is " covered with a slight brown down, which, without being " actually a moustache, yet gives a certain virile aspect to her " physiognomy."—All this is from the last section of the article by M. Alexis de Valon in the *Revue des Deux Mondes,* the whole of the preceding forty-five pages of the article having consisted of a pretty skilful and vivid narrative of the adventures of Donna Catalina, as the writer had been able to conceive them from the rude autobiographic original, with the aid of M. de Ferrer's editorial elucidations. How far he adhered to the original, and how far he dressed it up into a romance suitable for modern French tastes, no one can tell who has not seen M. de Ferrer's own book.

De Quincey, I am pretty sure, had never seen that book. There is not, so far as I know, a copy of it in Edinburgh now ; and there can hardly have been a copy of it in Edinburgh in De Quincey's time. His sole or chief authority, I believe, when he wrote his paper for *Tait's Magazine,* was the previous paper by M. Alexis de Valon in the *Revue des Deux Mondes.* But it is fair to give his own account of the matter. In an introductory paragraph prefixed to the first instalment of the story in *Tait* for May 1847, and vouching for its authenticity, he wrote :—

" No memoir exists, or personal biography, that is so trebly
" authenticated by proofs and attestations, direct and collateral.
" From the archives of the Royal Marine at Seville, from the
" autobiography of the heroine, from contemporary chroniclers,
" and from several official sources scattered in and out of Spain,
" some of them ecclesiastical, the amplest proofs have been
" drawn, and may yet be greatly extended, of the extraordinary
" events here recorded.   M. de Ferrer, a Spaniard of much
" research, and originally incredulous as to the facts, published
" about seventeen years ago a selection from the leading docu-
" ments, accompanied by his *palinode* as to their accuracy.   His
" materials have been since used for the basis of more than one
" narrative, not inaccurate, in French, German, and Spanish
" journals of high authority.   It is seldom that the French
" writers err by prolixity.   They have done so in this case.   The
" present narrative, which contains no one sentence derived
" from any foreign one, has the great advantage of close com-
" pression ; my own pages, after equating the size, being as 1
" to 3 of the shortest continental form.   In the mode of narra-
" tion I am vain enough to flatter myself that the reader will
" find little reason to hesitate between us.   Mine will, at least,
" weary nobody ; which is more than can be always said for
" the continental versions."—O, Mr. De Quincey ! your own
complete paper in *Tait's Magazine* is decidedly longer than its
predecessor in the *Revue des Deux Mondes ;* and, whatever
continental versions of the story of Donna Catalina, in German
or Spanish journals, may have preceded that one, and whatever
others may have come out in French journals in the interval of
two months between the publication of that one and the preparation of your own, you were bound, in my opinion, to mention that one in particular !—In the reprint of 1854 he does
mention it.   In that reprint the Introductory Paragraph of
1847 was cancelled, and what had to be told of "the history of
the history" was relegated to a more formal *Postscript.*   On
referring to that Postscript, printed a few pages back, the reader
will find De Quincey playing with the fact that the "Confessions of a Biscayan Fire-Eater" had some special interest for

himself, as the author of the "Confessions of an English Opium-Eater," and then restating in detail the case for the authenticity of Kate's memoirs. There had been a controversy on the subject, he says, after their first publication ; but, the researches of De Ferrer and others having been conclusive, the narrative had at last been adopted as "historically established," and had been "reported at length by journals of the highest credit " in Spain and Germany, and by a Parisian journal so cautious " and so distinguished for its ability as the *Revue des Deux* " *Mondes.*" Better late than never, though still not up to the proper mark ! What follows is more significant. "I must not " leave the impression upon my readers," he says, "that this " complex body of documentary evidence has been searched " and appraised by myself. Frankly I acknowledge that, on " the sole occasion when any opportunity offered itself for such " a labour, I shrank from it as too fatiguing." This is De Quincey's way of saying that, to as late as 1854, he had never had an opportunity of examining the original of Kate's memoirs in M. de Ferrer's book, and had therefore reprinted his story of her adventures much as it stood in his Magazine papers of 1847.

My own final impression of the whole matter is that De Quincey, having read the article in the *Revue des Deux Mondes* in February or March 1847, said to himself, "This is a capital subject ; I will do it over again," and that there and then,— the prospect of thirty or forty· guineas for a paper spreading over two or three numbers acting then as a sufficient allurement for one of the most exquisite minds that ever toiled in periodical literature,—·he *proceeded* to do it over again, with little or nothing else than the article in the *Revue des Deux Mondes* for his material.

Incident for incident, situation for situation, from beginning to end, the story in the two papers is one and the same. Necessarily also the phraseology of the one corresponds to that of the other to a great extent throughout, though here De Quincey's craft in language enabled him to make good his assertion that *his* narrative contained "no one sentence derived from any foreign one." As an example at once of the identity of substance and the diversity of expression take that ghastly scene of the discovery by Kate and her two companions, as they were crossing the Andes, of the frozen body of a hunter, gun in hand, seated on a rock in one of the high snowy solitudes :—

Revue des Deux Mondes.	*De Quincey.*
Les voyageurs étaient arrivés à un endroit où s'élèvent comme des vagues sombres, au milieu des neiges, d'enormes blocs de rochers. L'héroïne chercha vainement, à l'abri de ces pierres, quelques-uns de ces buissons qui leur avaient permis parfois d'allumer un petit foyer ; toute végétation avait disparu ; à ces hauteurs, l'homme seul a droit de vivre. Alors, ne sachant que faire ni quel parti prendre, elle imagina, pour mieux s'orienter, de grimper par un des blocs de pierre d'où son regard embrasserait un horizon plus étendu. Elle se hissa péniblement, atteignit le sommet le plus élevé de ces monticules et jeta les yeux autour d'elle. Tout à coup elle poussa un cri et courut de nouveau vers ses compagnons. Assis et appuyé contre un rocher voisin, un homme lui était apparu ! Quel pouvait être ce voyageur ? C'était un libérateur peut-être, et sans doute il n'était pas seul ! L'annonce de ce secours inattendu rendit du courage aux deux moribonds ; ils se levèrent et suivirent Catalina. Arrivés à	They had reached a billowy scene of rocky masses, large and small, looking shockingly black on their perpendicular sides as they rose out of the vast snowy expanse. Upon the highest of these that was accessible, Kate mounted to look around her, and she saw—oh, rapture at such an hour !—a man sitting on a shelf of rock, with a gun by his side. Joyously she shouted to her comrades, and ran down to communicate the good news. Here was a sportsman, watching, perhaps, for an eagle ; and now they would have relief. One man's cheek kindled with the hectic of sudden joy, and he rose eagerly to march. The other was fast sinking under the fatal sleep that frost sends before herself as her merciful minister of death ; but, hearing in his dream the tidings of relief, and assisted by his friends, he also staggeringly arose. It could not be three minutes' walk, Kate thought, to the station of the sportsman. That thought supported them all. Under Kate's guidance, who had taken a sailor's glance at the

vingt pas de l'endroit désigné, ils aperçurent l'étranger, qui n'avait pas bougé de place. Il était assis, à demi caché derrière une pointe de rocher, dans la position d'un tirailleur qui guette ou d'un chasseur à l'affût.—Qui vive ! cria Catalina en soulevant son arquebuse avec effort. L'étranger ne répondit pas, ne bougea pas et ne parut pas avoir entendu — Qui vive ! répéta Catalina. Cette seconde sommation fut aussi vaine que la première. Les trois voyageurs s'avancèrent lentement, avec précaution, en longeant le rocher, et arrivèrent enfin à deux pas du guetteur silencieux qui leur tournait le dos. —Eh ! l'ami, dit Catalina en lui frappant sur l'épaule, dormez-vous ?—Mais à peine avait-elle prononcé ces mots, qu'elle recula de trois pas en pâlissant d'épouvante. Au toucher de Catalina, l'homme assis avait roulé sur la neige comme une masse inerte. C'était un cadavre gelé, raide comme une statue ; son visage était bleu et sa bouche entr'ouverte par un affreux sourire.

bearings, they soon unthreaded the labyrinth of rocks so far as to bring the man within view. He had not left his resting-place : their steps on the soundless snow, naturally, he could not hear ; and, as their road brought them upon him from the rear, still less could he see them. Kate hailed him ; but so keenly was he absorbed in some speculation, or in the object of his watching, that he took no notice of them, not even moving his head. Coming close behind him, Kate touched his shoulder, and said, "My friend, are you sleeping ?" Yes, he *was* sleeping—sleeping the sleep from which there is no awaking ; and, the slight touch of Kate having disturbed the equilibrium of the corpse, down it rolled on the snow : the frozen body rang like a hollow iron cylinder ; the face uppermost, and blue with mould, mouth open, teeth ghastly and bleaching in the frost, and a frightful grin upon the lips.

Throughout the whole of De Quincey's narrative there is this kind of parallelism with his original in the *Revue des Deux Mondes*, sometimes closer, but sometimes more lax. He had the art of De Quinceyfying whatever he borrowed ; and his SPANISH MILITARY NUN is, in reality, as we have already said, a De Quinceyfied translation from the French. But much is

involved in the word "De Quinceyfied." Not only are there
passages in which we see him throwing ironical side-glances at
the French original he is using, and refusing its version, or any
French version, of the facts and circumstances ; not only are
there digressions, in which De Quincey leaves the track of the
original altogether, to amuse himself and his readers for some
moments with some crank or whimsy before returning to it ;
but the key of playful wit in which he has set the whole narrative of the Nun's life and adventures from its very start in the
first few sentences, and the humour with which some of the
situations and the sketches of some of the characters are
suffused, are entirely De Quincey's.—Above all, the Catalina of
his story emerges as a much higher being than the Catalina of
the French original.   "I love this Kate, blood-stained as she
is," is one of his ejaculations at a point where he signifies his
difference from the French estimate of her ; and, if ever that wild
Spanish eccentric, that masculine nun-adventuress from Biscay,
with her black eyes and black hair, the tinge of brown down on
her upper lip, and the sword by her side, shall take permanent
hold of the imagination of those who read books, it will be
because her portrait, after having been several times attempted
by rougher hands, was repainted more sympathetically by this
greater artist.

   At the same time, M. Alexis de Valon deserves the credit of
having, in his fashion, told his story well. We have to go to
him, in fact, for the exact chronology of Kate's life.   Born in
1592, she escaped from the nunnery of St. Sebastian on the
18th of March 1607, when she was in her fifteenth year.   It
was in the following year that, after her intermediate adventures
in other Spanish towns, she embarked for Spanish America.
Her various adventures there extended over a period of sixteen
or seventeen years ; and, when she returned to Spain in November 1624, as the famous detected woman-soldier, she was thirty-
two years of age.   The decree for the pension bestowed upon her
by the Spanish King, Philip IV., and said to be still extant at
Seville, was signed in August 1625.   It was during the subsequent ten years of her vague residence in Spain and visits to

Italy that several likenesses of her were taken, and those observations of her personal appearance and habits were made which M. de Ferrer gathered up. She was forty-three years of age when, in the year 1635, she took that fatal voyage back to America which ended in her mysterious disappearance on a stormy night at the landing-place of Vera Cruz on the Mexican coast, when all the other passengers got safely ashore and were surprised that she was not among them. De Quincey had formed a conjecture of his own, he says, on the subject of this mysterious disappearance ; but, as he does not give it, we may quote that of her French biographer. "No need to say," M. Alexis de Valon writes, "that this mysterious disappearance "occasioned the most contradictory suppositions. Had Cata "lina, passionate for a return to a life of wandering, fled again "into the wilds? How then should no farther traces of her "have been discovered? Or, in the dark of that stormy night, "was she drowned in disembarking, no one observing the "accident? This opinion seems the most reasonable, and yet "her body was not found in the harbour. A shark, no doubt, "had swallowed Catalina : many persons more respectable "than she have had no other sepulture."

The reader will understand now who that Frenchman was whom De Quincey, without naming him, takes to task several times in the course of his story, and once so severely, for insufficient appreciation of the character of the Spanish Military Nun. He was M. Alexis de Valon, the author of that article in the *Revue des Deux Mondes* for 15th February 1847 of the matter of which De Quincey's story in *Tait's Edinburgh Magazine* for May, June, and July of the same year was a De Quinceyfied reproduction. "A De Quinceyfied reproduction," we repeat, but with the certainty that the reader will now perceive how important the "De Quinceyfying" was in that particular which we have already specified as the most essential and characteristic of all,—to wit the substitution throughout De Quincey's version of the story of a far higher and more poetical conception of the character of the wild Biscayan vagrant than had been ventured on in the French version. One can go back now with increased interest to that paragraph (pp. 62-66) where De Quincey, commenting on one passage of his French original, takes occasion to declare polemically, once for all, this fundamental difference of his own mood throughout the narrative from that of his unnamed French authority. "*Restée seule, l'aventurière se mit à genoux, se prit à pleurer et pria Dieu avec ferveur, sans doute pour la première fois de sa vie*" ("Left alone, the wanderer knelt down, took to weeping, and prayed to God with fervour, doubtless for the first time in her life"): so M. Alexis de Valon had written, in his description of Kate in her terrible solitude on the heights of the Andes after the deaths of her two companions. For the last phrase De Quincey is down upon him in an instant. He is "a Frenchman, who sadly misjudges Kate, looking at her through a Parisian opera-glass"; and, as for himself, not only does he believe that Kate had prayed many times before without mentioning the fact, but he will champion Kate in many other matters against all Frenchmen and all gainsayers whatever. It is here that he breaks out, "*I* love this Kate, bloodstained as she is," and that he proceeds to an ethical dissertation in her behalf, winding up with the assertion that "Kate *was* noble in many things," possessing "qualities that God loves either in man or woman," and with the wish that she were still alive "to give a punch on the head to that fellow who traduces her." This difference in De Quincey's conception of his heroine from that of the French critic of her Memoirs is maintained to the very end, but is perhaps nowhere more conspicuous than in the contrast between the two accounts of the mysterious disappearance of the heroine at last in the harbour of Vera Cruz. "Fell overboard, and probably eaten by a shark!" is substantially, as we have seen, our last glimpse of Kate in the French account of her life. De Quincey refuses a close so precise and so prosaic. He will not tell even his own hypothesis on the subject, but rises into the mystic, and leaves us there. "This nun sailed " again from Spain to America, and she found—the rest which " all of us find. But where it was, could never be made known " to the father of Spanish camps, that sat in Madrid ; nor to

" Kate's spiritual father, that sat in Rome. Known it is to the
" great Father of all, that once whispered to Kate on the Andes;
" but else it has been a secret for more than two centuries ; and
" to man it remains a secret for ever and ever ! "—The reader
may choose between the two moods, and the two versions of
Kate's story which they respectively inspire ; and all is subject,
of course, to any re-inquiry that may yet be moved, after M.
de Ferrer, into the historical authenticity of Kate's professed
Autobiography.—D. M.

THE ENGLISH MAIL-COACH

L

INTRODUCTION

IN October 1849 there appeared in Blackwood's Magazine an article entitled THE ENGLISH MAIL-COACH, OR THE GLORY OF MOTION. There was no intimation that it was to be continued ; but in December 1849 there followed in the same Magazine an article in two sections, headed by a paragraph explaining that it was by the author of the previous article in the October number, and was to be taken in connexion with that article. One of the sections of this second article was entitled THE VISION OF SUDDEN DEATH, and the other DREAM-FUGUE ON THE ABOVE THEME OF SUDDEN DEATH. When De Quincey revised the papers in 1854 for republication in Volume IV. of the Collective Edition of his writings, he brought the whole under the one general title of THE ENGLISH MAIL-COACH, dividing the text, as at present, into three sections or chapters, the first with the sub-title *The Glory of Motion,* the second with the sub-title *The Vision of Sudden Death,* and the third with the sub-title *Dream-Fugue, founded on the preceding theme of Sudden Death.* Great care was bestowed on the revision. Passages that had appeared in the magazine articles were omitted; new sentences were inserted; and the language was re-touched throughout. Running mention of some of the more important of these changes will be found in our footnotes; and it has been thought right, in one instance at least, to give, in the form of one of the longer Appended Notes,—as has been already done on similar occasion in one of the Appended Notes to the Essay ON MURDER CONSIDERED AS ONE OF THE FINE ARTS,—a specimen of the cancelled matter.   For, while the rule for an editor ought to be to keep his author's text always in the exact state in which the author himself finally left it, yet, the literary tastes and methods of such a writer as De Quincey being themselves a subject of legitimate study, there may be some advantage in exhibiting him now and then, if it can be done by some convenient aside, in his moments of self-criticism and self-correction.

Written in De Quincey's sixty-fifth year, THE ENGLISH MAIL-COACH is certainly one of his most original and striking productions.   It is interesting more particularly as an example of his power in a peculiar sort of English prose-writing, and indeed as an assertion of peculiar notions of his as to the liberties and capabilities of English Prose in general.

A very common, if not a prevalent, opinion is that Prose and Verse are separated from each other by a great gulf, and that their rights and functions are totally different.   Prose, it is thought, ought always to be simple, easy, lucid, and readable without much effort; and it ought to undertake therefore only such business as may consist in plain statements of fact, or arguments addressed to the cool understanding, or stern rebuke and invective, or the light fancies and witty and humorous pleasantries that are welcome in ordinary conversation, refraining from whatever transcends these bounds and would lift the mind into higher and grander moods. When the mind is profoundly moved, when deep feeling or powerful imagination takes possession of it, when the voice begins to swell with the consciousness of a greater and finer burden than usual, then, and on that indication, it is thought, one ought to leave the habitation of Prose altogether, put the key in one's pocket, walk across the bridge to the palace of Verse or Poetry on the other side of the gulf, and shut oneself up there till the phrenzy is over. This, or something like this, I repeat, is the common apprehension. There cannot, I believe, be a greater mistake, or one more disastrous to true literature. It may be confuted, in the first place, I believe, by observation of the actual state of the facts as respects the relations of Prose to Verse. Although, when rhythm is definitely regularised into metre, there is then set up a separation and gate of transit between Prose and Verse, marked mechanically in our typographic custom of printing verse in lines, yet in the very fact that Prose still retains within it that power of various rhythm out of which Verse had its origin, and which may be regarded as incipient Verse, or Verse not yet

restricted and regularised, is there not a guarantee
that the transition from Prose to Verse may be often
optional rather than necessary, and that much excellent
matter of those very kinds which most tempt to the
transition may be cogitated and expressed more freely,
and more effectively for some purposes, without making the transition?   Prose and Verse have a large
territory of property in common, and are best conceived, as I have ventured to suggest elsewhere, not as
two entirely separate spheres or circles, but as two
spheres or circles intersecting and interpenetrating
through extensive portions of both their bulks, and
absolutely disconnected only in two extreme and out-
standing crescents,—a left or lower crescent, let us
say, belonging to prose only, and a right or upper
crescent, let us say, belonging to verse only.   But,
further, how much of what is greatest in English
Literature we must sacrifice and condemn if the
opinion in question is accepted!   Not to go back on
such old prose-grandeurs as those of Milton, Sir
Thomas Browne, and Jeremy Taylor,—which, indeed,
the advocates of the opinion point to as corroborating
it, citing them as specimens of English prose yet lum-
bering and in chaos, and waiting for Dryden to set it
right and teach it syntax,—what shall we say of such
later prose eloquence as that of Burke, Chalmers, and
others of our orators, or of some of the splendours of
Carlyle and of Ruskin?   It would not be difficult to
prove, I think, that the very time in English Literary
History when English verse-literature itself most

languished, ceasing as it did to a great extent to be poetry at all, and possessed as it was to a great extent with the notion that anything very clever or pungent in verse is poetry, was that time when English Prose desisted most rigidly from its older liberty of poetic range and function, and that the visible restoration of something of that liberty to English Prose in our present century is part of the general literary movement which has also re-ennobled English Verse.

It is one of the most marked of De Quincey's distinctions, at all events, that he exemplified, and even systematically championed, the long disused liberty of English prose. He did this in two ways,—a minor way, and a major way.

The minor way consisted in his permitting himself, in any article whatever that he might be writing, to follow freely any suggestion of his fancy, and so to rise or fall in his style according to the variations of his matter. He could be simple and easy when he chose, short-sentenced and colloquial even to the verge of slang; but he protested against the cowardice of refusing an intricate, or pathetic, or sublime conception because it would necessitate longer exertion and wheel of wing for its adequate management and expression, higher involutions and harmonies of paragraph and sentence. He tells us how he once put the case to Charles Lamb, one of the defects of whose fine genius, he thought, was that it refused every opportunity of rising out of its habitual style of simple and witty grace, and shrank from every form of the continuous, the sustained, the elaborate. "If, "as a musician, as the leader of a mighty orchestra," he said to Lamb, "you had this theme offered you— "'Belshazzar the King gave a great feast to a "thousand of his lords,'—or this, 'And on a certain "day Marcus Cicero stood up, and in a set speech "rendered thanks to Caius Cæsar for Quintus Ligarius "pardoned and Marcus Marcellus restored'—surely "no man would deny that in such a case simplicity, "though in a passive sense not lawfully absent, must "stand aside as totally insufficient for the *positive* "part." Had De Quincey never written another word on the subject, these two examples, it seems to me, must by themselves win him the case with all who can understand their significance, and must kill dead any opposite notion that may have been in their minds.

The frequency with which De Quincey acted on this principle in his own writings, thinking nothing too high and rare for prose, and allowing himself the language of pomp and poetical and musical elevation whenever the theme or idea required it, was his minor way, as I have called it, of vindicating for Prose a liberty to the utmost of its will. And what was the major way? It was the express practice through a considerable portion of his writings of a special kind of Prose Art whose very characteristic it was that it burst and defied all tradition of the prosaic. He called it "impassioned prose"; and, in

the general preface to the Collective British Edition
of his writings, where he propounded a classification
of them as they had already appeared, or were
appearing, in the Collective American Edition, he
invited especial attention to this class of them,—illus-
trating "modes of impassioned prose" for which he
thought there had been hardly any precedent,—as
entitled, by their aim and conception, if not by
their execution, to far higher rank than the rest.
Without excluding from the class passages that
might be found scattered through his miscellaneous
writings, and indeed hinting that there might be an
inclusion of such, he cited as the most conspicuous
and sustained examples of the class his CONFESSIONS
OF AN ENGLISH OPIUM-EATER, and a special and still
unfinished series of fragments intended to be a sequel
to that work under the title of SUSPIRIA DE PRO-
FUNDIS ("SIGHS FROM THE DEPTHS"). It was by his
CONFESSIONS OF AN ENGLISH OPIUM-EATER that he
had first introduced himself to the public in 1821; and
he was employed in 1854, 1855, and 1856, in recasting
that work and enlarging it to the dimensions of one
whole volume of the Edition of his Collected Writings.
At what time he wrote the extant fragments which
he called SUSPIRIA DE PROFUNDIS is less certain;
they were probably written at different times; but
he had begun the publication of them in Blackwood's
Magazine in 1845, and he reports in 1856 that not
more than about a third of all that he meant to
include in that series had yet been printed. For

what *had* been printed of the SUSPIRIA he claimed, even more emphatically than for the CONFESSIONS, the character of being representative specimens of his peculiar style of "impassioned prose." But, in reality, in neither case is the 'designation "impassioned prose" the best that could have been chosen. When one refers to the writings themselves, one finds that they consist chiefly of renderings of the visionary scenery and visionary incidents that come in dreams, or might be supposed to come in dreams, and especially in the dreams of one in whom the faculty of dreaming had been developed to extraordinary and abnormal potency by some artificial influence, such as that of opium. Hence a fitter name than "impassioned prose" for this class of De Quincey's writings, on the whole, would be imaginative prose, prose phantasy, or, if the name had not been thrown unnecessarily into disrepute, prose-poetry. Why this last name has incurred disrepute of late it might be hard to say. Had not Bacon, when he defined poetry as "feigned history," expressly asserted that it might be "styled as well in prose as in verse"; and has not every subsequent English theorist on poetry worthy of any respect retained Bacon's axiom,—John Stuart Mill, for example, rejecting with disdain, as the very "vulgarest" of all definitions of poetry (such is his expression), "that which confounds poetry with metrical composition"? In a matter of mere naming, however, prejudice may be humoured; and, as "prose phantasy" means the same thing as "prose poetry," let "prose phantasy" be the name here adopted in substitution for De Quincey's own.

THE ENGLISH MAIL-COACH is a specimen of De Quincey in his mood and craft of prose phantasy. Originally, indeed, it belonged to the series of the SUSPIRIA DE PROFUNDIS. "This little paper, accord-" ing to my original intention, formed part," he tells us, "of the 'Suspiria de Profundis,' from which, for " a momentary purpose, I did not scruple to detach " it, and to publish it apart, as sufficiently intelligible " even when dislocated from its place in a larger "whole." Had Christopher North tired of the "Suspiria," or had he at least bargained with De Quincey that this should not be one of them, by representing to him that ordinary magazine readers would have difficulty in imagining how a story of an English Mail-Coach could be a sigh from the depths? All the same, it retained its original character, and *is* a prose phantasy. Through a considerable portion of the First Section of the paper, indeed, the writer plays with his subject amusingly, fetching up merely incidental memories of the old coaching days and their humours; and it is not till towards the close that he quite settles down to the task which he had prescribed for himself. Then it is that we are actually spirited back by De Quincey's descriptive genius to those old coaching days of which he has hitherto been only chatting, the days between Trafalgar and Waterloo, and that, seated with him on the box-seat of one of the fast mails from the

London Post Office, we accompany him on his night-
journey on one of the great English roads, our coach-
lamps burning, the horses at gallop, the wind blowing
in our faces, trees and hedges and hamlets rushing
past us in the darkness, our own lamp-lit course
through the darkness impetuous as that of a fiery
arrow, and broken only at the successive inns where
we stop to change horses, and where, having shouted
from the coach-top "Badajoz" or "Salamanca" or
the name of whatever has been that last victory the
news of which we are carrying, we descend to exchange
salutations and huzzas with the crowd of guests,
stable-men, and gathered villagers! Reading all this,
we do feel that we are reading a prose-poem, in
which De Quincey has fully redeemed the promise of
his double title to it in the phrases "*The Glory of
Motion*" and "*Going Down with Victory*," and has
made these phrases immortal. The Second Section
of the paper, entitled "*The Vision of Sudden Death*,"
and purporting to be a recollection of a strange coach-
accident at night on a solitary country road in one of
De Quincey's old journeys to the north, is equally a
prose-poem, but in a more tragic key, and with a
fascination of mournful horror in it that makes the
reader hold his breath. Then follows, in the Third
Section of the paper, that "*Dream-Fugue, founded on
the preceding theme of Sudden Death*," which winds up
the whole. To my mind it is the least satisfactory
portion of the whole, — fine word - music, indeed,
but failing in that quality of instant stroke on the

optical sense, and so of instant self-interpretation, which we have a right to expect in a prose phantasy, however mystic and subtle the meaning, and which is necessary to secure for such a thing a permanent place in the memory. Not the less it is a very notable part of the trilogy; and, as it is avowedly an exercise by De Quincey in that extreme kind of prose phantasy which seeks to reproduce in words the fluctu-ating visions of the world of dreams, and to connect them with the character and waking life of the dreamer, it possesses at least the value that one may attach to a daring literary experiment.

De Quincey was aware that his *Dream-Fugue* had not given entire satisfaction on its first appearance in *Blackwood* in 1849. Hence, when reprinting it in 1854, in Volume IV. of his Collected Works, together with the two preceding sections of THE ENGLISH MAIL-COACH, he inserted in the preface to that volume an explanation of this last and most peccant section of the paper, and of the relations of the three sections of the paper to each other. It would be unfair to him, and to readers of the paper now, to let it re-appear without that accompaniment. As, however, it presupposes acquaintance with the paper itself in all its three parts, and would hardly be intelligible with-out such acquaintance, it will be best to reserve it till after the whole has been read and has made its own impression. It will be given, therefore, in the last of our Appended Notes.—D. M.

THE ENGLISH MAIL-COACH

SECTION THE FIRST

THE GLORY OF MOTION

SOME twenty or more years before I matriculated at Oxford,[1] Mr Palmer, at that time M.P. for Bath, had accomplished two things, very hard to do on our little planet, the Earth, however cheap they may be held by eccentric people in comets—he had invented mail-coaches, and he had married the daughter[2] of a duke. He was, therefore, just twice as great a man as Galileo, who did certainly invent (or, which is the same thing,[3] discover)[4] the satellites of Jupiter, those

---

[1] As De Quincey went to Oxford in 1803, "twenty or more years" before that would be about 1780. The precise date of the first mail-coach journey from London on Palmer's system was, however, 24th August 1784.—See Appended Note, *Mr. Palmer and his Mail-Coach System.*—M.

[2] Lady Madeline Gordon.

[3] "*The same thing:*"—Thus, in the calendar of the Church Festivals, the discovery of the true cross (by Helen, the mother of Constantine) is recorded (and, one might think, with the express consciousness of sarcasm) as the *Invention* of the Cross.

[4] The original text in *Blackwood* ran thus,—"Galileo, who certainly invented (or *discovered*) the satellites of Jupiter"; and

very next things extant to mail-coaches in the two
capital pretensions of speed and keeping time, but,
on the other hand, who did *not* marry the daughter
of a duke.

These mail-coaches, as organised by Mr Palmer,
are entitled to a circumstantial notice from myself,
having had so large a share in developing the
anarchies of my subsequent dreams; an agency which
they accomplished, 1st, through velocity, at that time
unprecedented—for they first revealed the glory of
motion[1]; 2dly, through grand effects for the eye
between lamp-light and the darkness upon solitary
roads; 3dly, through animal beauty and power so
often displayed in the class of horses selected for this
mail service; 4thly, through the conscious presence
of a central intellect, that, in the midst of vast distances[2]—of storms, of darkness, of danger—overruled
all obstacles into one steady co-operation to a national
result.   For my own feeling, this post-office service
spoke as by some mighty orchestra, where a thousand
instruments, all disregarding each other, and so far in
danger of discord, yet all obedient as slaves to the

it was in the reprint of 1854 that the expression was changed into
its present form and the footnote "*The same thing*" added.—M.

[1] In *Blackwood* there were at this point these words, now
omitted,—"suggesting, at the same time, an under-sense, not
unpleasurable, of possible though indefinite danger."—M.

[2] "*Vast distances:*"—One case was familiar to mail-coach
travellers, where two mails in opposite directions, north and south,
starting at the same minute from points six hundred miles apart,
met almost constantly at a particular bridge which bisected the
total distance.

supreme *baton* of some great leader, terminate in a perfection of harmony like that of heart, brain, and lungs, in a healthy animal organisation. But, finally, that particular element in this whole combination which most impressed myself, and through which it is that to this hour Mr Palmer's mail-coach system tyrannises over my dreams by terror and terrific beauty, lay in the awful *political* mission which at that time it fulfilled. The mail-coach it was that distributed over the face of the land, like the opening of apocalyptic vials, the heart-shaking news of Trafalgar, of Salamanca, of Vittoria, of Waterloo.[1] These were the harvests that, in the grandeur of their reaping, redeemed the tears and blood in which they had been sown. Neither was the meanest peasant so much below the grandeur and the sorrow of the times as to confound battles such as these, which were gradually moulding the destinies of Christendom, with the vulgar conflicts of ordinary warfare, so often no more than gladiatorial trials of national prowess. The victories of England in this stupendous contest rose of themselves as natural *Te Deums* to heaven; and it was felt by the thoughtful that such victories, at such a crisis of general prostration, were not more beneficial to ourselves than finally to France, our enemy, and to the nations of all western or central Europe, through whose pusill-

---

[1] Battle of Trafalgar, Nelson's last victory, 21st October 1805; Battle of Salamanca, 22d July 1812; Battle of Vittoria, 21st June 1813; Battle of Waterloo, 18th June 1815.—M.

animity it was that the French domination had
prospered.

The mail-coach, as the national organ for publishing these mighty events thus diffusively influential,
became itself a spiritualised and glorified object to
an impassioned heart; and naturally, in the Oxford
of that day, *all* hearts were impassioned, as being all
(or nearly all) in *early* manhood. In most universities
there is one single college; in Oxford there were
five-and-twenty, all of which were peopled by young
men, the *élite* of their own generation; not boys, but
men; none under eighteen.[1] In some of these many
colleges, the custom permitted the student to keep
what are called "short terms;" that is, the four
terms of Michaelmas, Lent, Easter, and Act, were kept
by a residence, in the aggregate, of ninety-one days,
or thirteen weeks. Under this interrupted residence,
it was possible that a student might have a reason
for going down to his home four times in the year.
This made eight journeys to and fro. But, as these
homes lay dispersed through all the shires of the
island, and most of us disdained all coaches except
his majesty's mail, no city out of London could pretend to so extensive a connection with Mr Palmer's
establishment as Oxford. Three mails, at the least,

[1] This sentence originally appeared in *Blackwood* in this form,—
"There were, perhaps, of us gownsmen, two thousand *resident* in
Oxford, and dispersed through five-and-twenty colleges"; and
there was a footnote explaining that besides the *resident* students
and fellows there were many *non-residents*, keeping their names
on the books but coming to Oxford but occasionally.—M.

I remember as passing every day through Oxford, and benefiting by my personal patronage—viz., the Worcester, the Gloucester, and the Holyhead mail. Naturally, therefore, it became a point of some interest with us, whose journeys revolved[1] every six weeks on an average, to look a little into the executive details of the system. With some of these Mr Palmer had no concern ; they rested upon bye-laws enacted by posting-houses for their own benefit, and upon other bye-laws, equally stern, enacted by the inside passengers for the illustration of their own haughty exclusiveness. These last were of a nature to rouse our scorn, from which the transition was not very long to systematic mutiny. Up to this time, say 1804, or 1805 (the year of Trafalgar), it had been the fixed assumption of the four inside people (as an old tradition of all public carriages derived from the reign of Charles II.), that they, the illustrious quaternion, constituted a porcelain variety of the human race, whose dignity would have been compromised by exchanging one word of civility with the three miserable delf-ware outsides. Even to have kicked an outsider, might have been held to attaint the foot concerned in that operation ; so that, perhaps, it would have required an act of Parliament to restore its purity of blood. What words, then, could express the horror, and the sense of treason, in that case, which *had* happened, where all three outsides

---

[1] *Revolve* was a favourite word with De Quincey, in the sense of " return," " come back."—M.

(the trinity of Pariahs[1]) made a vain attempt to sit down at the same breakfast-table or dinner-table with the consecrated four? I myself witnessed such an attempt; and on that occasion a benevolent old gentleman endeavoured to soothe his three holy associates, by suggesting that, if the outsides were indicted for this criminal attempt at the next assizes, the court would regard it as a case of lunacy, or *delirium tremens*, rather than of treason. England owes much of her grandeur to the depth of the aristocratic element in her social composition, when pulling against her strong democracy. I am not the man to laugh at it. But sometimes, undoubtedly, it expressed itself in comic shapes. The course taken with the infatuated outsiders, in the particular attempt which I have noticed, was, that the waiter, beckoning them away from the privileged *salle-à-manger*, sang out, "This way, my good men," and then enticed these good men away to the kitchen. But that plan had not always answered. Sometimes, though rarely, cases occurred where the intruders, being stronger than usual, or more vicious than usual, resolutely refused to budge, and so far carried their point, as to have a separate table arranged for themselves in a corner of the general room. Yet, if an Indian screen could be found ample enough to plant them out from the very eyes of the high table,

---

[1] This word *Pariah* for "social outcast" (from the name of the lowest of the Hindoo ranks) was a favourite word in De Quincey's vocabulary, for which he often found very serious use.—M.

or *duis*, it then became possible to assume as a fiction
of law—that the three delf fellows, after all, were not
present. They could be ignored by the porcelain men,
under the maxim, that objects not appearing, and not
existing, are governed by the same logical construction.[1]

Such being, at that time, the usages of mail-
coaches, what was to be done by us of young Oxford?
We, the most aristocratic of people, who were addicted
to the practice of looking down superciliously even
upon the insides themselves as often very questionable
characters—were we, by voluntarily going outside, to
court indignities ?   If our dress and bearing sheltered
us, generally, from the suspicion of being "raff" (the
name at that period for "snobs," [2]) we really *were*
such constructively, by the place we assumed. If
we did not submit to the deep shadow of eclipse, we
entered at least the skirts of its penumbra. And
the analogy of theatres was valid against us, where
no man can complain of the annoyances incident to
the pit or gallery, having his instant remedy in paying
the higher price of the boxes.   But the soundness of
this analogy we disputed.   In the case of the theatre,
it cannot be pretended that the inferior situations
have any separate attractions, unless the pit may be

---

[1] *De non apparentibus, etc.* [*De non apparentibus et non exist-
entibus eadem est lex*].

[2] "*Snobs*," and its antithesis, "*nobs*," arose among the internal
factions of shoemakers perhaps ten years later. Possibly enough,
the terms may have existed much earlier ; but they were then first
made known, picturesquely and effectively, by a trial at some assizes
which happened to fix the public attention.

supposed to have an advantage for the purposes of
the critic or the dramatic reporter. But the critic
or reporter is a rarity. For most people, the sole
benefit is in the price. Now, on the contrary, the
outside of the mail had its own incommunicable
advantages.   These we could not forego.[1]   The
higher price we would willingly have paid, but not
the price connected with the condition of riding
inside ; which condition we pronounced insufferable.
The air, the freedom of prospect, the proximity to
the horses, the elevation of seat—these were what
we required ; but, above all, the certain anticipation
of purchasing occasional opportunities of driving.

Such was the difficulty which pressed us ; and
under the coercion of this difficulty, we instituted a
searching inquiry into the true quality and valuation
of the different apartments about the mail.   We
conducted this inquiry on metaphysical principles ;
and it was ascertained satisfactorily, that the roof of
the coach, which by some weak men had been called
the attics, and by some the garrets, was in reality the
drawing-room ; in which drawing-room the box was
the chief ottoman or sofa ; whilst it appeared that
the *inside*, which had been traditionally regarded as
the only room tenantable by gentlemen, was, in fact,
the coal-cellar in disguise.

Great wits jump. The very same idea had not
long before struck the celestial intellect of China.

---

[1] The word *forgo* again mis-spelt. See previous footnote, vol.
. p. 41.--M.

Amongst the presents carried out by our first embassy to that country was a state-coach. It had been specially selected as a personal gift by George III.; but the exact mode of using it was an intense mystery to Pekin. The ambassador, indeed (Lord Macartney), had made some imperfect explanations upon this point; but, as his excellency communicated these in a diplomatic whisper, at the very moment of his departure, the celestial intellect was very feebly illuminated, and it became necessary to call a cabinet council on the grand state question, "Where was the Emperor to sit?" The hammer-cloth happened to be unusually gorgeous; and partly on that consideration, but partly also because the box offered the most elevated seat, was nearest to the moon, and undeniably went foremost, it was resolved by acclamation that the box was the imperial throne, and for the scoundrel who drove, he might sit where he could find a perch. The horses, therefore, being harnessed, solemnly his imperial majesty ascended his new English throne under a flourish of trumpets, having the first lord of the treasury on his right hand, and the chief jester on his left. Pekin gloried in the spectacle; and in the whole flowery people, constructively present by representation, there was but one discontented person, and *that* was the coachman. This mutinous individual audaciously shouted, "Where am *I* to sit?" But the privy council, incensed by his disloyalty, unanimously opened the door, and kicked him into the inside. He had all the inside places to himself; but such is the rapacity of ambition, that he was still dissatisfied. "I say," he cried out in an extempore petition, addressed to the emperor through the window—"I say, how am I to catch hold of the reins?"—"Anyhow," was the imperial answer; "don't trouble *me*, man, in my glory. How catch the reins? Why, through the windows, through the keyholes—*any*how." Finally this contumacious coachman lengthened the check-strings into a sort of jury-reins, communicating with the horses; with these he drove as steadily as Pekin had any right to expect. The emperor returned after the briefest of circuits; he descended in great pomp from his throne, with the severest resolution never to remount it. A public thanksgiving was ordered for his majesty's happy escape from the disease of broken neck; and the state-coach was dedicated thenceforward as a votive offering to the god Fo, Fo—whom the learned more accurately called Fi, Fi.[1]

A revolution of this same Chinese character did young Oxford of that era effect in the constitution of mail-coach society. It was a perfect French revolution; and we had good reason to say, *ça ira*.[2] In fact, it soon became *too* popular. The "public"—

[1] This paragraph is a caricature of a story told in Staunton's Account of the Earl of Macartney's Embassy to China in 1792. —M.

[2] *Ça ira* ("This will do," "This is the go"), a proverb of the French Revolutionists when they were hanging the aristocrats in the streets, etc., and the burden of one of the popular revolutionary songs—"Ça ira, ça ira, ça ira."—M.

a well known character, particularly disagreeable, though slightly respectable, and notorious for affecting the chief seats in synagogues—had at first loudly opposed this revolution ; but when the opposition showed itself to be ineffectual, our disagreeable friend went into it with headlong zeal. At first it was a sort of race between us ; and, as the public is usually from thirty to fifty years old, naturally we of young Oxford, that averaged about twenty, had the advantage. Then the public took to bribing, giving fees to horse-keepers, etc., who hired out their persons as warming-pans on the box-seat. *That*, you know, was shocking to all moral sensibilities. Come to bribery, said we, and there is an end to all morality, Aristotle's, Zeno's, Cicero's, or anybody's. And, besides, of what use was it ? For *we* bribed also. And as our bribes, to those of the public, were as five shillings to six-pence, here again young Oxford had the advantage. But the contest was ruinous to the principles of the stables connected with the mails. This whole corporation was constantly bribed, rebribed, and often sur-rebribed ; a mail-coach yard was like the hustings in a contested election ; and a horse-keeper, ostler, or helper, was held by the philosophical at that time to be the most corrupt character in the nation.

There was an impression upon the public mind, natural enough from the continually augmenting velocity of the mail, but quite erroneous, that an outside seat on this class of carriages was a post of danger. On the contrary, I maintained that, if a man had become nervous from some gipsy prediction in his childhood, allocating to a particular moon now approaching some unknown danger, and he should inquire earnestly, "Whither can I fly, for shelter? Is a prison the safest retreat? or a lunatic hospital? or the British Museum?" I should have replied, "Oh, no; I'll tell you what to do. Take lodgings for the next forty days on the box of his majesty's mail. Nobody can touch you there. If it is by bills at ninety days after date that you are made unhappy—if noters and protesters are the sort of wretches whose astrological shadows darken the house of life—then note you what I vehemently protest—viz., that no matter though the sheriff and under-sheriff in every county should be running after you with his *posse*, touch a hair of your head he cannot whilst you keep house, and have your legal domicile on the box of the mail. It is felony to stop the mail; even the sheriff cannot do that. And an *extra* touch of the whip to the leaders (no great matter if it grazes the sheriff) at any time guarantees your safety." In fact, a bedroom in a quiet house seems a safe enough retreat, yet it is liable to its own notorious nuisances—to robbers by night, to rats, to fire. But the mail laughs at these terrors. To robbers, the answer is packed up and ready for delivery in the barrel of the guard's blunderbuss. Rats again! there *are* none about mail-coaches, any more than snakes in Von Troil's Iceland;[1] except, indeed, now

[1] "*Von Troil's Iceland:*"—The allusion is to a well-known chap-

and then a parliamentary rat, who always hides his shame in what I have shown to be the " coal cellar." And as to fire, I never knew but one in a mail-coach, which was in the Exeter mail, and caused by an obstinate sailor bound to Devonport. Jack, making light of the law and the law-giver that had set their faces against his offence, insisted on taking up a forbidden seat [1] in the rear of the roof, from which he could exchange his own yarns with those of the guard. No greater offence was then known to mail-

---

ter in Von Troil's work, entitled, " Concerning the Snakes of Iceland." The entire chapter consists of these six words—" *There are no snakes in Iceland.*"

[1] " *Forbidden seat :* "—The very sternest code of rules was enforced upon the mails by the Post-office. Throughout England, only three outsides were allowed, of whom one was to sit on the box, and the other two immediately behind the box ; none, under any pretext, to come near the guard ; an indispensable caution ; since else, under the guise of passenger, a robber might by any one of a thousand advantages—which sometimes are created, but always are favoured, by the animation of frank social intercourse— have disarmed the guard. Beyond the Scottish border, the regulation was so far relaxed as to allow of *four* outsides, but not relaxed at all as to the mode of placing them. One, as before, was seated on the box, and the other three on the front of the roof, with a determinate and ample separation from the little insulated chair of the guard. This relaxation was conceded by way of compensating to Scotland her disadvantages in point of population. England, by the superior density of her population, might always count upon a large fund of profits in the fractional trips of chance passengers riding for short distances of two or three stages. In Scotland, this chance counted for much less. And therefore, to make good the deficiency, Scotland was allowed a compensatory profit upon one *extra* passenger.

coaches; it was treason, it was *læsa majestas*, it was by tendency arson; and the ashes of Jack's pipe, falling amongst the straw of the hinder boot containing the mail-bags, raised a flame which (aided by the wind of our motion) threatened a revolution in the republic of letters. Yet even this left the sanctity of the box unviolated. In dignified repose, the coachman and myself sat on, resting with benign composure upon our knowledge that the fire would have to burn its way through four inside passengers before it could reach ourselves. I remarked to the coachman, with a quotation from Virgil's " Æneid " really too hackneyed—

> " Jam proximus ardet
> Ucalegon."

But, recollecting that the Virgilian part of the coachman's education might have been neglected, I interpreted so far as to say, that perhaps at that moment the flames were catching hold of our worthy brother and inside passenger, Ucalegon. The coachman made no answer, which is my own way when a stranger addresses me either in Syriac or in Coptic, but by his faint sceptical smile he seemed to insinuate that he knew better; for that Ucalegon, as it happened, was not in the way-bill, and therefore could not have been booked.

No dignity is perfect which does not at some point ally itself with the mysterious. The connection of the mail with the state and the executive government—a connection obvious, but yet not strictly defined—gave to the whole mail establishment an official grandeur which did us service on the roads, and invested us with seasonable terrors. Not the less impressive were those terrors, because their legal limits were imperfectly ascertained. Look at those turnpike gates; with what deferential hurry, with what an obedient start, they fly open at our approach! Look at that long line of carts and carters ahead, audaciously usurping the very crest of the road. Ah! traitors, they do not hear us as yet; but, as soon as the dreadful blast of our horn reaches them with proclamation of our approach, see with what frenzy of trepidation they fly to their horses' heads, and deprecate our wrath by the precipitation of their crane-neck quarterings. Treason they feel to be their crime; each individual carter feels himself under the ban of confiscation and attainder; his blood is attainted through six generations; and nothing is wanting but the headsman and his axe, the block and the saw-dust, to close up the vista of his horrors. What! shall it be within benefit of clergy to delay the king's message on the high road? —to interrupt the great respirations, ebb and flood, *systole* and *diastole*, of the national intercourse?—to endanger the safety of tidings, running day and night between all nations and languages? Or can it be fancied, amongst the weakest of men, that the bodies of the criminals will be given up to their widows for Christian burial? Now the doubts which were raised as to our powers did more to wrap them in terror, by wrapping them in uncertainty, than could have been effected by the sharpest definitions of the law from the Quarter Sessions. We, on our parts (we, the collective mail, I mean), did our utmost to exalt the idea of our privileges by the insolence with which we wielded them. Whether this insolence rested upon law that gave it a sanction, or upon conscious power that haughtily dispensed with that sanction, equally it spoke from a potential station, and the agent, in each particular insolence of the moment, was viewed reverentially, as one having authority.

Sometimes after breakfast his majesty's mail would become frisky ; and in its difficult wheelings amongst the intricacies of early markets, it would upset an apple-cart, a cart loaded with eggs, etc. Huge was the affliction and dismay, awful was the smash. I, as far as possible, endeavoured in such a case to represent the conscience and moral sensibilities of the mail ; and, when wildernesses of eggs were lying poached under our horses' hoofs, then would I stretch forth my hands in sorrow, saying (in words too celebrated at that time, from the false echoes[1] of Marengo), " Ah ! wherefore have we not time to weep over you ?" which was evidently impossible, since,

---

[1] "*False echoes :*"—Yes, false ! for the words ascribed to Napoleon, as breathed to the memory of Desaix, never were uttered at all. They stand in the same category of theatrical fictions as the cry of the foundering line-of-battle ship Vengeur, as the vaunt of General Cambronne at Waterloo, " *La Garde meurt, mais ne se rend pas,*" or as the repartees of Talleyrand.

in fact, we had not time to laugh over them. Tied to post-office allowance, in some cases of fifty minutes for eleven miles, could the royal mail pretend to undertake the offices of sympathy and condolence? Could it be expected to provide tears for the accidents of the road? If even it seemed to trample on humanity, it did so, I felt, in discharge of its own more peremptory duties.

Upholding the morality of the mail, *à fortiori* I upheld its rights; as a matter of duty, I stretched to the uttermost its privilege of imperial precedency, and astonished weak minds by the feudal powers which I hinted to be lurking constructively in the charters of this proud establishment. Once I remember being on the box of the Holyhead mail, between Shrewsbury and Oswestry, when a tawdry thing from Birmingham, some "Tallyho" or "High-flyer," all flaunting with green and gold, came up alongside of us. What a contrast to our royal simplicity of form and colour in this plebeian wretch! The single ornament on our dark ground of chocolate colour was the mighty shield of the imperial arms, but emblazoned in proportions as modest as a signet-ring bears to a seal of office. Even this was displayed only on a single panel, whispering, rather than proclaiming, our relations to the mighty state; whilst the beast from Birmingham, our green-and-gold friend from false, fleeting, perjured Brummagem, had as much writing and painting on its sprawling flanks as would have puzzled a decipherer from the tombs of

Luxor. For some time this Birmingham machine ran along by our side—a piece of familiarity that already of itself seemed to me sufficiently jacobinical. But all at once a movement of the horses announced a desperate intention of leaving us behind. "Do you see *that*?" I said to the coachman.—"I see," was his short answer. He was wide awake, yet he waited longer than seemed prudent; for the horses of our audacious opponent had a disagreeable air of freshness and power. But his motive was loyal; his wish was, that the Birmingham conceit should be full-blown before he froze it. When *that* seemed right, he unloosed, or, to speak by a stronger word, he *sprang*, his known resources : he slipped our royal horses like cheetahs, or hunting-leopards, after the affrighted game. How they could retain such a reserve of fiery power after the work they had accomplished, seemed hard to explain. But on our side, besides the physical superiority, was a tower of moral strength, namely, the king's name, "which they upon the adverse faction wanted." Passing them without an effort, as it seemed, we threw them into the rear with so lengthening an interval between us, as proved in itself the bitterest mockery of their presumption; whilst our guard blew back a shattering blast of triumph, that was really too painfully full of derision.

I mention this little incident for its connection with what followed. A Welsh rustic, sitting behind me, asked if I had not felt my heart burn within me

during the progress of the race ? I said, with philosophic calmness, *No ;* because we were not racing
with a mail, so that no glory could be gained. In
fact, it was sufficiently ·mortifying that such a
Birmingham thing should dare to challenge us. The
Welshman replied, that he didn't see *that ;* for that
a cat might look at a king, and a Brummagem coach
might lawfully race the Holyhead mail. "*Race* us,
if you like," I replied, " though even *that* has an air
of sedition, but not *beat* us. This would have been
treason ; and for its own sake I am glad that the
'Tallyho' was disappointed." So dissatisfied did
the Welshman seem with this opinion, that at last I
was obliged to tell him a very fine story from one
of our elder dramatists—viz., that once, in some far
oriental kingdom, when the sultan of all the land,
with his princes, ladies, and chief omrahs, were flying
their falcons, a hawk suddenly flew at a majestic
eagle ; and in defiance of the eagle's natural advantages, in contempt also of the eagle's traditional
royalty, and before the whole assembled field of
astonished spectators from Agra and Lahore, killed
the eagle on the spot. Amazement seized the sultan
at the unequal contest, and burning admiration for
its unparalleled result. He commanded that the
hawk should be brought before him ; he caressed
the bird with enthusiasm ; and he ordered that, for
the commemoration of his matchless courage, a
diadem of gold and rubies should be solemnly placed
on the hawk's head ; but then that, immediately

after this solemn coronation, the bird should be led
off to execution, as the most valiant indeed of traitors,
but not the less a traitor, as having dared to rise
rebelliously against his liege lord and anointed sove-
reign, the eagle. "Now," said I to the Welshman,
"to you and me, as men of refined sensibilities, how
painful it would have been that this poor Brummagem
brute, the 'Tallyho,' in the impossible case of a
victory over us, should have been crowned with
Birmingham tinsel, with paste diamonds, and Roman
pearls, and then led off to instant execution." The
Welshman doubted if that could be warranted by
law. And when I hinted at the 6th of Edward
Longshanks, chap. 18, for regulating the precedency
of coaches, as being probably the statute relied on
for the capital punishment of such offences, he replied
drily, that if the attempt to pass a mail really were
treasonable, it was a pity that the "Tallyho"
appeared to have so imperfect an acquaintance with
law.

The modern modes of travelling cannot compare
with the old mail-coach system in grandeur and power.
They boast of more velocity, not, however, as a consciousness, but as a fact of our lifeless knowledge,
resting upon *alien* evidence ; as, for instance, because
somebody *says* that we have gone fifty miles in the
hour, though we are far from feeling it as a personal
experience, or upon the evidence of a result, as that
actually we find ourselves in York four hours after
leaving London. Apart from such an assertion, or

such a result, I myself am little aware of the pace. But, seated on the old mail-coach, we needed no evidence out of ourselves to indicate the velocity. On this system the word was, *Non magna loquimur*, as upon railways, but *vivimus*. Yes, "magna *vivimus ;*" we do not make verbal ostentation of our grandeurs, we realise our grandeurs in act, and in the very experience of life. The vital experience of the glad animal sensibilities made doubts impossible on the question of our speed ; we heard our speed, we saw it, we felt it as a thrilling ; and this speed was not the product of blind insensate agencies, that had no sympathy to give, but was incarnated in the fiery eyeballs of the noblest amongst brutes, in his dilated nostril, spasmodic muscles, and thunder-beating hoofs. The sensibility of the horse, uttering itself in the maniac light of his eye, might be the last vibration of such a movement ; the glory of Salamanca might be the first. But the intervening links that connected them, that spread the earthquake of battle into the eyeball of the horse, were the heart of man and its electric thrillings—kindling in the rapture of the fiery strife, and then propagating its own tumults by contagious shouts and gestures to the heart of his servant the horse.

But now, on the new system of travelling, iron tubes and boilers have disconnected man's heart from the ministers of his locomotion. Nile nor Trafalgar has power to raise an extra bubble in a steam-kettle. The galvanic cycle is broken up for ever ; man's imperial nature no longer sends itself forward through the electric sensibility of the horse ; the inter-agencies are gone in the mode of communication between the horse and his master, out of which grew so many aspects of sublimity under accidents of mists that hid, or sudden blazes that revealed, of mobs that agitated, or midnight solitudes that awed.   Tidings, fitted to convulse all nations, must henceforwards travel by culinary process; and the trumpet that once announced from afar the laurelled mail, heart-shaking, when heard screaming on the wind, and proclaiming itself through the darkness to every village or solitary house on its route, has now given way for ever to the pot-wallopings of the boiler.

Thus have perished multiform openings for public expressions of interest, scenical yet natural, in great national tidings ; for revelations of faces and groups that could not offer themselves amongst the fluctuating mobs of a railway station.   The gatherings of gazers about a laurelled mail had one centre, and acknowledged one sole interest.   But the crowds attending at a railway station have as little unity as running water, and own as many centres as there are separate carriages in the train.

How else, for example, than as a constant watcher for the dawn, and for the London mail that in summer months entered about daybreak amongst the lawny thickets of Marlborough forest, couldst thou, sweet Fanny of the Bath road, have become the glorified inmate of my dreams ?   Yet Fanny, as the loveliest

young woman for face and person that perhaps in my
whole life I have beheld, merited the station which
even now, from a distance of forty years, she holds
in my dreams; yes, though by links of natural asso-
ciation she brings along with her a troop of dreadful
creatures, fabulous and not fabulous, that are more
abominable to the heart, than Fanny and the dawn
are delightful.

Miss Fanny of the Bath road, strictly speaking,
lived at a mile's distance from that road; but came
so continually to meet the mail, that I on my frequent
transits rarely missed her, and naturally connected
her image with the great thoroughfare where only I
had ever seen her. Why she came so punctually, I
do not exactly know; but I believe with some burden
of commissions to be executed in Bath, which had
gathered to her own residence as a central rendezvous
for converging them. The mail-coachman who drove
the Bath mail, and wore the royal livery,[1] happened
to be Fanny's grandfather. A good man he was,
that loved his beautiful granddaughter; and, loving
her wisely, was vigilant over her deportment in any

---

[1] " *Wore the royal livery :*"—The general impression was, that
the royal livery belonged of right to the mail-coachmen as their
professional dress. But that was an error. To the guard it *did*
belong, I believe, and was obviously essential as an official warrant,
and as a means of instant identification for his person, in the discharge of his important public duties. But the coachman, and
especially if his place in the series did not connect him immediately
with London and the General Post-office, obtained the scarlet coat
only as an honorary distinction after long (or, if not long, trying
and special) service.

case where young Oxford might happen to be concerned. Did my vanity then suggest that I myself,
individually, could fall within the line of his terrors?
Certainly not, as regarded any physical pretensions
that I could plead; for Fanny (as a chance passenger
from her own neighbourhood once told me) counted
in her train a hundred and ninety-nine professed
admirers, if not open aspirants to her favour; and
probably not one of the whole brigade but excelled
myself in personal advantages. Ulysses even, with
the unfair advantage of his accursed bow, could
hardly have undertaken that amount of suitors. So
the danger might have seemed slight—only that
woman is universally aristocratic; it is amongst her
nobilities of heart that she *is* so. Now, the aristocratic distinctions in my favour might easily with Miss
Fanny have compensated my physical deficiencies.
Did I then make love to Fanny? Why, yes; about
as much love as one *could* make whilst the mail was
changing horses—a process which, ten years later,
did not occupy above eighty seconds; but *then*—viz.,
about Waterloo—it occupied five times eighty. Now,
four hundred seconds offer a field quite ample enough
for whispering into a young woman's ear a great deal
of truth, and (by way of parenthesis) some trifle of
falsehood. Grandpapa did right, therefore, to watch
me. And yet, as happens too often to the grand-
papas of earth, in a contest with the admirers of
granddaughters, how vainly would he have watched
me had I meditated any evil whispers to Fanny!

She, it is my belief, would have protected herself
against any man's evil suggestions. But he, as the
result showed, could not have intercepted the opportunities for such suggestions. Yet, why not? Was
he not active? Was he not blooming? Blooming
he was as Fanny herself.

> "Say, all our praises why should lords——"

Stop, that's not the line.

> "Say, all our roses why should girls engross?"

The coachman showed rosy blossoms on his face
deeper even than his granddaughter's—*his* being
drawn from the ale cask, Fanny's from the fountains
of the dawn. But, in spite of his blooming face,
some infirmities he had; and one particularly in
which he too much resembled a crocodile. This lay
in a monstrous inaptitude for turning round. The
crocodile, I presume, owes that inaptitude to the
absurd *length* of his back; but in our grandpapa it
arose rather from the absurd *breadth* of his back,
combined, possibly, with some growing stiffness in
his legs. Now, upon this crocodile infirmity of his
I planted a human advantage for tendering my
homage to Miss Fanny. In defiance of all his
honourable vigilance, no sooner had he presented to
us his mighty Jovian back (what a field for displaying to mankind his royal scarlet!), whilst inspecting
professionally the buckles, the straps, and the silvery
turrets[1] of his harness, than I raised Miss Fanny's

---

[1] " *Turrets:* "—As one who loves and venerates Chaucer for

hand to my lips, and, by the mixed tenderness and
respectfulness of my manner, caused her easily to
understand how happy it would make me to rank
upon her list as No. 10 or 12, in which case a few
casualties amongst her lovers (and observe, they
hanged liberally in those days) might have promoted
me speedily to the top of the tree ; as, on the other
hand, with how much loyalty of submission I
acquiesced by anticipation in her award, supposing
that she should plant me in the very rear-ward of
her favour, as No. 199 + 1.   Most truly I loved this
beautiful and ingenuous girl ; and had it not been
for the Bath mail, timing all courtships by post-office
allowance, heaven only knows what might have
come of it.   People talk of being over head and ears
in love ; now, the mail was the cause that I sank
only over ears in love, which, you know, still left a
trifle of brain to overlook the whole conduct of the
affair.[1]

Ah, reader ! when I look back upon those days,
it seems to me that all things change—all things

his unrivalled merits of tenderness, of picturesque characterisation,
and of narrative skill, I noticed with great pleasure that the word
torrettes is used by him to designate the little devices through
which the reins are made to pass ["toretz fyled rounde" occurs in
line 1294 of the *Knightes Tale ;* where, however, the reference is
not to horse-trappings].   This same word, in the same exact sense,
I heard uniformly used by many scores of illustrious mail-coachmen, to whose confidential friendship I had the honour of being
admitted in my younger days.

[1] This paragraph was considerably condensed by De Quincey in
1854 from its original in *Blackwood* in 1849.—M.

perish. " Perish the roses and the palms of kings : " perish even the crowns and trophies of Waterloo : thunder and lightning are not the thunder and lightning which I remember. Roses are degenerating. The Fannies of our island—though this I say with reluctance—are not visibly improving; and the Bath road is notoriously superannuated. Crocodiles, you will say, are stationary. Mr Waterton tells me that the crocodile does *not* change ; that a cayman, in fact, or an alligator, is just as good for riding upon as he was in the time of the Pharaohs. *That* may be ; but the reason is, that the crocodile does not live fast—he is a slow coach. I believe it is generally understood among naturalists, that the crocodile is a blockhead. It is my own impression that the Pharaohs were also blockheads. Now, as the Pharaohs and the crocodile domineered over Egyptian society, this accounts for a singular mistake that prevailed through innumerable generations on the Nile. The crocodile made the ridiculous blunder of supposing man to be meant chiefly for his own eating. Man, taking a different view of the subject, naturally met that mistake by another : he viewed the crocodile as a thing sometimes to worship, but always to run away from. And this continued until Mr Waterton[1] changed the relations between the

[1] "*Mr Waterton :*"—Had the reader lived through the last generation, he would not need to be told that some thirty or thirty-five years back, Mr Waterton, a distinguished country gentleman of ancient family in Northumberland [Charles Water-

animals.   The mode of escaping from the reptile he
showed to be, not by running away, but by leaping
on its back, booted and spurred.   The two animals
had misunderstood each other.   The use of the
crocodile has now been cleared up—viz., to be
ridden ; and the final cause of man is, that he may
improve the health of the crocodile by riding him
a fox-hunting before breakfast.   And it is pretty
certain that any crocodile, who has been regularly
hunted through the season, and is master of the
weight he carries, will take a six-barred gate now as
well as ever he would have done in the infancy of
the pyramids.

If, therefore, the crocodile does *not* change, all
things else undeniably *do :* even the shadow of the
pyramids grows less.   And often the restoration in
vision of Fanny and the Bath road, makes me too
pathetically sensible of that truth.   Out of the
darkness, if I happen to call back the image of
Fanny, up rises suddenly from a gulf of forty years
a rose in June ; or, if I think for an instant of the
rose in June, up rises the heavenly face of Fanny.
One after the other, like the antiphonies in the

ston, naturalist, born 1782, died 1865], publicly mounted and
rode in top-boots a savage old crocodile, that was restive and very
impertinent, but all to no purpose.   The crocodile jibbed and tried
to kick, but vainly.   He was no more able to throw the squire,
than Sinbad was to throw the old scoundrel who used his back
without paying for it, until he discovered a mode (slightly
immoral, perhaps, though some think not) of murdering the old
fraudulent jockey, and so circuitously of unhorsing him.

choral service, rise Fanny and the rose in June, then back again the rose in June and Fanny. Then come both together, as in a chorus—roses and Fannies, Fannies and roses, without end, thick as blossoms in paradise. Then comes a venerable crocodile, in a royal livery of scarlet and gold, with sixteen capes; and the crocodile is driving four-in-hand from the box of the Bath mail. And suddenly we upon the mail are pulled up by a mighty dial, sculptured with the hours, that mingle with the heavens and the heavenly host. Then all at once we are arrived at Marlborough forest, amongst the lovely households[1] of the roe-deer; the deer and their fawns retire into the dewy thickets; the thickets are rich with roses; once again the roses call up the sweet countenance of Fanny; and she, being the granddaughter of a crocodile, awakens a dreadful host of semi-legendary animals—griffins, dragons, basilisks, sphinxes—till at length the whole vision of fighting images crowds into one towering armorial shield, a vast emblazonry of human charities and human loveliness that have perished, but quartered heraldically with unutterable and demoniac natures, whilst over all rises, as a

---

[1] "*Households:*"—Roe-deer do not congregate in herds like the fallow or the red deer, but by separate families, parents and children; which feature of approximation to the sanctity of human hearths, added to their comparatively miniature and graceful proportions, conciliates to them an interest of peculiar tenderness, supposing even that this beautiful creature is less characteristically impressed with the grandeurs of savage and forest life.

surmounting crest, one fair female hand, with the forefinger pointing, in sweet, sorrowful admonition, upwards to heaven, where is sculptured the eternal writing which proclaims the frailty of earth and her children.[1]

GOING DOWN WITH VICTORY.

But the grandest chapter of our experience, within the whole mail-coach service, was on those occasions when we went down from London with the news of victory. A period of about ten years stretched from Trafalgar to Waterloo; the second and third years of which period (1806 and 1807) were comparatively sterile; but the other nine (from 1805 to 1815 inclusively) furnished a long succession of victories; the least of which, in such a contest of Titans, had an inappreciable value of position—partly for its absolute interference with the plans of our enemy, but still more from its keeping alive through central Europe the sense of a deep-seated vulnerability in France. Even to tease the coasts of our enemy, to mortify them by continual blockades, to insult them by capturing if it were but a baubling schooner under the eyes of their arrogant armies, repeated from time to time a sullen proclamation of power lodged in one

[1] This paragraph is but about one-fifth of the length of the corresponding paragraph as it appeared originally in *Blackwood*, De Quincey's taste having led him, on revision in 1854, to cancel the other four-fifths as forced or irrelevant.—See Appended Note, *Cancelled Paragraph.*—M.

quarter to which the hopes of Christendom turned in secret. How much more loudly must this proclamation have spoken in the audacity [1] of having bearded the *élite* of their troops, and having beaten them in pitched battles! Five years of life it was worth paying down for the privilege of an outside place on a mail-coach, when carrying down the first tidings of any such event. And it is to be noted that, from our insular situation, and the multitude of our frigates disposable for the rapid transmission of intelligence, rarely did any unauthorised rumour steal away a prelibation from the first aroma of the regular despatches. The government news was generally the earliest news.

From eight P.M., to fifteen or twenty minutes later, imagine the mails assembled on parade in

---

[1] "*Audacity:*"—Such the French accounted it ; and it has struck me that Soult would not have been so popular in London, at the period of her present Majesty's coronation [28th June 1838], or in Manchester, on occasion of his visit to that town [July 1838], if they had been aware of the insolence with which he spoke of us in notes written at intervals from the field of Waterloo. As though it had been mere felony in our army to look a French one in the face, he said in more notes than one, dated from two to four P.M. on the field of Waterloo, "Here are the English—we have them ; they are caught *en flagrant delit.*" Yet no man should have known us better ; no man had drunk deeper from the cup of humiliation than Soult had in 1809, when ejected by us with headlong violence from Oporto, and pursued through a long line of wrecks to the frontier of Spain ; subsequently at Albuera, in the bloodiest of recorded battles [16th May 1811], to say nothing of Toulouse [10th April 1814], he should have learned our pretensions.

Lombard Street, where, at that time,[1] and not in St
Martin's-le-Grand, was seated the General Post-
office.[2]   In what exact strength we mustered I do
not remember ; but, from the length of each separate
attelage, we filled the street, though a long one, and
though we were drawn up in double file.   On *any*
night the spectacle was beautiful.   The absolute perfection of all the appointments about the carriages
and the harness, their strength, their brilliant clean-
liness, their beautiful simplicity—but, more than all,
the royal magnificence of the horses—were what
might first have fixed the attention.   Every carriage,
on every morning in the year, was taken down to
an official inspector for examination—wheels, axles,
linchpins, pole, glasses, lamps, were all critically
probed and tested.   Every part of every carriage
had been cleaned, every horse had been groomed,
with as much rigour as if they belonged to a private
gentleman ; and that part of the spectacle offered
itself always.   But the night before us is a night of
victory ; and, behold ! to the ordinary display, what
a heart-shaking addition !—horses, men, carriages, all
are dressed in laurels and flowers, oak-leaves and
ribbons.   The guards, as being officially his Majesty's
servants, and of the coachmen such as are within the
privilege of the post-office, wear the royal liveries of
course ; and as it is summer (for all the *land* victories

---

[1] "*At that time :*"—I speak of the era previous to Waterloo.

[2] The present General Post-office in St. Martin's-le-Grand was
opened 23d Sept. 1829.—M.

were naturally won in summer), they wear, on this fine evening, these liveries exposed to view, without any covering of upper coats. Such a costume, and the elaborate arrangement of the laurels in their hats, dilate their hearts, by giving to them openly a personal connection with the great news, in which already they have the general interest of patriotism. That great national sentiment surmounts and quells all sense of ordinary distinctions. Those passengers who happen to be gentlemen are now hardly to be distinguished as such except by dress; for the usual reserve of their manner in speaking to the attendants has on this night melted away. One heart, one pride, one glory, connects every man by the transcendent bond of his national blood. The spectators, who are numerous beyond precedent, express their sympathy with these fervent feelings by continual hurrahs. Every moment are shouted aloud by the post-office servants, and summoned to draw up, the great ancestral names of cities known to history through a thousand years—Lincoln, Winchester, Portsmouth, Gloucester, Oxford, Bristol, Manchester, York, Newcastle, Edinburgh, Glasgow, Perth, Stirling, Aberdeen—expressing the grandeur of the empire by the antiquity of its towns, and the grandeur of the mail establishment by the diffusive radiation of its separate missions. Every moment you hear the thunder of lids locked down upon the mail-bags. That sound to each individual mail is the signal for drawing off, which process is the finest part of the

entire spectacle. Then come the horses into play.
Horses! can these be horses that bound off with the
action and gestures of leopards? What stir!—what
sea-like ferment!—what a thundering of wheels!—
what a trampling of hoofs!—what a sounding of
trumpets!—what farewell cheers—what redoubling
peals of brotherly congratulation, connecting the
name of the particular mail—"Liverpool for ever!"
—with the name of the particular victory—"Badajoz
for ever!" or "Salamanca for ever!" The half-
slumbering consciousness that, all night long, and all
the next day—perhaps for even a longer period—
many of these mails, like fire racing along a train of
gunpowder, will be kindling at every instant new
successions of burning joy, has an obscure effect of
multiplying the victory itself, by multiplying to the
imagination into infinity the stages of its progressive
diffusion. A fiery arrow seems to be let loose, which
from that moment is destined to travel, without in-
termission, westwards for three hundred [1] miles—

---

[1] "*Three hundred:*"—Of necessity, this scale of measurement,
to an American, if he happens to be a thoughtless man, must sound
ludicrous. Accordingly, I remember a case in which an American
writer indulges himself in the luxury of a little fibbing, by ascribing to an Englishman a pompous account of the Thames, constructed
entirely upon American ideas of grandeur, and concluding in something like these terms:—"And, sir, arriving at London, this
mighty father of rivers attains a breadth of at least two furlongs,
having, in its winding course, traversed the astonishing distance of
one hundred and seventy miles." And this the candid American
thinks it fair to contrast with the scale of the Mississippi. Now,
it is hardly worth while to answer a pure fiction gravely, else one

northwards for six hundred; and the sympathy of our Lombard Street friends at parting is exalted a hundredfold by a sort of visionary sympathy with the yet slumbering sympathies which in so vast a succession we are going to awake.

Liberated from the embarrassments of the city, and issuing into the broad uncrowded avenues of the northern suburbs, we soon begin to enter upon our natural pace of ten miles an hour. In the broad light of the summer evening, the sun, perhaps, only just at the point of setting, we are seen from every

might say that no Englishman out of Bedlam ever thought of looking in an island for the rivers of a continent; nor, consequently, could have thought of looking for the peculiar grandeur of the Thames in the length of its course, or in the extent of soil which it drains; yet, if he *had* been so absurd, the American might have recollected that a river, not to be compared with the Thames even as to volume of water—viz., the Tiber—has contrived to make itself heard of in this world for twenty-five centuries to an extent not reached as yet by any river, however corpulent, of his own land. The glory of the Thames is measured by the destiny of the population to which it ministers, by the commerce which it supports, by the grandeur of the empire in which, though far from the largest, it is the most influential stream. Upon some such scale, and not by a transfer of Columbian standards, is the course of our English mails to be valued. The American may fancy the effect of his own valuations to our English ears, by supposing the case of a Siberian glorifying his country in these terms:—" These wretches, sir, in France and England, cannot march half a mile in any direction without finding a house where food can be had and lodging; whereas, such is the noble desolation of our magnificent country, that in many a direction for a thousand miles, I will engage that a dog shall not find shelter from a snow-storm, nor a wren find an apology for breakfast."

storey of every house.   Heads of every age crowd
to the windows—young and old understand the
language of our victorious symbols—and rolling
volleys of sympathising cheers run along us, behind
us, and before us.   The beggar, rearing himself
against the wall, forgets his lameness—real or assumed
—thinks not of his whining trade, but stands erect,
with bold exulting smiles, as we pass him.   The
victory has healed him, and says, Be thou whole!
Women and children, from garrets alike and cellars,
through infinite London, look down or look up with
loving eyes upon our gay ribbons and our martial
laurels; sometimes kiss their hands; sometimes hang
out, as signals of affection, pocket-handkerchiefs,
aprons, dusters, anything that, by catching the
summer breezes, will express an aerial jubilation.
On the London side of Barnet, to which we draw
near within a few minutes after nine, observe that
private carriage which is approaching us.   The weather
being so warm, the glasses are all down; and one
may read, as on the stage of a theatre, everything
that goes on within.   It contains three ladies—one
likely to be "mamma," and two of seventeen or
eighteen, who are probably her daughters.   What
lovely animation, what beautiful unpremeditated
pantomime, explaining to us every syllable that
passes, in these ingenuous girls!   By the sudden
start and raising of the hands, on first discovering
our laurelled equipage!—by the sudden movement
and appeal to the elder lady from both of them—

and by the heightened colour on their animated countenances, we can almost hear them saying, " See, see! Look at their laurels! Oh, mamma! there has been a great battle in Spain; and it has been a great victory." In a moment we are on the point of passing them. We passengers—I on the box, and the two on the roof behind me—raise our hats to the ladies; the coachman makes his professional salute with the whip; the guard even, though punctilious on the matter of his dignity as an officer under the crown, touches his hat. The ladies move to us, in return, with a winning graciousness of gesture; all smile on each side in a way that nobody could misunderstand, and that nothing short of a grand national sympathy could so instantaneously prompt. Will these ladies say that we are nothing to *them?* Oh, no; they will not say *that.* They cannot deny— they do not deny—that for this night they are our sisters; gentle or simple, scholar or illiterate servant, for twelve hours to come, we on the outside have the honour to be their brothers. Those poor women, again, who stop to gaze upon us with delight at the entrance of Barnet, and seem, by their air of weariness, to be returning from labour—do you mean to say that they are washerwomen and charwomen? Oh, my poor friend, you are quite mistaken. I assure you they stand in a far higher rank; for this one night they feel themselves by birth-right to be daughters of England, and answer to no humbler title.

Every joy, however, even rapturous joy—such is

the sad law of earth—may carry with it grief, or fear of grief, to some.   Three miles beyond Barnet, we see approaching us another private carriage, nearly repeating the circumstances of the former case. Here, also, the glasses are all down—here, also, is an elderly lady seated ; but the two daughters are missing ; for the single young person sitting by the lady's side, seems to be an attendant—so I judge from her dress, and her air of respectful reserve. The lady is in mourning ; and her countenance expresses sorrow.   At first she does not look up ; so that I believe she is not aware of our approach, until she hears the measured beating of our horses' hoofs. Then she raises her eyes to settle them painfully on our triumphal equipage.   Our decorations explain the case to her at once ; but she beholds them with apparent anxiety, or even with terror.   Some time before this, I, finding it difficult to hit a flying mark, when embarrassed by the coachman's person and reins intervening, had given to the guard a "Courier" evening paper, containing the gazette, for the next carriage that might pass.   Accordingly he tossed it in, so folded that the huge capitals expressing some such legend as—GLORIOUS VICTORY, might catch the eye at once.   To see the paper, however, at all, interpreted as it was by our ensigns of triumph, explained everything ; and, if the guard were right in thinking the lady to have received it with a gesture of horror, it could not be doubtful that she had suffered some deep personal affliction in connection with this Spanish war.

Here, now, was the case of one who, having formerly suffered, might, erroneously perhaps, be distressing herself with anticipations of another similar suffering. That same night, and hardly three hours later, occurred the reverse case. A poor woman, who too probably would find herself, in a day or two, to have suffered the heaviest of afflictions by the battle, blindly allowed herself to express an exultation so unmeasured in the news and its details, as gave to her the appearance which amongst Celtic Highlanders is called *fey*.[1] This was at some little town where we changed horses an hour or two after midnight. Some fair or wake had kept the people up out of their beds, and had occasioned a partial illumination of the stalls and booths, presenting an unusual but very impressive effect. We saw many lights moving about as we drew near ; and perhaps the most striking scene on the whole route was our reception at this place. The flashing of torches and the beautiful radiance of blue lights (technically, Bengal lights) upon the heads of our horses ; the fine effect of such a showery and ghostly illumination falling upon our flowers and glittering laurels ;[2] whilst all around ourselves, that

---

[1] *Fey*, fated, doomed to die : not a Celtic word, but an Anglo-Saxon word (*fǽege*) preserved in Lowland Scotch. "You are surely *fey*" would be said in Scotland to a person observed to be in extravagantly high spirits, or in any mood surprisingly beyond the bounds of his ordinary temperament, the notion being that the excitement is supernatural, and a presage of his approaching death or of some other calamity about to befall him.—M.

[2] "*Glittering laurels :*"—I must observe, that the colour of *green*

formed a centre of light, the darkness gathered on
the rear and flanks in massy blackness ; these optical
splendours, together with the prodigious enthusiasm
of the people, composed a picture at once scenical and
affecting, theatrical and holy. As we staid for three
or four minutes, I alighted ; and immediately from a
dismantled stall in the street, where no doubt she
had been presiding through the earlier part of the
night, advanced eagerly a middle-aged woman. The
sight of my newspaper it was that had drawn her
attention upon myself. The victory which we were
carrying down to the provinces on *this* occasion, was
the imperfect one of Talavera—imperfect for its
results, such was the virtual treachery of the Spanish
general, Cuesta, but not imperfect in its ever-memorable
heroism.[1] I told her the main outline of the battle.
The agitation of her enthusiasm had been so conspicuous when listening, and when first applying for
information, that I could not but ask her if she had
not some relative in the Peninsular army. Oh, yes ;
her only son was there. In what regiment ? He
was a trooper in the 23d Dragoons. My heart sank
within me as she made that answer. This sublime
regiment, which an Englishman should never mention
without raising his hat to their memory, had made
the most memorable and effective charge recorded in

suffers almost a spiritual change and exaltation under the effect of
Bengal lights.

[1] Battle of Talavera, in Spain, but close to the Portuguese
frontier, fought by Wellington (then Sir Arthur Wellesley) 27th
and 28th July 1809.—M.

military annals. They leaped their horses—*over* a trench where they could, *into* it and with the result of death or mutilation when they could *not*. What proportion cleared the trench is nowhere stated. Those who *did*, closed up and went down upon the enemy with such divinity of fervour (I use the word *divinity* by design : the inspiration of God must have prompted this movement to those whom even then He was calling to His presence), that two results followed. As regarded the enemy, this 23d Dragoons, not, I believe, originally three hundred and fifty strong, paralysed a French column, six thousand strong, then ascended the hill, and fixed the gaze of the whole French army. As regarded themselves, the 23d were supposed at first to have been barely not annihilated ; but eventually, I believe, about one in four survived. And this, then, was the regiment— a regiment already for some hours glorified and hallowed to the ear of all London, as lying stretched, by a large majority, upon one bloody aceldama—in which the young trooper served whose mother was now talking in a spirit of such joyous enthusiasm. Did I tell her the truth ? Had I the heart to break up her dreams ? No. To-morrow, said I to myself —to-morrow, or the next day, will publish the worst. For one night more, wherefore should she not sleep in peace ? After to-morrow, the chances are too many that peace will forsake her pillow. This brief respite, then, let her owe to *my* gift and *my* forbearance. But, if I told her not of the bloody price that had been paid, not, therefore, was I silent on the contributions from her son's regiment to that day's service and glory. I showed her not the funeral banners under which the noble regiment was sleeping. I lifted not the overshadowing laurels from the bloody trench in which horse and rider lay mangled together. But I told her how these dear children of England, officers and privates, had leaped their horses over all obstacles as gaily as hunters to the morning's chase. I told her how they rode their horses into the mists of death (saying to myself, but not saying to *her*), and laid down their young lives for thee, O mother England ! as willingly—poured out their noble blood as cheerfully—as ever, after a long day's sport, when infants, they had rested their wearied heads upon their mother's knees, or had sunk to sleep in her arms. Strange it is, yet true, that she seemed to have no fears for her son's safety, even after this knowledge that the 23d Dragoons had been memorably engaged ; but so much was she enraptured by the knowledge that *his* regiment, and therefore that *he*, had rendered conspicuous service in the dreadful conflict—a service which had actually made them, within the last twelve hours, the foremost topic of conversation in London — so absolutely was fear swallowed up in joy—that, in the mere simplicity of her fervent nature, the poor woman threw her arms round my neck, as she thought of her son, and gave to *me* the kiss which secretly was meant for *him*.

THE ENGLISH MAIL-COACH

THE VISION OF SUDDEN DEATH [1]

WHAT is to be taken as the predominant opinion of man, reflective and philosophic, upon SUDDEN DEATH? It is remarkable that, in different conditions of society, sudden death has been variously regarded as the consummation of an earthly career most fervently to be desired, or, again, as that consummation which is with most horror to be deprecated. Cæsar the Dictator, at his last dinner party (*cœna*), on the very evening before his assassination, when the minutes of his earthly career were numbered, being asked what death, in *his* judgment, might be pronounced the most eligible, replied, "That which should be most sudden."   On the other hand, the divine Litany

---

[1] In *Blackwood* for December 1849 there was prefixed to this Paper a paragraph within brackets, explaining its connexion with the preceding Section, which had appeared in October, and also its connexion with the subsequent "Dream-Fugue." Of the substance of this paragraph account has already been taken in the Introduction.—M.

of our English Church, when breathing forth suppli-
cations, as if in some representative character for the
whole human race prostrate before God, places such
a death in the very van of horrors :—"From lightning and tempest; from plague, pestilence, and
famine; from battle and murder, and from SUDDEN
DEATH—*Good Lord, deliver us.*" Sudden death is
here made to crown the climax in a grand ascent of
calamities; it is ·ranked among the last of curses;
and yet, by the noblest of Romans, it was ranked
as the first of blessings.   In that difference, most
readers will see little more than the essential difference between Christianity and Paganism.   But this,
on consideration, I doubt.   The Christian Church
may be right in its estimate of sudden death; and
it is a natural feeling, though after all it may also be
an infirm one, to wish for a quiet dismissal from life
—as that which *seems* most reconcilable with meditation, with penitential retrospects, and with the
humilities of farewell prayer.   There does not, however, occur to me any direct scriptural warrant for
this earnest petition of the English Litany, unless
under a special construction of the word "sudden."
It seems a petition—indulged rather and conceded
to human infirmity, than exacted from human piety.
It is not so much a doctrine built upon the eternities
of the Christian system, as a plausible opinion built
upon special varieties of physical temperament.   Let
that, however, be as it may, two remarks suggest
themselves as prudent restraints upon a doctrine,

which else *may* wander, and *has* wandered, into an uncharitable superstition. The first is this : that many people are likely to exaggerate the horror of a sudden death, from the disposition to lay a false stress upon words or acts, simply because by an accident they have become *final* words or acts. If a man dies, for instance, by some sudden death when he happens to be intoxicated, such a death is falsely regarded with peculiar horror ; as though the intoxication were suddenly exalted into a blasphemy. But *that* is unphilosophic. The man was, or he was not, *habitually* a drunkard. If not, if his intoxication were a solitary accident, there can be no reason for allowing special emphasis to this act, simply because through misfortune it became his final act. Nor, on the other hand, if it were no accident, but one of his *habitual* transgressions, will it be the more habitual or the more a transgression, because some sudden calamity, surprising him, has caused this habitual transgression to be also a final one. Could the man have had any reason even dimly to foresee his own sudden death, there would have been a new feature in his act of intemperance—a feature of presumption and irreverence, as in one that, having known himself drawing near to the presence of God, should have suited his demeanour to an expectation so awful. But this is no part of the case supposed. And the only new element in the man's act is not any element of special immorality, but simply of special misfortune.

The other remark has reference to the meaning of the word *sudden*. Very possibly Cæsar and the Christian Church do not differ in the way supposed; that is, do not differ by any difference of doctrine as between Pagan and Christian views of the moral temper appropriate to death, but perhaps they are contemplating different cases. Both contemplate a violent death, a Βιαθανατος—death that is Βιαιος, or, in other words, death that is brought about, not by internal and spontaneous change, but by active force having its origin from without.[1] In this meaning the two authorities agree. Thus far they are in harmony. But the difference is, that the Roman by the word "sudden" means *unlingering;* whereas the Christian Litany by "sudden death" means a death *without warning*, consequently without any available summons to religious preparation. The poor mutineer, who kneels down to gather into his heart the bullets from twelve firelocks of his pitying comrades, dies by a most sudden death in Cæsar's sense; one shock, one mighty spasm, one (possibly *not* one) groan, and all is over. But, in the sense of the Litany, the mutineer's death is far from sudden; his offence originally, his imprisonment, his trial, the interval between his sentence and its execution, having all furnished him with separate warnings of his fate— having all summoned him to meet it with solemn preparation.

[1] *Biaios*, Greek for "forcible" or "violent": hence *Biath-aantos*, violent death. —M.

Here at once, in this sharp verbal distinction, we comprehend the faithful earnestness with which a holy Christian Church pleads on behalf of her poor departing children, that God would vouchsafe to them the last great privilege and distinction possible on a death-bed—viz., the opportunity of untroubled preparation for facing this mighty trial. Sudden death, as a mere variety in the modes of dying, where death in some shape is inevitable, proposes a question of choice which, equally in the Roman and the Christian sense, will be variously answered according to each man's variety of temperament. Meantime, one aspect of sudden death there is, one modification, upon which no doubt can arise, that of all martyrdoms it is the most agitating—viz., where it surprises a man under circumstances which offer (or which seem to offer) some hurrying, flying, inappreciably minute chance of evading it. Sudden as the danger which it affronts, must be any effort by which such an evasion can be accomplished. Even *that*, even the sickening necessity for hurrying in extremity where all hurry seems destined to be vain, even that anguish is liable to a hideous exasperation in one particular case—viz., where the appeal is made not exclusively to the instinct of self-preservation, but to the conscience, on behalf of some other life besides your own, accidentally thrown upon *your* protection. To fail, to collapse in a service merely your own, might seem comparatively venial; though, in fact, it is far from venial. But to fail in a case where Providence has suddenly

thrown into your hands the final interests of another
—a fellow-creature shuddering between the gates of
life and death; this, to a man of apprehensive conscience, would mingle the misery of an atrocious-
criminality with the misery of a bloody calamity.
You are called upon, by the case supposed, possibly
to die; but to die at the very moment when, by any
even partial failure, or effeminate collapse of your
energies, you will be self-denounced as a murderer.
You had but the twinkling of an eye for your
effort, and that effort might have been unavailing;
but to have risen to the level of such an effort,
would have rescued you, though not from dying,
yet from dying as a traitor to your final and farewell duty.[1]

The situation here contemplated exposes a dreadful
ulcer, lurking far down in the depths of human
nature. It is not that men generally are summoned
to face such awful trials. But potentially, and in
shadowy outline, such a trial is moving subterran-
eously in perhaps all men's natures. Upon the
secret mirror of our dreams such a trial is darkly
projected, perhaps, to every one of us. That dream,
so familiar to childhood, of meeting a lion, and,
through languishing prostration in hope and the
energies of hope, that constant sequel of lying down
before the lion, publishes the secret frailty of human
nature—reveals its deep-seated falsehood to itself—

---

[1] The expression in this paragraph is much modified from the
original in *Blackwood*.—M.

records its abysmal treachery. Perhaps not one of us escapes that dream; perhaps, as by some sorrowful doom of man, that dream repeats for every one of us, through every generation, the original temptation in Eden. Every one of us, in this dream, has a bait offered to the infirm places of his own individual will; once again a snare is presented for tempting him into captivity to a luxury of ruin; once again, as in aboriginal Paradise, the man falls by his own choice; again, by infinite iteration, the ancient earth groans to Heaven, through her secret caves, over the weakness of her child: "Nature, from her seat, sighing through all her works," again "gives signs of wo that all is lost;" and again the counter sigh is repeated to the sorrowing heavens for the endless rebellion against God. It is not without probability that in the world of dreams every one of us ratifies for himself the original transgression. In dreams, perhaps under some secret conflict of the midnight sleeper, lighted up to the consciousness at the time, but darkened to the memory as soon as all is finished, each several child of our mysterious race completes for himself the treason of the aboriginal fall.[1]

*　　*　　*　　*　　*

[1] In the original *Blackwood* article there was no break of asterisks at this point, the next paragraph running on with this opening sentence, "As I drew near to the Manchester post-office, I found that it was considerably past midnight; but to my great relief, as it was important for me to be in Westmoreland by the morning, I saw by the huge saucer eyes of the mail, blazing through the gloom of overhanging houses, that my chance was not

The incident, so memorable in itself by its features of horror, and so scenical by its grouping for the eye, which furnished the text for this reverie upon *Sudden Death*, occurred to myself in the dead of night, as a solitary spectator, when seated on the box of the Manchester and Glasgow mail, in the second or third summer after Waterloo.   I find it necessary to relate the circumstances, because they are such as could not have occurred unless under a singular combination of accidents.   In those days, the oblique and lateral communications with many rural post-offices were so arranged, either through necessity or through defect of system, as to make it requisite for the main north-western mail (*i.e.*, the *down* mail), on reaching Manchester, to halt for a number of hours; how many, I do not remember; six or seven, I think; but the result was, that, in the ordinary course, the mail recommenced its journey northwards about midnight. Wearied with the long detention at a gloomy hotel, I walked out about eleven o'clock at night for the sake of fresh air; meaning to fall in with the mail and resume my seat at the post-office.   The night, however, being yet dark, as the moon had scarcely risen, and the streets being at that hour empty, so as to offer no opportunities for asking the road, I lost my way; and did not reach the post-office until it was considerably past midnight; but, to my great

yet lost." The break of asterisks, and the insertion of several sentences after the break before resuming as above, were after-thoughts for the reprint of 1854.—M.

relief (as it was important for me to be in Westmoreland by the morning), I saw in the huge saucer eyes
of the mail, blazing through the gloom, an evidence
that my chance was not yet lost.   Past the time it
was ; but, by some rare accident, the mail was not
even yet ready to start.   I ascended to my seat on
the box, where my cloak was still lying as it had
lain at the Bridgewater Arms.   I had left it there in
imitation of a nautical discoverer, who leaves a bit of
bunting on the shore of his discovery, by way of
warning off the ground the whole human race, and
notifying to the Christian and the heathen worlds,
with his best compliments, that he has hoisted his
pocket-handkerchief once and for ever upon that virgin
soil ; thenceforward claiming the *jus dominii* to the
top of the atmosphere above it, and also the right of
driving shafts to the centre of the earth below it ; so
that all people found after this warning, either aloft
in upper chambers of the atmosphere, or groping in
subterraneous shafts, or squatting audaciously on the
surface of the soil, will be treated as trespassers—
kicked, that is to say, or decapitated, as circumstances
may suggest, by their very faithful servant, the owner
of the said pocket-handkerchief.   In the present case,
it is probable that my cloak might not have been
respected, and the *jus gentium* might have been cruelly
violated in my person—for, in the dark, people
commit deeds of darkness, gas being a great ally of
morality—but it so happened that, on this night,
there was no other outside passenger ; and thus the

crime, which else was but too probable, missed
for want of a criminal.[1]

Having mounted the box, I took a small quantity
of laudanum, having already travelled two hundred
and fifty miles—viz., from a point seventy miles
beyond London. In the taking of laudanum there
was nothing extraordinary. But by accident it drew
upon me the special attention of my assessor on the
box, the coachman. And in *that* also there was
nothing extraordinary. But by accident, and with
great delight, it drew my own attention to the fact
that this coachman was a monster in point of bulk,
and that he had but one eye. In fact, he had been
foretold by Virgil as

"Monstrum horrendum, informe, ingens, cui lumen ademptum."

He answered to the conditions in every one of the
items:—1. a monster he was; 2. dreadful; 3. shapeless;
4. huge; 5. who had lost an eye. But why should
that delight me ? Had he been one of the Calendars
in the "Arabian Nights," and had paid down his
eye as the price of his criminal curiosity, what right
had *I* to exult in his misfortune ? I did *not* exult; I
delighted in no man's punishment, though it were even
merited. But these personal distinctions (Nos. 1, 2,
3, 4, 5) identified in an instant an old friend of mine,
whom I had known in the south for some years as
the most masterly of mail-coachmen. He was the
man in all Europe that could (if *any* could) have

[1] A whole paragraph of the original is omitted here, De Quincey's
taste rejecting it on revision ; nor is it worth resuscitating.—M.

relie iven six-in-hand full gallop over *Al Sirat*—that
larl dreadful bridge of Mahomet, with no side battlements,
of and of *extra* room not enough for a razor's edge—
t leading right across the bottomless gulf. Under this
eminent man, whom in Greek I cognominated Cyclops
diphrélates (Cyclops the charioteer), I, and others known
to me, studied the diphrelatic art. Excuse, reader, a
word too elegant to be pedantic.[1] As a pupil, though
I paid extra fees, it is to be lamented that I did not
stand high in his esteem. It showed his dogged
honesty (though, observe, not his discernment), that
he could not see my merits. Let us excuse his
absurdity in this particular, by remembering his want
of an eye. Doubtless *that* made him blind to my
merits. In the art of conversation, however, he
admitted that I had the whip-hand of him. On this
present occasion, great joy was at our meeting. But
what was Cyclops doing here? Had the medical
men recommended northern air, or how? I collected,
from such explanations as he volunteered, that he
had an interest at stake in some suit-at-law now

---

[1] For the last two sentences the original in *Blackwood* had
these four :—"I used to call him *Cyclops Mastigophorus*, Cyclops
the whip-bearer, until I observed that his skill made whips useless,
except to fetch off an impertinent fly from a leader's head ; upon
which I changed his Grecian name to Cyclops *diphrélates* (Cyclops
the charioteer). I, and others known to me, studied under him the
diphrelatic art. Excuse, reader, a word too elegant to be pedantic.
And also take this remark from me as a *gage d'amitié*—that no
word ever was or *can* be pedantic which, by supporting a distinction,
supports the accuracy of logic, or which fills up a chasm for the
understanding."—M.

pending at Lancaster; so that probably he had got himself transferred to this station, for the purpose of connecting with his professional pursuits an instant readiness for the calls of his lawsuit.

Meantime, what are we stopping for? Surely we have now waited long enough. Oh, this procrastinating mail, and this procrastinating post-office! Can't they take a lesson upon that subject from *me?* Some people have called *me* procrastinating. Yet you are witness, reader, that I was here kept waiting for the post-office. Will the post-office lay its hand on its heart, in its moments of sobriety, and assert that ever it waited for me? What are they about? The guard tells me that there is a large extra accumulation of foreign mails this night, owing to irregularities caused by war, by wind, by weather, in the packet service, which as yet does not benefit at all by steam. For an *extra* hour, it seems, the post-office has been engaged in threshing out the pure wheaten correspondence of Glasgow, and winnowing it from the chaff of all baser intermediate towns. But at last all is finished. Sound your horn, guard. Manchester, good-by; we've lost an hour by your criminal conduct at the post-office: which, however, though I do not mean to part with a serviceable ground of complaint, and one which really *is* such for the horses, to me secretly is an advantage, since it compels us to look sharply for this lost hour amongst the next eight or nine, and to recover it (if we can) at the rate of one mile extra per hour. Off we are at last, and at eleven miles an hour; and for the moment I detect no changes in the energy or in the skill of Cyclops.

From Manchester to Kendal, which virtually (though not in law) is the capital of Westmoreland, there were at this time seven stages of eleven miles each. The first five of these, counting from Manchester, terminate in Lancaster, which is therefore fifty-five miles north of Manchester, and the same distance exactly from Liverpool. The first three stages terminate in Preston (called, by way of distinction from other towns of that name, *proud* Preston), at which place it is that the separate roads from Liverpool and from Manchester to the north become confluent.[1] Within these first three stages lay the foundation, the progress, and termination of our night's adventure. During the first stage, I found out that Cyclops was mortal : he was liable to the shocking affection of sleep—a thing which previously I had never suspected. If a man indulges in the vicious habit of sleeping, all the skill in aurigation of Apollo himself, with the horses of Aurora to execute his notions, avail him nothing. "Oh, Cyclops!" I exclaimed, "thou art mortal. My

---

[1] "*Confluent :*"—Suppose a capital Y (the Pythagorean letter): Lancaster is at the foot of this letter ; Liverpool at the top of the *right* branch ; Manchester at the top of the *left ;* proud Preston at the centre, where the two branches unite. It is thirty-three miles along either of the two branches ; it is twenty-two miles along the stem—viz., from Preston in the middle, to Lancaster at the root. There's a lesson in geography for the reader.

friend, thou snorest." Through the first eleven
miles, however, this infirmity—which I grieve to
say that he shared with the whole Pagan Pantheon
—betrayed itself only by brief snatches. On waking
up, he made an apology for himself, which, instead of
mending matters, laid open a gloomy vista of coming
disasters. The summer assizes, he reminded me,
were now going on at Lancaster : in consequence of
which, for three nights and three days, he had not
lain down in a bed. During the day, he was waiting
for his own summons as a witness on the trial in
which he was interested ; or else, lest he should be
missing at the critical moment, was drinking with
the other witnesses, under the pastoral surveillance
of the attorneys. During the night, or that part of
it which at sea would form the middle watch, he was
driving. This explanation certainly accounted for his
drowsiness, but in a way which made it much more
alarming ; since now, after several days' resistance to
this infirmity, at length he was steadily giving way.
Throughout the second stage he grew more and more
drowsy. In the second mile of the third stage, he
surrendered himself finally and without a struggle
to his perilous temptation. All his past resistance
had but deepened the weight of this final oppression.
Seven atmospheres of sleep rested upon him ; and to
consummate the case, our worthy guard, after singing
" Love amongst the Roses " for perhaps thirty times,
without invitation, and without applause, had in
revenge moodily resigned himself to slumber—not so

deep, doubtless, as the coachman's, but deep enough
for mischief. And thus at last, about ten miles
from Preston, it came about that I found myself left
in charge of his Majesty's London and Glasgow mail,
then running at the least twelve miles an hour.

What made this negligence less criminal than else
it must have been thought, was the condition of the
roads at night during the assizes. At that time, all
the law business of populous Liverpool, and also of
populous Manchester, with its vast cincture of populous rural districts, was called up by ancient usage
to the tribunal of Lilliputian Lancaster. To break
up this old traditional usage required, 1. a conflict
with powerful established interests; 2. a large system
of new arrangements; and 3. a new parliamentary
statute. But as yet this change was merely in con-
templation. As things were at present, twice in the
year[1] so vast a body of business rolled northwards,
from the southern quarter of the county, that for a
fortnight at least it occupied the severe exertions of
two judges in its despatch. The consequence of this
was, that every horse available for such a service,
along the whole line of road, was exhausted in
carrying down the multitudes of people who were
parties to the different suits. By sunset, therefore,
it usually happened that, through utter exhaustion
amongst men and horses, the road sank into profound

---

[1] "*Twice in the year:*"—There were at that time only two
assizes even in the most populous counties—viz., the Lent Assizes,
and the Summer Assizes.

silence. Except the exhaustion in the vast adjacent county of York from a contested election, no such silence succeeding to no such fiery uproar was ever witnessed in England.

On this occasion, the usual silence and solitude prevailed along the road. Not a hoof nor a wheel was to be heard. And to strengthen this false luxurious confidence in the noiseless roads, it happened also that the night was one of peculiar solemnity and peace. For my own part, though slightly alive to the possibilities of peril, I had so far yielded to the influence of the mighty calm as to sink into a profound reverie. The month was August, in the middle of which lay my own birth-day—a festival to every thoughtful man suggesting solemn and often sigh-born [1] thoughts. The county was my own native county—upon which, in its southern section, more than upon any equal area known to man past or present, had descended the original curse of labour in its heaviest form, not mastering the bodies only of men, as of slaves, or criminals in mines, but working through the fiery will. Upon no equal space of earth was, or ever had been, the same energy of human power put forth daily. At this particular season also of the assizes, that dreadful hurricane of flight and pursuit, as it might have seemed to a stranger, which swept to and from Lancaster àll day long,

---

[1] "*Sigh-born:*"—I owe the suggestion of this word to an obscure remembrance of a beautiful phrase in "Giraldus Cambrensis"— viz., *suspiriosæ cogitationes.*

hunting the county up and down, and regularly sub-
siding back into silence about sunset, could not fail
(when united with this permanent distinction of
Lancashire as the very metropolis and citadel of
labour) to point the thoughts pathetically upon that
counter vision of rest, of saintly repose from strife
and sorrow, towards which, as to their secret haven,
the profounder aspirations of man's heart are in
solitude continually travelling.   Obliquely upon our
left we were nearing the sea, which also must,
under the present circumstances, be repeating the
general state of halcyon repose.   The sea, the atmosphere, the light, bore each an orchestral part in this
universal lull.   Moonlight, and the first timid tremblings of the dawn, were by this time blending; and
the blendings were brought into a still more exquisite
state of unity by a slight silvery mist, motionless
and dreamy, that covered the woods and fields, but
with a veil of equable transparency.   Except the feet
of our own horses, which, running on a sandy margin
of the road, made but little disturbance, there was
no sound abroad.   In the clouds, and on the earth,
prevailed the same majestic peace; and in spite of all
that the villain of a schoolmaster has done for the
ruin of our sublimer thoughts, which are the thoughts
of our infancy, we still believe in no such nonsense
as a limited atmosphere.   Whatever we may swear
with our false feigning lips, in our faithful hearts we
still believe, and must for ever believe, in fields of
air traversing the total gulf between earth and the

central heavens. Still, in the confidence of children
that tread without fear *every* chamber in their father's
house, and to whom no door is closed, we, in that
Sabbatic vision which sometimes is revealed for an
hour upon nights like this, ascend with easy steps
from the sorrow-stricken fields of earth, upwards to
the sandals of God.

Suddenly, from thoughts like these, I was awakened
to a sullen sound, as of some motion on the distant
road.   It stole upon the air for a moment ; I listened
in awe ; but then it died away.   Once roused, however, I could not but observe with alarm the
quickened motion of our horses.   Ten years' experience
had made my eye learned in the valuing of motion ;
and I saw that we were now running thirteen miles
an hour.   I pretend to no presence of mind.   On the
contrary, my fear is, that I am miserably and shame-
fully deficient in that quality as regards action.
The palsy of doubt and distraction hangs like some
guilty weight of dark unfathomed remembrances upon
my energies, when the signal is flying for *action*.
But, on the other hand, this accursed gift I have, as
regards *thought*, that in the first step towards the
possibility of a misfortune, I see its total evolution ;
in the radix of the series I see too certainly and
too instantly its entire expansion ; in the first syllable
of the dreadful sentence, I read already the last.   It
was not that I feared for ourselves.   *Us*, our bulk
and impetus charmed against peril in any collision.
And I had ridden through too many hundreds of

perils that were frightful to approach, that were matter of laughter to look back upon, the first face of which was horror—the parting face a jest—for any anxiety to rest upon *our* interests. The mail was not built, I felt assured, nor bespoke, that could betray *me* who trusted to its protection. But any carriage that we could meet would be frail and light in comparison of ourselves. And I remarked this ominous accident of our situation. We were on the wrong side of the road. But then, it may be said, the other party, if other there was, might also be on the wrong side; and two wrongs might make a right. *That* was not likely. The same motive which had drawn *us* to the right-hand side of the road—viz., the luxury of the soft beaten sand, as contrasted with the paved centre—would prove attractive to others. The two adverse carriages would therefore, to a certainty, be travelling on the same side; and from this side, as not being ours in law, the crossing over to the other would, of course, be looked for from *us*.[1] Our lamps, still lighted, would give the impression of vigilance on our part. And every creature that met us, would rely upon *us* for quartering.[2] All this, and

[1] It is true that, according to the law of the case as established by legal precedents, all carriages were required to give way before Royal equipages, and therefore before the mail as one of them. But this only increased the danger, as being a regulation very imperfectly made known, very unequally enforced, and therefore often embarrassing the movements on both sides.

[2] "*Quartering :*"—This is the technical word, and, I presume, derived from the French *cartayer*, to evade a rut or any obstacle.

if the separate links of the anticipation had been a thousand times more, I saw, not discursively, or by effort, or by succession, but by one flash of horrid simultaneous intuition.

Under this steady though rapid anticipation of the evil which *might* be gathering ahead, ah! what a sullen mystery of fear, what a sigh of wo, was that which stole upon the air, as again the far-off sound of a wheel was heard! A whisper it was—a whisper from, perhaps, four miles off—secretly announcing a ruin that, being foreseen, was not the less inevitable; that, being known, was not, therefore, healed. What could be done—who was it 'that could do it—to check the storm-flight of these maniacal horses? Could I not seize the reins from the grasp of the slumbering coachman? You, reader, think that it would have been in *your* power to do so. And I quarrel not with your estimate of yourself. But, from the way in which the coachman's hand was viced between his upper and lower thigh, this was impossible. Easy, was it? See, then, that bronze equestrian statue. The cruel rider has kept the bit in his horse's mouth for two centuries. Unbridle him, for a minute, if you please, and wash his mouth with water. Easy, was it? Unhorse me, then, that imperial rider; knock me those marble feet from those marble stirrups of Charlemagne.

The sounds ahead strengthened, and were now too clearly the sounds of wheels. Who and what could it be? Was it industry in a taxed cart? Was it youthful gaiety in a gig? Was it sorrow that loitered, or joy that raced? For as yet the snatches of sound were too intermitting, from distance, to decipher the character of the motion. Whoever were the travellers, something must be done to warn them. Upon the other party rests the active responsibility, but upon *us*—and, wo is me! that *us* was reduced to my frail opium-shattered self—rests the responsibility of warning. Yet, how should this be accomplished? Might I not sound the guard's horn? Already, on the first thought, I was making my way over the roof to the guard's seat. But this, from the accident which I have mentioned, of the foreign mails' being piled upon the roof, was a difficult and even dangerous attempt to one cramped by nearly three hundred miles of outside travelling. And, fortunately, before I had lost much time in the attempt, our frantic horses swept round an angle of the road, which opened upon us that final stage where the collision must be accomplished, and the catastrophe sealed. All was apparently finished. The court was sitting; the case was heard; the judge had finished; and only the verdict was yet in arrear.

Before us lay an avenue, straight as an arrow, six hundred yards, perhaps, in length; and the umbrageous trees, which rose in a regular line from either side, meeting high overhead, give to it the character of a cathedral aisle. These trees lent a deeper solemnity to the early light; but there was still light enough to perceive, at the further end of this Gothic aisle, a frail reedy gig, in which were seated a young man, and by his side a young lady.   Ah, young sir ! what are you about?   If it is requisite that you should whisper your communications to this young lady—though really I see nobody, at an hour and on a road so solitary, likely to overhear you—is it therefore requisite that you should carry your lips forward to hers?   The little carriage is creeping on at one mile an hour ; and the parties within it being thus tenderly engaged, are naturally bending down their heads.   Between them and eternity, to all human calculation, there is but a minute and a-half.   Oh heavens ! what is it that I shall do?   Speaking or acting, what help can I offer?   Strange it is, and to a mere auditor of the tale might seem laughable, that I should need a suggestion from the " Iliad " to prompt the sole resource that remained.   Yet so it was.   Suddenly I remembered the shout of Achilles, and its effect.   But could I pretend to shout like the son of Peleus, aided by Pallas?   No : but then I needed not the shout that should alarm all Asia militant ; such a shout would suffice as might carry terror into the hearts of two thoughtless young people, and one gig-horse.   I shouted—and the young man heard me not.   A second time I shouted—and now he heard me, for now he raised his head.

Here, then, all had been done that, by me, *could* be done : more on *my* part was not possible.   Mine had been the first step ; the second was for the young man ; the third was for God.   If, said I, this stranger

is a brave man, and if, indeed, he loves the young
girl at his side—or, loving her not, if he feels the
obligation, pressing upon every man worthy to be
called a man, of doing his utmost for a woman con-
fided to his protection—he will, at least, make some
effort to save her. If *that* fails, he will not perish
the more, or by a death more cruel, for having made
it; and he will die as a brave man should, with his
face to the danger, and with his arm about the woman
that he sought in vain to save. But, if he makes no
effort, shrinking, without a struggle, from his duty,
he himself will not the less certainly perish for this
baseness of poltroonery. He will die no less: and
why not? Wherefore should we grieve that there is
one craven less in the world? No; *let* him perish,
without a pitying thought of ours wasted upon him;
and, in that case, all our grief will be reserved for
the fate of the helpless girl who now, upon the least
shadow of failure in *him*, must, by the fiercest of
translations—must, without time for a prayer—must,
within seventy seconds, stand before the judgment-
seat of God.

But craven he was not: sudden had been the call
upon him, and sudden was his answer to the call.
He saw, he heard, he comprehended, the ruin that
was coming down: already its gloomy shadow
darkened above him; and already he was measuring
his strength to deal with it. Ah! what a vulgar
thing does courage seem, when we see nations buying
it and selling it for a shilling a-day: ah! what a

sublime thing does courage seem, when some fearful summons on the great deeps of life carries a man, as if running before a hurricane, up to the giddy crest of some tumultuous crisis, from which lie two courses, and a voice says to him audibly, " One way lies hope; take the other, and mourn for ever!"   How grand a triumph, if, even then, amidst the raving of all around him, and the frenzy of the danger, the man is able to confront his situation—is able to retire for a moment into solitude with God, and to seek his counsel from *Him!*

For seven seconds, it might be, of his seventy, the stranger settled his countenance stedfastly upon us, as if to search and value every element in the conflict before him.   For five seconds more of his seventy he sat immovably, like one that mused on some great purpose.   For five more, perhaps, he sat with eyes upraised, like one that prayed in sorrow, under some extremity of doubt, for light that should guide him to the better choice.   Then suddenly he rose; stood upright; and by a powerful strain upon the reins, raising his horse's fore-feet from the ground, he slewed him round on the pivot of his hind-legs, so as to plant the little equipage in a position nearly at right angles to ours.   Thus far his condition was not improved; except as a first step had been taken towards the possibility of a second.   If no more were done, nothing was done; for the little carriage still occupied the very centre of our path, though in an altered direction.   Yet even now it may not be too late:

fifteen of the seventy seconds may still be unexhausted; and one almighty bound may avail to clear the ground. Hurry, then, hurry! for the flying moments—*they* hurry. Oh, hurry, hurry, my brave young man! for the cruel hoofs of our horses—*they* also hurry! Fast are the flying moments, faster are the hoofs of our horses. But fear not for *him*, if human energy can suffice ; faithful was he that drove to his terrific duty; faithful was the horse to *his* command. One blow, one impulse given with voice and hand, by the stranger, one rush from the horse, one bound as if in the act of rising to a fence, landed the docile creature's fore-feet upon the crown or arching centre of the road. The larger half of the little equipage had then cleared our over-towering shadow : *that* was evident even to my own agitated sight. But it mattered little that one wreck should float off in safety, if upon the wreck that perished were embarked the human freightage. The rear part of the carriage—was *that* certainly beyond the line of absolute ruin ? What power could answer the question ? Glance of eye, thought of man, wing of angel, which of these had speed enough to sweep between the question and the answer, and divide the one from the other ? Light does not tread upon the steps of light more indivisibly, than did our all-conquering arrival upon the escaping efforts of the gig. *That* must the young man have felt too plainly. His back was now turned to us ; not by sight could he any longer communicate with the peril ; but by the dreadful rattle of our harness, too truly had his ear been instructed—that all was finished as regarded any further effort of *his*. Already in resignation he had rested from his struggle ; and perhaps in his heart he was whispering, "Father, which art in heaven, do Thou finish above what I on earth have attempted." Faster than ever mill-race we ran past them in our inexorable flight.[1] Oh, raving of hurricanes that must have sounded in their young ears at the moment of our transit ! Even in that moment the thunder of collision spoke aloud. Either with the swingle-bar, or with the haunch of our near leader, we had struck the off-wheel of the little gig, which stood rather obliquely, and not quite so far advanced, as to be accurately parallel with the near-wheel. The blow, from the fury of our passage, resounded terrifically. I rose in horror, to gaze upon the ruins we might have caused. From my elevated station I looked down, and looked back upon the scene, which in a moment told its own tale, and wrote all its records on my heart for ever.

Here was the map of the passion that now had finished.[2] The horse was planted immovably, with

[1] Among the many modifications of the original wording made by De Quincey in revising these paragraphs for the reprint in his Collected Works may be noted, as particularly characteristic, his substitution of this form of the present sentence for the original form ; which was "We ran past them faster than ever mill-race in our inexorable flight." His sensitiveness to fit sound, at such a moment of wild rapidity, suggested the inversion.—M.

[2] This sentence, "Here was the map," etc. is an insertion in the reprint ; and one observes how artistically it causes the due

his fore-feet upon the paved crest of the central road. He of the whole party might be supposed untouched by the passion of death. The little cany carriage— partly, perhaps, from the violent torsion of the wheels in its recent movement, partly from the thundering blow we had given to it—as if it sympathised with human horror, was all alive with tremblings and shiverings. The young man trembled not, nor shivered. He sat like a rock. But *his* was the steadiness of agitation frozen into rest by horror. As yet he dared not to look round ; for he knew that, if anything remained to do, by him it could no longer be done. And as yet he knew not for certain if their safety were accomplished. But the lady——

But the lady——! Oh, heavens ! will that spectacle ever depart from my dreams, as she rose and sank upon her seat, sank and rose, threw up her arms wildly to heaven, clutched at some visionary object in the air, fainting, praying, raving, despairing ? Figure to yourself, reader, the elements of the case ; suffer me to recall before your mind the circumstances of that unparalleled situation. From the silence and deep peace of this saintly summer night—from the pathetic blending of this sweet moonlight, dawnlight, dreamlight — from the manly tenderness of this flattering, whispering, murmuring love—suddenly as from the woods and fields—suddenly as from the chambers of the air opening in revelation—suddenly

pause between the horror as still in rush of transaction and the look at the wreck when the crash was past.—M.

as from the ground yawning at her feet, leaped upon her, with the flashing of cataracts, Death the crowned phantom, with all the equipage of his terrors, and the tiger roar of his voice.

The moments were numbered; the strife was finished; the vision was closed. In the twinkling of an eye, our flying horses had carried us to the termination of the umbrageous aisle; at right angles we wheeled into our former direction, the turn of the road carried the scene out of my eyes in an instant, and swept it into my dreams for ever.

THE ENGLISH MAIL-COACH

DREAM-FUGUE:

FOUNDED ON THE PRECEDING THEME OF SUDDEN DEATH

> "Whence the sound
> Of instruments, that made melodious chime,
> Was heard, of harp and organ ; and who moved
> Their stops and chords, was seen ; his volant touch
> Instinct through all proportions, low and high,
> Fled and pursued transverse the resonant fugue."
>
> *Par. Lost*, Bk. XI.

Tumultuosissimamente.

PASSION of sudden death ! that once in youth I read and interpreted by the shadows of thy averted signs ![1]—rapture of panic taking the shape (which amongst tombs in churches I have seen) of woman bursting her sepulchral bonds—of woman's Ionic form bending forward from the ruins of her grave

---

[1] "*Averted signs :*"—I read the course and changes of the lady's agony in the succession of her involuntary gestures ; but it must be remembered that I read all this from the rear, never once catching the lady's full face, and even her profile imperfectly.

with arching foot, with eyes upraised, with clasped
adoring hands—waiting, watching, trembling, praying for the trumpet's call to rise from dust for ever!
Ah, vision too fearful of shuddering humanity on the
brink of almighty abysses!—vision that didst start
back, that didst reel away, like a shrivelling scroll
from before the wrath of fire racing on the wings of
the wind! Epilepsy so brief of horror, wherefore is
it that thou canst not die? Passing so suddenly into
darkness, wherefore is it that still thou sheddest thy
sad funeral blights upon the gorgeous mosaics of
dreams? Fragment of music too passionate, heard
once, and heard no more, what aileth thee, that thy
deep rolling chords come up at intervals through all
the worlds of sleep, and after forty years, have lost
no element of horror?

I.

Lo, it is summer—almighty summer! The everlasting gates of life and summer are thrown open
wide; and on the ocean, tranquil and verdant as a
savannah, the unknown lady from the dreadful vision
and I myself are floating—she upon a fairy pinnace,
and I upon an English three-decker. Both of us are
wooing gales of festal happiness within the domain
of our common country, within that ancient watery
park, within that pathless chase of ocean, where
England takes her pleasure as a huntress through
winter and summer, from the rising to the setting

sun. Ah, what a wilderness of floral beauty was hidden, or was suddenly revealed, upon the tropic islands through which the pinnace moved! And upon her deck what a bevy of human flowers— young women how lovely, young men how noble, that were dancing together, and slowly drifting towards *us* amidst music and incense, amidst blossoms from forests and gorgeous corymbi[1] from vintages, amidst natural carolling, and the echoes of sweet girlish laughter. Slowly the pinnace nears us, gaily she hails us, and silently she disappears beneath the shadow of our mighty bows. But then, as at some signal from heaven, the music, and the carols, and the sweet echoing of girlish laughter—all are hushed. What evil has smitten the pinnace, meeting or over-taking her? Did ruin to our friends couch within our own dreadful shadow? Was our shadow the shadow of death? I looked over the bow for an answer, and, behold! the pinnace was dismantled; the revel and the revellers were found no more; the glory of the vintage was dust; and the forests with their beauty were left without a witness upon the seas. "But where," and I turned to our crew— "where are the lovely women that danced beneath the awning of flowers and clustering corymbi? Whither have fled the noble young men that danced with *them?*" Answer there was none. But suddenly the man at the mast-head, whose countenance darkened with alarm, cried out, "Sail on the weather

[1] *Corymbus*, a cluster of fruit or flowers.—M.

beam ! Down she comes upon us : in seventy seconds she also will founder."

II.

I looked to the weather side, and the summer had departed. The sea was rocking, and shaken with gathering wrath. Upon its surface sat mighty mists, which grouped themselves into arches and long cathedral aisles. Down one of these, with the fiery pace of a quarrel from a cross-bow,[1] ran a frigate right athwart our course. "Are they mad ?" some voice exclaimed from our deck. "Do they woo their ruin ?" But in a moment, as she was close upon us, some impulse of a heady current or local vortex gave a wheeling bias to her course, and off she forged without a shock. As she ran past us, high aloft amongst the shrouds stood the lady of the pinnace. The deeps opened ahead in malice to receive her, towering surges of foam ran after her, the billows were fierce to catch her. But far away she was borne into desert spaces of the sea : whilst still by sight I followed her, as she ran before the howling gale, chased by angry sea-birds and by maddening billows ; still I saw her, as at the moment when she ran past us, standing amongst the shrouds, with her

---

[1] *Quarrel*, a cross-bow bolt, an arrow with a four-square head ; connected with *quadratus*, made square. Richardson's Dictionary gives this example from Robert Brunne :—

"A quarrelle lete he flie,
And smote him in the schank."—M.

white draperies streaming before the wind. There she stood, with hair dishevelled, one hand clutched amongst the tackling—rising, sinking, fluttering, trembling, praying—there for leagues I saw her as she stood, raising at intervals one hand to heaven, amidst the fiery crests of the pursuing waves and the raving of the storm; until at last, upon a sound from afar of malicious laughter and mockery, all was hidden for ever in driving showers; and afterwards, but when I know not, nor how.

III.

Sweet funeral bells from some incalculable distance, wailing over the dead that die before the dawn, awakened me as I slept in a boat moored to some familiar shore. The morning twilight even then was breaking; and, by the dusky revelations which it spread, I saw a girl, adorned with a garland of white roses about her head for some great festival, running along the solitary strand in extremity of haste. Her running was the running of panic; and often she looked back as to some dreadful enemy in the rear. But when I leaped ashore, and followed on her steps to warn her of a peril in front, alas! from me she fled as from another peril, and vainly I shouted to her of quicksands that lay ahead. Faster and faster she ran; round a promontory of rocks she wheeled out of sight; in an instant I also wheeled round it, but only to see the treacherous sands gathering above her head.   Already her person was buried; only the fair young head and the diadem of white roses around it were still visible to the pitying heavens; and, last of all, was visible one white marble arm.   I saw by the early twilight this fair young head, as it was sinking down to darkness—saw this marble arm, as it rose above her head and her treacherous grave, tossing, faltering, rising, clutching, as at some false deceiving hand stretched out from the clouds—saw this marble arm uttering her dying hope, and then uttering her dying despair.   The head, the diadem, the arm—these all had sunk; at last over these also the cruel quicksand had closed; and no memorial of the fair young girl remained on earth, except my own solitary tears, and the funeral bells from the desert seas, that, rising again more softly, sang a requiem over the grave of the buried child, and over her blighted dawn.

I sat, and wept in secret the tears that men have ever given to the memory of those that died before the dawn, and by the treachery of earth, our mother. But suddenly the tears and funeral bells were hushed by a shout as of many nations, and by a roar as from some great king's artillery, advancing rapidly along the valleys, and heard afar by echoes from the mountains.   "Hush!" I said, as I bent my ear earthwards to listen—"hush!—this either is the very anarchy of strife, or else "—and then I listened more profoundly, and whispered as I raised my head —"or else, oh heavens! it is *victory* that is final, victory that swallows up all strife."

IV.

Immediately, in trance, I was carried over land and sea to some distant kingdom, and placed upon a triumphal car, amongst companions crowned with laurel. The darkness of gathering midnight, brooding over all the land, hid from us the mighty crowds that were weaving restlessly about ourselves as a centre: we heard them, but saw them not. Tidings had arrived, within an hour, of a grandeur that measured itself against centuries; too full of pathos they were, too full of joy, to utter themselves by other language than by tears, by restless anthems, and *Te Deums* reverberated from the choirs and orchestras of earth. These tidings we that sat upon the laurelled car had it for our privilege to publish amongst all nations. And already, by signs audible through the darkness, by snortings and tramplings, our angry horses, that knew no fear of fleshly weariness, upbraided us with delay. Wherefore *was* it that we delayed? We waited for a secret word, that should bear witness to the hope of nations, as now accomplished for ever. At midnight the secret word arrived; which word was—Waterloo and Recovered Christendom! The dreadful word shone by its own light; before us it went; high above our leaders' heads it rode, and spread a golden light over the paths which we traversed. Every city, at the presence of the secret word, threw open its gates. The rivers were conscious as we crossed. All the forests, as we ran along their margins, shivered in homage to the secret word. And the darkness comprehended it.

Two hours after midnight we approached a mighty Minster. Its gates, which rose to the clouds, were closed. But when the dreadful word, that rode before us, reached them with its golden light, silently they moved back upon their hinges; and at a flying gallop our equipage entered the grand aisle of the cathedral. Headlong was our pace; and at every altar, in the little chapels and oratories to the right hand and left of our course, the lamps, dying or sickening, kindled anew in sympathy with the secret word that was flying past. Forty leagues we might have run in the cathedral, and as yet no strength of morning light had reached us, when before us we saw the aerial galleries of organ and choir. Every pinnacle of the fretwork, every station of advantage amongst the traceries, was crested by white-robed choristers, that sang deliverance; that wept no more tears, as once their fathers had wept; but at intervals that sang together to the generations, saying,

"Chant the deliverer's praise in every tougue,"

and receiving answers from afar,

"Such as once in heaven and earth were sung."

And of their chanting was no end; of our headlong pace was neither pause nor slackening.[1]

Thus, as we ran like torrents—thus, as we swept

---

[1] "Slackening" substituted in the reprint of 1854 for "remission" in the original *Blackwood* article of 1849.—M.

with bridal rapture over the Campo Santo[1] of the cathedral graves—suddenly we became aware of a vast necropolis rising upon the far-off horizon—a city of sepulchres, built within the saintly cathedral for the warrior dead that rested from their feuds on earth. Of purple granite was the necropolis; yet, in the first minute, it lay like a purple stain upon the horizon, so mighty was the distance. In the second minute it trembled through many changes, growing into terraces and towers of wondrous altitude, so mighty was the pace. In the third minute already, with our dreadful gallop, we were entering its suburbs. Vast sarcophagi rose on every side, having towers and turrets that, upon the limits of the central aisle, strode forward with haughty intrusion, that ran back with mighty shadows into answering recesses. Every sarcophagus showed many bas-reliefs—bas-reliefs of battles and of battle-fields; battles from forgotten ages—battles from yesterday—battle-fields

[1] "*Campo Santo :*"—It is probable that most of my readers will be acquainted with the history of the Campo Santo (or cemetery) at Pisa, composed of earth brought from Jerusalem from a bed of sanctity, as the highest prize which the noble piety of crusaders could ask or imagine. To readers who are unacquainted with England, or who (being English) are yet unacquainted with the cathedral cities of England, it may be right to mention that the graves within-side the cathedrals often form a flat pavement over which carriages and horses *might* run; and perhaps a boyish remembrance of one particular cathedral, across which I had seen passengers walk and burdens carried, as about two centuries back they were through the middle of St. Paul's in London, may have assisted my dream.

that, long since, nature had healed and reconciled to
herself with the sweet oblivion of flowers—battle-fields
that were yet angry and crimson with carnage. Where
the terraces ran, there did *we* run ; where the towers
curved, there did *we* curve. With the flight of
swallows our horses swept round every angle. Like
rivers in flood, wheeling round headlands — like
hurricanes that ride into the secrets of forests—
faster than ever light unwove the mazes of darkness,
our flying equipage carried earthly passions, kindled
warrior instincts, amongst the dust that lay around
us—dust oftentimes of our noble fathers that had
slept in God from Créci to Trafalgar. And now
had we reached the last sarcophagus, now were we
abreast of the last bas-relief, already had we recovered
the arrow-like flight of the illimitable central aisle,
when coming up this aisle to meet us we beheld afar
off a female child, that rode in a carriage as frail as
flowers. The mists, which went before her, hid the
fawns that drew her, but could not hide the shells
and tropic flowers with which she played—but could
not hide the lovely smiles by which she uttered her
trust in the mighty cathedral, and in the cherubim
that looked down upon her from the mighty shafts
of its pillars. Face to face she was meeting us ; face
to face she rode, as if danger there were none.
"Oh, baby !" I exclaimed, "shalt thou be the ransom
for Waterloo ? Must we, that carry tidings of great
joy to every people, be messengers of ruin to thee !"
In horror I rose at the thought ; but then also, in

horror at the thought, rose one that was sculptured on a bas-relief—a Dying Trumpeter. Solemnly from the field of battle he rose to his feet; and, unslinging his stony trumpet, carried it, in his dying anguish, to his stony lips—sounding once, and yet once again; proclamation that, in *thy* ears, oh baby! spoke from the battlements of death. Immediately deep shadows fell between us, and aboriginal silence. The choir had ceased to sing. The hoofs of our horses, the dreadful rattle of our harness, the groaning of our wheels, alarmed the graves no more. By horror the bas-relief had been unlocked unto life. By horror we, that were so full of life, we men and our horses, with their fiery fore-legs rising in mid air to their everlasting gallop, were frozen to a bas-relief. Then a third time the trumpet sounded; the seals were taken off all pulses; life, and the frenzy of life, tore into their channels again; again the choir burst forth in sunny grandeur, as from the muffling of storms and darkness; again the thunderings of our horses carried temptation into the graves. One cry burst from our lips, as the clouds, drawing off from the aisle, showed it empty before us—" Whither has the infant fled?—is the young child caught up to God?" Lo! afar off, in a vast recess, rose three mighty windows to the clouds; and on a level with their summits, at height insuperable to man, rose an altar of purest alabaster. On its eastern face was trembling a crimson glory. A glory was it from the reddening dawn that now streamed *through* the

windows ? Was it from the crimson robes of the
martyrs painted *on* the windows ? Was it from the
bloody bas-reliefs of earth ? There, suddenly, within
that crimson radiance, rose the apparition of a
woman's head, and then of a woman's figure. The
child it was—grown up to woman's height.[1] Clinging
to the horns of the altar, voiceless she stood—sinking,
rising, raving, despairing ; and behind the volume of
incense, that, night and day, streamed upwards from
the altar, dimly was seen the fiery font, and the
shadow of that dreadful being who should have
baptized her with the baptism of death. But by
her side was kneeling her better angel, that hid his
face with wings ; that wept and pleaded for *her ;*
that prayed when *she* could *not ;* that fought with
Heaven by tears for *her* deliverance ; which also, as
he raised his immortal countenance from his wings,
I saw, by the glory in his eye, that from Heaven he
had won at last.

V.

Then was completed the passion of the mighty
fugue. The golden tubes of the organ, which as yet
had but muttered at intervals—gleaming amongst
clouds and surges of incense—threw up, as from
fountains unfathomable, columns of heart-shattering

---

[1] The two sentences here ending stood thus in the original in
Blackwood :—"Whencesoever it were—there, within that crimson
radiance, suddenly appeared a female head, and then a female
figure. It was the child, now grown up to a woman's height."—M.

music. Choir and anti-choir were filling fast with unknown voices. Thou also, Dying Trumpeter!—with thy love that was victorious, and thy anguish that was finishing—didst enter the tumult; trumpet and echo—farewell love, and farewell anguish—rang through the dreadful *sanctus*.[1] Oh, darkness of the grave! that from the crimson altar and from the fiery font wert visited and searched by the effulgence in the angel's eye—were these indeed thy children? Pomps of life, that, from the burials of centuries, rose again to the voice of perfect joy, did ye indeed mingle with the festivals of Death?[2] Lo! as I looked back for seventy leagues through the mighty cathedral, I saw the quick and the dead that sang together to God, together that sang to the generations of man. All the hosts of jubilation, like armies that ride in pursuit, moved with one step. Us, that, with laurelled heads, were passing from the cathedral, they overtook, and, as with a garment, they wrapped us round with thunders greater than our own. As brothers we moved together; to the dawn that advanced—to the stars that fled; rendering thanks to God in the highest—that, having hid His face through one generation behind thick clouds of War, once again was ascending—from the Campo Santo of Waterloo was ascending—in the visions of Peace; rendering thanks for thee, young girl! whom, having over-shadowed with His ineffable passion of death, suddenly

---

[1] Four sentences of the original in *Blackwood* omitted here.—M.

[2] Sentences again omitted that were in the original.—M.

did God relent ; suffered thy angel to turn aside His
arm ; and even in thee, sister unknown ! shown to
me for a moment only to be hidden for ever, found
an occasion to glorify His goodness.   A thousand
times, amongst the phantoms of sleep, have I seen
thee entering the gates of the golden dawn—with
the secret word riding before thee—with the armies
of the grave behind thee ; seen thee sinking, rising,
raving, despairing ; a thousand times in the worlds
of sleep have seen thee followed by God's angel
through storms ; through desert seas ; through the
darkness of quicksands ; through dreams, and the
dreadful revelations that are in dreams—only that
at the last, with one sling of His victorious arm, He
might snatch thee back from ruin, and might emblazon in thy deliverance the endless resurrections
of His love ![1]

---

[1] This last sentence, like all the rest of the paragraph, is much
modified from the original in *Blackwood.*   There it stood thus :—
"A thousand times, amongst the phantoms of sleep, has he shown
thee to me, standing before the golden dawn, and ready to enter
its fgates—with the dreadful Word going before thee—with the
armies of the grave behind thee ; shown thee to me, sinking, rising,
fluttering, fainting, but then suddenly reconciled, adoring: a
thousand times has he followed thee in the worlds of sleep—
through storms ; through desert seas ; through the darkness of
quicksands ; through fugues and the persecution of fugues ;
through dreams, and the dreadful resurrections that are in dreams
—only that at the last, with one motion of his victorious arm,
he might record and emblazon the endless resurrections of his
love !"—M.

APPENDED NOTES

MR. PALMER AND HIS NEW MAIL-COACH SYSTEM

MR. JOHN PALMER, a native of Bath, and from about 1768 the energetic proprietor of the Theatre Royal in that city, had been led, by the wretched state in those days of the means of inter-communication between Bath and London, and his own conse-quent difficulties in arranging for a punctual succession of good actors at his theatre, to turn his attention to the improvement of the whole system of Post-Office conveyance, and of locomotive machinery generally, in the British Islands. The following extract from a biographic sketch of him in Volume LXXXVIII., Part II., of *The Gentleman's Magazine*, will give some concep-tion of his procedure in pursuit of his purpose :—"Mr. Palmer, in the course of his frequent journeys, saw and felt the imper-fections of the posts, and was also convinced of the possibility of their reformation. Inspired, as it were, with this idea, he prepared his mind by degrees for the accomplishment of his object, beginning with an examination of all the Posts and Post-Offices in the kingdom ; and now it was that he found an Herculean labour, and, as it afterwards turned out, an Augean stable, requiring much more than the strength of a Hercules to cleanse it. In every part of the kingdom he found abuses of such an extent and magnitude as would not possibly be credited but by one who thus minutely analysed them. But how to remedy and bring into order this vast, irregular, and complicated machine was a task which, the more he viewed and considered, the more he was deterred from attempting. At last he made up his mind determinately to traverse the whole kingdom by stage-coaches wheresoever they were established, to observe the state of the roads, the time they each occupied in performing their journeys in winter and summer, how they were conducted, how they might be better regulated and made suitable for the conveyance of the mails.   In his journeys over the kingdom he generally travelled, for better observation and information from the coachmen, on the outside ; and he repeatedly witnessed the delay and danger to passengers from the frequent stoppages at public-houses, the drunkenness and brutality of drivers, decayed coaches and horses, and from the immense weights they occasionally were loaded with : often having witnessed coaches breaking down, and cattle dying on the road."—The result was a scheme for superseding, on the great roads at least, the then existing system of sluggish and irregular stage-coaches, the property of private persons and companies, by a new system of government coaches, in connexion with the Post-Office, carrying the mails, and also a regulated number of passengers, with clock-work precision, at a rate of comparative speed, which he hoped should ulti-mately be not less than ten miles an hour.   The opposition to the scheme was, of course, enormous ; coach-proprietors, inn-keepers, the Post-Office officials themselves, were all against Mr. Palmer; he was voted a crazy enthusiast and a public bore. Pitt, however, when the scheme was submitted to him, recognised its feasibility ; on the 8th of August 1784 the first mail-coach on Mr. Palmer's plan started from London at 8 o'clock in the morning and reached Bristol at 11 o'clock at night ; and from that day, coach after coach on the same plan having been put upon the roads, the success of the new system was assured.— Mr. Palmer himself having been appointed Surveyor and Comp-troller-General of the Post-Office, and having in that capacity so perfected the mail-arrangements that, while the whole country was feeling the benefit, the net revenue to the Govern-ment from the Post-Office had risen from £150,000 a year to many times that sum, one might have expected for his later years nothing but national gratitude.   But, though he had taken rank as an eminent public man, M.P. for Bath and what not, opposition still dogged him; and from about 1806 to 1813 he was engaged in a contest with Parliament on the subject of the remuneration due to him for his Post-Office and Mail-Coach reform. By his contract with the Government that remuneration was to consist of 2½ per cent for life on all the *increase* of the Post-Office revenue that should be effected by his system, —his receipts to be nothing should there be no increase. After a great deal of discussion, of which there are copious records in Parliamentary Papers of the time, Parliament repudiated the bargain; and Mr. Palmer's claims were discharged in full by a single compensation-grant of £50,000. He lived some little while after this settlement with him, and died at Brighton on the 16th of August 1818.—De Quincey, in the first paragraph of his paper, makes it one of Mr. Palmer's distinctions that he "had married the daughter of a duke"; and in a footnote to that paragraph the lady's name is given as "Lady Madeline Gordon" (ante p. 159). From an old Debrett, however, I learn that Lady Madelina Gordon, second daughter of Alexander, fourth Duke of Gordon, was first married, on the 3d of April 1789, to Sir Robert Sinclair, Bart., and next, on the 25th of November 1805, to *Charles Palmer, of Lockley Park, Berks, Esq.* If Debrett is right, her second husband was not the John Palmer of Mail-Coach celebrity, and De Quincey is wrong.—D. M.

CANCELLED PARAGRAPH

It has been mentioned in the footnote at p. 188 that De Quincey, in revising his *Blackwood* article of October 1849 for republication in Volume IV. of his Collected Works in 1854, shortened the paragraph immediately preceding that portion of the article which bears the sub-heading "GOING DOWN WITH VICTORY" into about one-fifth of its original bulk. The following is the entire paragraph as it stood in *Blackwood:*—

"Perhaps, therefore, the crocodile does *not* change, but all

" things else *do;* even the shadow of the Pyramids grows less.
" And often the restoration in vision of Fanny and the Bath
" road, makes me too pathetically sensible of that truth.   Out
" of the darkness, if I happen to call up the image of Fanny
" from thirty-five years back, arises suddenly a rose in June ;
" or, if I think for an instant of a rose in June, up rises the
" heavenly face of Fanny.   One after the other, like the anti-
" phonies in a choral service, rises Fanny and the rose in June,
" then back again the rose in June and Fanny.   Then come
" both together, as in a chorus ; roses and Fannies, Fannies
" and roses, without end—thick as blossoms in paradise.   Then
" comes a venerable crocodile, in a royal livery of scarlet and
" gold, or in a coat with sixteen capes ; and the crocodile is
" driving four-in-hand from the box of the Bath mail.   And
" suddenly we upon the mail are pulled up by a mighty dial,
" sculptured with the hours, and with the dreadful legend of
" Too Late.   Then all at once we are arrived in Marlborough
" forest, amongst the lovely households of the roe-deer : these
" retire into the dewy thickets ; the thickets are rich with
" roses ; the roses call up (as ever) the sweet countenance of
" Fanny, who, being the granddaughter of a crocodile, awakens
" a dreadful host of wild semi-legendary animals—griffins,
" dragons, basilisks, sphinxes—till at length the whole vision
" of fighting images crowds into one towering armorial shield,
" a vast emblazonry of human charities and human loveliness
" that have perished, but quartered heraldically with unutter-
" able horrors of monstrous and demoniac natures ; whilst over
" all rises, as a surmounting crest, one fair female hand, with
" the fore-finger pointing, in sweet, sorrowful admonition, up-
" wards to heaven, and having power (which, without experi-
" ence, I never could have believed) to awaken the pathos that
" kills in the very bosom of the horrors that madden the grief
" that gnaws at the heart, together with the monstrous creations
" of darkness that shock the belief, and make dizzy the reason
" of man.   This is the peculiarity that I wish the reader to
" notice, as having first been made known to me for a possi-
" bility by this early vision of Fanny on the Bath road.   The

" peculiarity consisted in the confluence of two different keys,
" though apparently repelling each other, into the music and
" governing principles of the same dream ; horror, such as pos-
" sesses the maniac, and yet, by momentary transitions, grief,
" such as may be supposed to possess the dying mother when
" leaving her infant children to the mercies of the cruel.
" Usually, and perhaps always, in an unshaken nervous system,
" these two modes of misery exclude each other—here first they
" met in horrid reconciliation. There was always a separate
" peculiarity in the quality of the horror. This was afterwards
" developed into far more revolting complexities of misery and
" incomprehensible darkness ; and perhaps I am wrong in
" ascribing any value as a *causative* agency to this particular
" case on the Bath road—possibly it furnished merely an *occa-*
" *sion* that accidentally introduced a mode of horrors certain,
" at any rate, to have grown up, with or without the Bath
" road, from more advanced stages of the nervous derangement.
" Yet, as the cubs of tigers or leopards, when domesticated,
" have been observed to suffer a sudden development of their
" latent ferocity under too eager an appeal to their playfulness
" —the gaieties of sport in *them* being too closely connected
" with the fiery brightness of their murderous instincts—so I
" have remarked that the caprices, the gay arabesques, and
" the lively floral luxuriations of dreams, betray a shocking
" tendency to pass into finer maniacal splendours. That gaiety,
" for instance, (for such at first it was,) in the dreaming faculty,
" by which one principal point of resemblance to a crocodile in
" the mail-coachman was soon made to clothe him with the
" form of a crocodile, and yet was blended with accessory cir-
" cumstances derived from his *human* functions, passed rapidly
" into a further development, no longer gay or playful, but
" terrific, the most terrific that besieges dreams, viz.—the
" horrid inoculation upon each other of incompatible natures.
" This horror has always been secretly felt by man ; it was felt
" even under pagan forms of religion, which offered a very
" feeble, and also a very limited gamut for giving expression to
" the human capacities of sublimity or of horror. We read it

" in the fearful composition of the sphinx. The dragon, again,
" is the snake inoculated upon the scorpion. The basilisk
" unites the mysterious malice of the evil eye, unintentional
" on the part of the unhappy agent, with the intentional venom
" of some other malignant natures. But these horrid com-
" plexities of evil agency are but *objectively* horrid ; they inflict
" the horror suitable to their compound nature ; but there is
" no insinuation that they *feel* that horror. Heraldry is so full
" of these fantastic creatures, that, in some zoologies, we find
" a separate chapter or a supplement dedicated to what is
" denominated heraldic zoology. And why not ? For these
" hideous creatures, however visionary, have a real traditionary
" ground in medieval belief—sincere and partly reasonable,
" though adulterating with mendacity, blundering, credulity,
" and intense superstition. But the dream-horror which I
" speak of is far more frightful. The dreamer finds housed
" within himself—occupying, as it were, some separate chamber
" in his brain—holding, perhaps, from that station a secret
" and detestable commerce with his own heart—some horrid
" alien nature. What if it were his own nature repeated,—
" still, if the duality were distinctly perceptible, even that—
" even this mere numerical double of his own consciousness
" —might be a curse too mighty to be sustained. But how, if
" the alien nature contradicts his own, fights with it, perplexes
" and confounds it ? How, again, if not one alien nature, but
" two, but three, but four, but five, are introduced within what
" once he thought the inviolable sanctuary of himself ? These,
" however, are horrors from the kingdom of anarchy and dark-
" ness, which, by their very intensity, challenge the sanctity
" of concealment, and gloomily retire from exposition. Yet it
" was necessary to mention them, because the first introduction
" to such appearances (whether causal, or merely casual) lay in
" the heraldic monsters, which monsters were themselves intro-
" duced (though playfully) by the transfigured coachman of the
" Bath mail."

Connected with this paragraph in the text was a footnote,
also now cancelled. It was attached to the words "however

visionary " as applied to the monstrous animals of heraldry, and ran as follows :—

" '*However visionary.*'—But *are* they always visionary ? " The unicorn, the kraken, the sea-serpent, are all, perhaps, " zoological facts. The unicorn, for instance, so far from being " a lie, is rather *too* true ; for, simply as a *monokeras*, he is " found in the Himalaya, in Africa, and elsewhere, rather too " often for the peace of what in Scotland would be called the " *intending* traveller. That which really *is* a lie in the account " of the unicorn—viz., his legendary rivalship with the lion— " which lie may God preserve, in preserving the mighty " imperial shield that embalms it—cannot be more destructive " to the zoological pretensions of the unicorn, than are to the " same pretensions in the lion our many popular crazes about " his goodness and magnanimity, or the old fancy (adopted by " Spenser, and noticed by so many among our elder poets) of " his graciousness to maiden innocence. The wretch is the " basest and most cowardly among the forest tribes ; nor has " the sublime courage of the English bull-dog ever been so " memorably exhibited as in his hopeless fight at Warwick " with the cowardly and cruel lion called Wallace. Another " of the traditional creatures, still doubtful, is the mermaid, " upon which Southey once remarked to me, that, if it had " been differently named, (as, suppose, a mer-ape,) nobody " would have questioned its existence any more than that of " sea-cows, sea-lions, etc. The mermaid has been discredited " by her human name and her legendary human habits. If " she would not coquette so much with melancholy sailors, " and brush her hair so assiduously on solitary rocks, she " would be carried on our books for as honest a reality, as " decent a female, as many that are assessed to the poor-rates."

Why did De Quincey, when revising his ENGLISH MAIL-COACH for Volume IV. of his Collected Writings, delete so elaborate a paragraph, with so elaborate an attached footnote ? Doubtless it was because he felt that such a long dissertation on heraldic monsters, "the horrid inoculation upon each other of incompatible natures," etc., all hung upon the mere mention

of the crocodile look of Fanny's grandfather, would be resented
by most readers as something foisted on its own account into
the heart of his Mail-Coach paper, and stopping the otherwise
genial current of the text.   He therefore sacrificed four-fifths of
the original paragraph, retaining only the one-fifth that would
easily cohere with the narrative.   The change was judicious ;
but the digression, with its curious theory of "the horrid
inoculation upon each other of incompatible natures," is characteristic of De Quincey, and is worth preserving in a detached
form.—D. M.

De Quincey's Explanation of his Dream-Fugue

The following is the passage on this subject referred to in
the Introduction as having been inserted in the preface to Vol.
IV. of De Quincey's Collected Works in 1854 :—

" 'The English Mail-Coach.'—This little paper, according
" to my original intention, formed part of the 'Suspiria de
" Profundis,' from which, for a momentary purpose, I did not
" scruple to detach it, and to publish it apart, as sufficiently
" intelligible even when dislocated from its place in a larger
" whole.   To my surprise, however, one or two critics, not
" carelessly in conversation, but deliberately in print, professed
" their inability to apprehend the meaning of the whole, or to
" follow the links of the connection between its several parts.
" I am myself as little able to understand where the difficulty
" lies, or to detect any lurking obscurity, as these critics found
" themselves to unravel my logic.   Possibly I may not be an
" indifferent and neutral judge in such a case.   I will therefore
" sketch a brief abstract of the little paper according to my
" original design, and then leave the reader to judge how far
" this design is kept in sight through the actual execution.

" Thirty-seven years ago, or rather more, accident made me,
" in the dead of night, and of a night memorably solemn, the
" solitary witness of an appalling scene, which threatened
" instant death in a shape the most terrific to two young people,

" whom I had no means of assisting, except in so far as I was
" able to give them a most hurried warning of their danger ;
" but even *that* not until they stood within the very shadow of
" the catastrophe, being divided from the most frightful of
" deaths by scarcely more, if more at all, than seventy seconds.

" Such was the scene, such in its outline, from which the
" whole of this paper radiates as a natural expansion. This
" scene is circumstantially narrated in Section the Second,
" entitled 'The Vision of Sudden Death.'

" But a movement of horror, and of spontaneous recoil from
" this dreadful scene, naturally carried the whole of that scene,
" raised and idealised, into my dreams, and very soon into a
" rolling succession of dreams. The actual scene, as looked
" down upon from the box of the mail, was transformed into a
" dream, as tumultuous and changing as a musical fugue. This
" troubled dream is circumstantially reported in Section the
" Third, entitled 'Dream-Fugue on the theme of Sudden
" Death.' What I had beheld from my seat upon the mail ;
" the scenical strife of action and passion, of anguish and fear,
" as I had there witnessed them moving in ghostly silence ;
" this duel between life and death narrowing itself to a point
" of such exquisite evanescence as the collision neared ; all
" these elements of the scene blended, under the law of associa-
" tion, with the previous and permanent features of distinction
" investing the mail itself : which features at that time lay—
" 1st, in velocity unprecedented ; 2dly, in the power and beauty
" of the horses ; 3dly, in the official connection with the
" government of a great nation ; and, 4thly, in the function,
" almost a consecrated function, of publishing and diffusing
" through the land the great political events, and especially
" the great battles during a conflict of unparalleled grandeur.
" These honorary distinctions are all described circumstantially
" in the First or introductory Section ('The Glory of Motion ').
" The three first were distinctions maintained at all times ; but
" the fourth and grandest belonged exclusively to the war with
" Napoleon ; and this it was which most naturally introduced
" Waterloo into the dream. Waterloo, I understood, was the

"particular feature of the 'Dream-Fugue' which my censors
"were least able to account for.   Yet surely Waterloo, which,
"in common with every other great battle, it had been our
"special privilege to publish over all the land, most naturally
"entered the dream under the licence of our privilege.   If not
"—if there be anything amiss—let the Dream be responsible.
"The Dream is a law to itself: and as well quarrel with a
"rainbow for showing, or for *not* showing, a secondary arch.
"So far as I know, every element in the shifting movements of
"the Dream derived itself either primarily from the incidents
"of the actual scene, or from secondary features associated
"with the mail.   For example, the cathedral aisle derived
"itself from the mimic combination of features which grouped
"themselves together at the point of approaching collision—
"viz., an arrow-like section of the road, six hundred yards
"long, under the solemn lights described, with lofty trees
"meeting overhead in arches.   The guard's horn, again—a
"humble instrument in itself—was yet glorified as the organ
"of publication for so many great national events.   And the
"incident of the Dying Trumpeter, who rises from a marble
"bas-relief, and carries a marble trumpet to his marble lips for
"the purpose of warning the female infant, was doubtless
"secretly suggested by my own imperfect effort to seize the
"guard's horn, and to blow a warning blast.   But the Dream
"knows best ; and the Dream, I say again, is the responsible
"party."

This is more interesting than convincing.   Despite the
information that the scene of Section Second of the paper was
the first in De Quincey's mind and that the rest came by
expansion forwards and backwards from that scene, the reader
will take the three sections in the order in which they now
stand ; and, what is more, he will not and cannot take the
Dream of the Third Section as an actual dream, responsible for
itself, but as an invented dream.—D. M.

SUSPIRIA DE PROFUNDIS:

BEING A SEQUEL TO THE

"CONFESSIONS OF AN ENGLISH OPIUM-EATER"

INTRODUCTION

As has been explained in the Introduction to THE ENGLISH MAIL-COACH, De Quincey had begun in 1845 a special series of contributions to Blackwood's Magazine under the title of SUSPIRIA DE PROFUNDIS : BEING A SEQUEL TO THE CONFESSIONS OF AN ENGLISH OPIUM-EATER. It seems clear that he intended this series to be a collection of fragments or papers, some perhaps already beside him in manuscript, but others still to be written, all of that species of prose-phantasy, and some more particularly in that vein of dream-phantasy, of which his CONFESSIONS OF AN OPIUM-EATER had been, as he believed, the first example set in English Literature. Hence the propriety of announcing the new series as a projected sequel to those celebrated earlier papers. For some reason or other, however, whether because De Quincey himself became fagged or dilatory, or because a long continuity of papers under the melancholy title of "Sighs from the Depths" did not suit the editorial arrangements of Blackwood, the series broke down. In the number of the Magazine for March 1845 there appeared, by way of opening the series, an "*Introductory Notice*" on the subject of

Dreaming in general, but especially of Opium-Dreaming, followed by an autobiographic paper entitled "*The Affliction of Childhood*," and a few separate and untitled paragraphs of lyrical prose; in the number for April in the same year there were a few more pages of autobiographical and lyrical paragraphs, undistinguished by any sub-titles, but offered together as a continuation of "Part I." of the SUSPIRIA DE PROFUNDIS; and in the number for June in the same year the said "Part I.," which had thus been going on already through two numbers, was announced as "concluded,"—the conclusion consisting of four independent short papers, sub-titled respectively "*The Palimpsest*," "*Levana and Our Ladies of Sorrow*," "*The Apparition of the Brocken*," and "*Savannah-la-Mar*." This last short paper purported to be also "Finale to Part I."; and there the series stopped,—Parts II. III. and IV. (for there were to be four Parts in all) never having found their way into *Blackwood*, or even into existence.

De Quincey, indeed, seems still to have secretly adhered for a time to his notion of making SUSPIRIA DE PROFUNDIS the collective name for a miscellany of such papers or shreds as might prove his unabated vigour in his later years in his old craft of English prose-phantasy. His fine little sketch called *The Daughter of Lebanon* purports to have been written for the SUSPIRIA; and we have his own word for the fact that THE ENGLISH MAIL-COACH itself was originally meant to be part of that series. When that paper got into in *Blackwood* 1849, however, it appeared independently, and without the least intimation of any connexion between it and the interrupted and unfinished SUSPIRIA set of papers of 1845. That set of magazine papers of 1845, calling itself "Part I." of the SUSPIRIA DE PROFUNDIS, remained, in fact, till De Quincey's death the only things of his that bore openly and avowedly the striking name which he had hoped, by gradual additions in the same vein, to leave much more comprehensively represented.

Before his death, indeed, he had, by his own act, diminished the quantity of his writings that could in future claim the striking name. When preparing in Edinburgh that Collective Edition of his works in fourteen volumes the publication of which extended from 1853 to 1860, he pillaged at his pleasure the *Blackwood* set of SUSPIRIA papers of 1845, whether that he might use some of them as stop-gaps when he wanted matter to fill out a volume to sufficient dimensions, or that he might distribute them more fitly through the volumes without continuing to call them SUSPIRIA. Thus, not only was *The Daughter of Lebanon* attached to the new and enlarged edition of the CONFESSIONS OF AN ENGLISH OPIUM-EATER which formed Volume V. of the collective issue, and not only was there no replacing of THE ENGLISH MAIL-COACH in its originally intended relationship; but so much of Part. I. of the SUSPIRIA as had appeared in the three numbers of *Blackwood* for March, April, and June 1845 was utilised, in recast shape, in new connexions,— *The Affliction of Childhood* and *The Apparition of the Brocken*, for example, being worked into the Volume of "Autobiographic Sketches"— that nothing tangible remained of what had once been that Part I. of the SUSPIRIA, except *The Introductory Notice* and some of the stray lyrical paragraphs, together with *The Palimpsest, Levana and our Ladies of Sorrow*, and *Savannah-la-Mar*. De Quincey had been revising and retouching these too ; but what he would have done with them if he had lived to extend the collective re-issue of his works to more than fourteen volumes can hardly be guessed. As it was, though there was frequent mention of the SUSPIRIA DE PROFUNDIS in the course of those volumes, with explanations of their peculiar intention, not a single paper appeared in the whole of the fourteen-volume Edition under that express title.

. When, however, the present proprietors of De Quincey's works augmented the collection of them by adding two more volumes, containing papers which De Quincey had left in a more or less revised state in the hands of the proprietors of the previous edition, and also other papers thought worthy of recovery from the periodicals in which they had originally appeared, they included all those still stray pieces for which SUSPIRIA DE PROFUNDIS seemed to be the name reserved. Accordingly, in Volume XVI. of the now standard edition of De Quincey there are forty-nine pages of matter bearing the general title of SUSPIRIA DE PROFUNDIS : BEING A SEQUEL TO THE

CONFESSIONS OF AN ENGLISH OPIUM-EATER, and consisting of separate short papers, sub-titled, in conformity with indications which De Quincey had left, severally thus :—(1) *Dreaming*, (2) *The Palimpsest of the Human Brain*, (3) *Levana and our Ladies of Sorrow*, (4) *Savannah-la-Mar*, (5) *Vision of Life*, (6) *Memorial Suspiria.* With these may be now re-associated that other little paper, entitled *The Daughter of Lebanon*, which belonged, in De Quincey's original intention, to the series of the SUSPIRIA. For, though he detached that paper from the rest in the collective issue of his writings superintended by himself, he detached it in such a way as still to declare its connexion with the rest. He annexed it, in fragmentary fashion, to his revised and enlarged edition of the CONFESSIONS OF AN ENGLISH OPIUM-EATER (forming Vol. V. of his own fourteen-volume issue, but now forming Vol. I. of the later sixteen-volume issue), thus distinctly offering it as one piece of sequel to the CONFESSIONS, and so reserving its rights to be re-included at any time among those other pieces of sequel to the same which he had schemed out under the name of SUSPIRIA DE PROFUNDIS.

The SUSPIRIA, as we now have them, consisting only of those few separate fragments which De Quincey left to be edited under that title, one is at liberty to arrange these in what may seem now their fittest and most natural order. They are reproduced here as follows :—

I. *Dreaming :*—There can be no doubt that this

paper should go first. It appeared originally in *Blackwood* with the title "Introductory Notice"; and, though De Quincey left the title changed into "Dreaming" in his revised MS. of the paper, its office is still that of an introduction to the others. It avowedly connects the SUSPIRIA DE PROFUNDIS with the CONFESSIONS OF AN ENGLISH OPIUM-EATER, and explains the nature of the connexion,—being in fact less a piece of prose-phantasy itself than an exposition of the origin of prose-phantasy in the phenomena of dreaming, and, in his own case, especially in opium-dreaming. A fine little exposition of that sort it is. The eloquent passage on the decay of the habit of solitude in modern life, and on the necessity of a retention of that habit by some means or other, in the interest of a percentage at least, if there is to be a continuance in the world of any of the higher powers and efforts of intellect, is particularly worthy of attention.

II. *The Palimpsest of the Human Brain:*—This paper appeared in *Blackwood* with the title "The Palimpsest" merely; but the expansion is De Quincey's own. The purpose is still mainly expository, so that the paper may be described as a little psychological dissertation; but it is a dissertation in De Quincey's own fashion, and dashed therefore with that faculty of poetic phantasy which it professes to elucidate.

III. *Vision of Life:*—The two meditative, and rather mystical, paragraphs bearing this title do not

occur among the SUSPIRIA set of papers called
"Part. I." in *Blackwood* of March, April, and June
1845, but seem to be a stray "chip" from De
Quincey's private preparations towards Part. II. of
the SUSPIRIA. Indeed, in the American Collective
Edition of his writings, they figure as two paragraphs
of the text of a longish continuous paper which is
expressly called "Part II." of this SEQUEL TO THE
CONFESSIONS OF AN ENGLISH OPIUM-EATER. My
impression is that De Quincey, as soon as he came to
work on his own British Collective Edition of his
writings, divided his available material of the Suspiria
kind for that edition between *two* sequels to his
OPIUM EATING CONFESSIONS,—viz. his continued
AUTOBIOGRAPHIC SKETCHES and the SUSPIRIA to be
still so called,—and that "chips" thrown off from the
AUTOBIOGRAPHIC SKETCHES in that edition remained
over for inclusion among the SUSPIRIA. But the
distinction seems to have troubled him.

IV. *Memorial Suspiria :*—Neither is this paper one
of the *Blackwood* set of 1845. It is found as an
integral portion of the above-mentioned "Part II." of
the SUSPIRIA as printed in the American Collective
Edition,—separated by only a few pages of autobiographic narrative from the two paragraphs now
entitled *Vision of Life.* It may be regarded, therefore,
as another "chip" transferred from the AUTOBIO-
GRAPHIC SKETCHES to the SUSPIRIA. But it is very
properly among these now, being really a piece of
prose-phantasy. It starts, indeed, with a meditative

idea,—the idea how dreadful it would be if one could look forward, from an early point in one's life, to all that was to happen in and during that life, foreseeing this or that calamity in it, and realising the shock beforehand.   But, having propounded this idea in the opening paragraph, he proceeds to illustrate it by a story of family sorrows that lay within his own recollection.   Hence the title *Memorial Suspiria*.   The story is full of pathos, and is told beautifully and dreamily.

. V. *Savannah-la-Mar :*—This is in a still higher key. It is the dream of a city in the tropics that has been submerged, with all its inhabitants, by an earthquake, and the ruins of which, overspreading the ocean-bed, are to be seen, on calm days, by passing mariners, deep down through the glassy water.   The dream is made to yield a powerful metaphysical meaning, in the proposition that what to man is time present does not exist for God, but that the future is God's present, and that hence arises the mystery of His working by earthquake, and also by grief.

VI. *The Daughter of Lebanon :*—More even than the last two pieces, this answers to what may be called the ideal of a prose-poem.   It is a dream of a Syrian woman, grievously wronged and deserted, so that there is no further hope for her in the world, but for whom her conversion to Christianity opens up a higher hope, and who welcomes her release, since there can be no other, by a peaceful Christian death.   Such is the substance, so far as a few words can tell the substance; but the story is kept vague and shadowy, and the effect is as of a dream-idyll set to music.

VII. *Levana and our Ladies of Sorrow :*—One reason for putting this piece last is that De Quincey himself calls attention to it as furnishing a key to the whole scheme of his SUSPIRIA DE PROFUNDIS had he been able to complete the series. See Appended Footnote, *De Quincey's Superseded Note to his Levana.* Another reason, however, is that this little paper is perhaps, all in all, the finest thing that De Quincey ever wrote. It is certainly the most perfect specimen he has left us of his peculiar art of English prose-poetry, and certainly also one of the most magnificent pieces of prose in the English or in any other language. It is, as I have ventured to say elsewhere, a permanent addition to the mythology of the human race; and, had De Quincey left us nothing else, it would have entitled him to immortality in our literature. On this ground, were there no other, it may fitly close these volumes of selections from him in his narrative and imaginative vein.—D. M.

SUSPIRIA DE PROFUNDIS:

BEING A SEQUEL TO THE

"CONFESSIONS OF AN ENGLISH OPIUM-EATER"

DREAMING

IN 1821, as a contribution to a periodical work,—in 1822, as a separate volume,—appeared the "Confessions of an English Opium-Eater."[1] The object of

[1] This famous publication first appeared as an article in two parts, with the title CONFESSIONS OF AN OPIUM-EATER, BEING AN EXTRACT FROM THE LIFE OF A SCHOLAR, in the *London Magazine* for September and October 1821, when De Quincey was thirty-six years of age. The popularity of the article caused the proprietors of the magazine, Messrs. Taylor and Hessey, to reprint it in 1822, in the form of a small duodecimo volume, revised by the author, and with the modified title of CONFESSIONS OF AN ENGLISH OPIUM-EATER. Of this original form of the CONFESSIONS there have been several later editions, the last and most beautiful being that of Messrs. Kegan Paul, Trench, and Co., in 1885, admirably edited, with interesting Appendices and Notes, by Mr. Richard Garnett. But, though it is to this original or 1822 form of the CONFESSIONS that De Quincey refers in the above sentence of the present paper, written in 1845, it is to be remembered that he did not leave the CONFESSIONS finally in that form. Returning to them in his seventieth year or thereabouts, when he

that work was to reveal something of the grandeur which belongs *potentially* to human dreams. Whatever may be the number of those in whom this faculty of dreaming splendidly can be supposed to lurk, there are not, perhaps, very many in whom it is developed. He whose talk is of oxen, will probably dream of oxen ; and the condition of human life, which yokes so vast a majority to a daily experience incompatible with much elevation of thought, oftentimes neutralises the tone of grandeur in the reproductive faculty of

was bringing out the collective Edinburgh issue of his writings in fourteen volumes, he so recast them, revised them, and enlarged them, that the CONFESSIONS OF AN ENGLISH OPIUM-EATER as republished in 1856, in the shape of Vol. V. of that issue (now Vol. I. of the later sixteen-volume issue), is quite a different book from the original CONFESSIONS of 1822. It contains, indeed, those original CONFESSIONS as its core, but it swells them out to nearly three times their original bulk, and exhibits innumerable changes besides, both in the matter and in the language, throughout. Mr. Garnett, while recognising, with his characteristically fine taste, the masterliness of this expansion by De Quincey in his old age of the first notable literary performance of his early manhood, signifies his preference on the whole, for certain purposes at least, of the briefer original or 1822 form of the CONFESSIONS, and gives his reasons for that preference in his Introduction to the above-named reprint of the CONFESSIONS in that form. No need to discuss that question in this footnote. Enough to remind readers of De Quincey of the not unimportant fact in English Bibliography that there are two distinct forms of the celebrated CONFESSIONS OF AN ENGLISH OPIUM-EATER,—the briefer and more compact form of the original edition of 1822, and the greatly enlarged and more diffuse form put forth by De Quincey himself in 1856, and then intended by him to supersede the other. It was to the earlier or 1822 form, however, we repeat, that De Quincey referred in this paper of 1845, the expanded form not being then in existence.—M.

dreaming, even for those whose minds are populous with solemn imagery. Habitually to dream magnificently, a man must have a constitutional determination to reverie. This in the first place, and even this, where it exists strongly, is too much liable to disturbance from the gathering agitation of our present English life. Already, what by the procession through fifty years of mighty revolutions amongst the kingdoms of the earth, what by the continual development of vast physical agencies,—steam in all its applications, light getting under harness as a slave for man, powers from heaven descending upon education and accelerations of the press, powers from hell (as it might seem, but these also celestial) coming round upon artillery and the forces of destruction,—the eye of the calmest observer is troubled; the brain is haunted as if by some jealousy of ghostly beings moving amongst us; and it becomes too evident that, unless this colossal pace of advance can be retarded (a thing not to be expected), or, which is happily more probable, can be met by counter forces of corresponding magnitude, forces in the direction of religion or profound philosophy, that shall radiate centrifugally against this storm of life so perilously centripetal towards the vortex of the merely human, left to itself, the natural tendency of so chaotic a tumult must be to evil; for some minds to lunacy, for others a reagency of fleshy torpor. How much this fierce condition of eternal hurry upon an arena too exclusively human in its interests is likely to defeat the grandeur which is latent in all men, may be seen in the ordinary effect from living too constantly in varied company. The word *dissipation*, in one of its uses, expresses that effect; the action of thought and feeling is consciously dissipated and squandered. To reconcentrate them into meditative habits, a necessity is felt by all observing persons for sometimes retiring from crowds. No man ever will unfold the capacities of his own intellect who does not at least checker his life with solitude. How much solitude, so much power. Or, if not true in that rigour of expression, to this formula undoubtedly it is that the wise rule of life must approximate.

Among the powers in man which suffer by this too intense life of the *social* instincts, none suffers more than the power of dreaming. Let no man think this a trifle. The machinery for dreaming planted in the human brain was not planted for nothing. That faculty, in alliance with the mystery of darkness, is the one great tube through which man communicates with the shadowy. And the dreaming organ, in connection with the heart, the eye, and the ear, compose the magnificent apparatus which forces the infinite into the chambers of a human brain, and throws dark reflections from eternities below all life upon the mirrors of that mysterious *camera obscura*—the sleeping mind.

But if this faculty suffers from the decay of solitude, which is becoming a visionary idea in England, on the other hand, it is certain that some merely physical agencies can and do assist the faculty of dreaming almost preternaturally. Amongst these is intense exercise ; to some extent at least, and for some persons ; but beyond all others is opium, which indeed seems to possess a *specific* power in that direction ; not merely for exalting the colours of dream-scenery, but for deepening its shadows ; and, above all, for strengthening the sense of its fearful *realities.*

The *Opium Confessions* were written with some slight secondary purpose of exposing this specific power of opium upon the faculty of dreaming, but much more with the purpose of displaying the faculty itself ; and the outline of the work travelled in this course. Supposing a reader acquainted with the true object of the Confessions as here stated, namely, the revelation of dreaming, to have put this question :

"But how came you to dream more splendidly than others ?"

The answer would have been—

"Because (*prœmissis prœmittendis*) I took excessive quantities of opium."

Secondly, suppose him to say, "But how came you to take opium in this excess ?"

The answer to *that* would be, "Because some early events in my life had left a weakness in one organ which required (or seemed to require) that stimulant."

Then, because the opium dreams could not always have been understood without a knowledge of these events, it became necessary to relate them. Now, these two questions and answers exhibit the *law* of the work; that is, the principle which determined its form, but precisely in the inverse or regressive order. The work itself opened with the narration of my early adventures.   These, in the natural order of succession, led to the opium as a resource for healing their consequences; and the opium as naturally led to the dreams.   But in the synthetic order of presenting the facts, what stood last in the succession of development stood first in the order of my purposes.

At the close of this little work, the reader was instructed to believe, and *truly* instructed, that I had mastered the tyranny of opium.   The fact is, that *twice* I mastered it, and by efforts even more prodigious in the second of these cases than in the first.   But one error I committed in both.   I did not connect with the abstinence from opium, so trying to the fortitude under *any* circumstances, that enormity of exercise which (as I have since learned) is the one sole resource for making it endurable.   I overlooked, in those days, the one *sine quâ non* for making ... triumph permanent.   Twice I sank, twice I rose again.   A third time I sank; partly from the cause mentioned (the oversight as to exercise), partly from other causes, on which it avails not now to trouble the reader.   I could moralise, if I chose; and perhaps *he* will moralise, whether I choose it or not.   But, in the mean time, neither of us is acquainted properly with the circumstances of the case : I, from natural bias of judgment, not altogether acquainted; and he (with his permission) not at all.

During this third prostration before the dark idol, and after some years, new and monstrous phenomena began slowly to arise. For a time, these were neglected as accidents, or palliated by such remedies as I knew of. But when I could no longer conceal from myself that these dreadful symptoms were moving forward for ever, by a pace steadily, solemnly, and equably increasing, I endeavoured with some feeling of panic, for a third time to retrace my steps. But I had not reversed my motions for many weeks, before I became profoundly aware that this was impossible. Or, in the imagery of my dreams, which translated everything into their own language, I saw through vast avenues of gloom those towering gates of ingress which hitherto had always seemed to stand open, now at last barred against my retreat, and hung with funeral crape.

As applicable to this tremendous situation (the situation of one escaping by some refluent current from the maelstrom roaring for him in the distance, who finds suddenly that this current is but an eddy, wheeling round upon the same maelstrom), I have since remembered a striking incident in a modern novel. A lady abbess of a convent, herself suspected of Protestant leanings, and in that way already disarmed of all effectual power, finds one of her own nuns (whom she knows to be innocent) accused of an offence leading to the most terrific of punishments. The nun will be immured alive, if she is found guilty ; and there is no chance that she will not, for the evidence against her is strong, unless something were made known that cannot be made known; and the judges are hostile. All follows in the order of the reader's fears. The witnesses depose; the evidence is without effectual contradiction; the conviction is declared; the judgment is delivered; nothing remains but to see execution done. At this crisis, the abbess, alarmed too late for effectual interposition, considers with herself that, according to the regular forms, there will be one single night open, during which the prisoner cannot be withdrawn from her own separate jurisdiction. This one night, therefore, she will use, at any hazard to herself, for the salvation of her friend. At midnight, when all is hushed in the convent, the lady traverses the passages which lead to the cells of prisoners. She bears a master-key under her professional habit. As this will open every door in every corridor, already, by anticipation, she feels the luxury of holding her emancipated friend within her arms. Suddenly she has reached the door; she descries a dusky object; she raises her lamp, and, ranged within the recess of the entrance, she beholds the funeral banner of the holy office, and the black robes of its inexorable officials.

I apprehend that, in a situation such as this, supposing it a real one, the lady abbess would not start, would not show any marks externally of consternation or horror. The case was beyond *that*. The sentiment which attends the sudden revelation that *all is lost* silently is gathered up into the heart; it is too deep for gestures or for words; and no part of it passes to the outside. Were the ruin conditional, or were it in any point doubtful, it would be natural to utter ejaculations, and to seek sympathy. But where the ruin is understood to be absolute, where sympathy cannot be consolation, and counsel cannot be hope, this is otherwise. The voice perishes; the gestures are frozen; and the spirit of man flies back upon its own centre. I, at least, upon seeing those awful gates closed and hung with draperies of woe, as for a death already past, spoke not, nor started, nor groaned. One profound sigh ascended from my heart, and I was silent for days.[1]

In the *Opium Confessions* I touched a little upon the extraordinary power connected with opium (after long use) of amplifying the dimensions of time. Space, also, it amplifies by degrees that are sometimes terrific. But time it is upon which the exalting and multiplying power of opium chiefly spends its operation. Time becomes infinitely elastic, stretching out to such immeasurable and vanishing termini, that it seems ridiculous to compute the sense of it, on waking, by expressions commensurate to human life. As in starry fields one computes by diameters of the earth's orbit, or of Jupiter's, so, in valuing the *virtual* time lived during some dreams, the measurement by

---

[1] To this point the paper is substantially a reprint of what appeared as the "Introductory Notice" to the first instalment of the SUSPIRIA DE PROFUNDIS in Blackwood's Magazine for March 1845.—M.

generations is ridiculous—by millennia is ridiculous;
by æons, I should say, if æons were more determinate,
would be also ridiculous.[1]

---

[1] This last paragraph is the somewhat abrupt substitution left by
De Quincey for the five closing paragraphs of the paper as it stood
originally in *Blackwood* for March 1845.   These five closing paragraphs were intended to prepare the reader for what immediately
followed in the same number of the magazine, in the shape of
that first section of "Part I." of the SUSPIRIA which bore the title
The Affliction of Childhood; and there was, of course, no need to
retain the paragraphs after *The Affliction of Childhood* had been
removed from among the SUSPIRIA altogether, for incorporation
with those AUTOBIOGRAPHIC SKETCHES which continued in a more
direct manner the narrative begun in the CONFESSIONS OF AN OPIUM-
EATER.—M.

You know perhaps, masculine reader, better than I can tell you, what is a *Palimpsest*. Possibly, you have one in your own library. But yet, for the sake of others who may *not* know, or may have forgotten, suffer me to explain it here, lest any female reader, who honours these papers with her notice, should tax me with explaining it once too seldom; which would be worse to bear than a simultaneous complaint from twelve proud men, that I had explained it three times too often. You therefore, fair reader, understand, that for *your* accommodation exclusively, I explain the meaning of this word. It is Greek; and our sex enjoys the office and privilege of standing counsel tò yours, in all questions of Greek. We are, under favour, perpetual and hereditary dragomans to you. So that if, by accident, you know the meaning of a Greek word, yet by courtesy to us, your counsel learned in that matter, you will always seem *not* to know it.

A palimpsest, then, is a membrane or roll cleansed of its manuscript by reiterated successions.

What was the reason that the Greeks and the Romans had not the advantage of printed books?

The answer will be, from ninety-nine persons in a hundred,—Because the mystery of printing was not then discovered. But this is altogether a mistake. The secret of printing must have been discovered many thousands of times before it was used, or *could* be used. The inventive powers of man are divine; and also his stupidity is divine, as Cowper so playfully illustrates in the slow development of the *sofa* through successive generations of immortal dulness. It took centuries of blockheads to raise a joint stool into a chair; and it required something like a miracle of genius, in the estimate of elder generations, to reveal the possibility of lengthening a chair into a *chaise-longue*, or a sofa. Yes, these were inventions that cost mighty throes of intellectual power. But still, as respects printing, and admirable as is the stupidity of man, it was really not quite equal to the task. of evading an object which stared him in the face with so broad a gaze. It did not require an Athenian intellect to read the main secret of printing in many scores of processes which the ordinary uses of life were *daily* repeating. To say nothing of analogous artifices amongst various mechanic artizans, all that is essential in printing must have been known to every nation that struck coins and medals. Not, therefore, any want of a printing art,—that is, of an art for multiplying impressions,—but the want of a cheap material for *receiving* such impressions, was the obstacle to an introduction of printed books, even as early as Pisistratus. The ancients *did* apply printing to records of silver and gold; to marble, and many other substances cheaper than gold or silver, they did *not*, since each monument required a *separate* effort of inscription. Simply this defect it was of a cheap material for receiving impresses, which froze in its very fountains the early resources of printing.

Some twenty years ago this view of the case was luminously expounded by Dr. Whately, and with the merit, I believe, of having first suggested it. Since then, this theory has received indirect confirmation. Now, out of that original scarcity affecting all materials proper for durable books, which continued up to times comparatively modern, grew the opening for palimpsests. Naturally, when once a roll of parchment or of vellum had done its office, by propagating through a series of generations what once had possessed an interest for *them*, but which, under changes of opinion or of taste, had faded to their feelings or had become obsolete for their undertakings, the whole *membrana* or vellum skin, the two-fold product of human skill, costly material, and costly freight of thought, which it carried, drooped in value concurrently—supposing that each were inalienably associated to the other. Once it had been the impress of a human mind which stamped its value upon the vellum; the vellum, though costly, had contributed but a secondary element of value to the total result. At length, however, this relation between the vehicle and its freight has gradually been undermined. The vellum, from having been the setting of the jewel, has risen at length to be the jewel itself; and the burden of thought, from having given the chief value to the vellum, has now become the chief obstacle to its value; nay, has totally extinguished its value, unless it can be dissociated from the connection. Yet, if this unlinking *can* be effected, then, fast as the inscription upon the membrane is sinking into rubbish, the membrane itself is reviving in its separate importance; and, from bearing a ministerial value, the vellum has come at last to absorb the whole value.

Hence the importance for our ancestors that the separation *should* be effected. Hence it arose in the middle ages, as a considerable object for chemistry, to discharge the writing from the roll, and thus to make it available for a new succession of thoughts. The soil, if cleansed from what once had been hot-house plants, but now were held to be weeds, would be ready to receive a fresh and more appropriate crop. In that object the monkish chemists succeeded; but after a fashion which seems almost incredible,—incredible not as regards the extent of their success, but as regards the delicacy of restraints under which it moved,—so equally adjusted was their success to the immediate interests of that period, and to the reversionary objects of our own. They did the thing; but not so radically as to prevent us, their posterity, from *un*doing it. They expelled the writing sufficiently to leave a field for the new manuscript, and yet not sufficiently to make the traces of the elder manuscript irrecoverable for us. Could magic, could

Hermes Trismegistus, have done more? What would you think, fair reader, of a problem such as this,—to write a book which should be sense for your own generation, nonsense for the next, should revive into sense for the next after that, but again become nonsense for the fourth; and so on by alternate successions, sinking into night or blazing into day, like the Sicilian river Arethusa, and the English river Mole[1]; or like the undulating motions of a flattened stone which children cause to skim the breast of a river, now diving below the water, now grazing its surface, sinking heavily into darkness, rising buoyantly into light, through a long vista of alternations? Such a problem, you say, is impossible. But really it is a problem not harder apparently than—to bid a generation kill, so that a subsequent generation may call back into life; bury, so that posterity may command to rise again. Yet *that* was what the rude chemistry of past ages effected when coming into combination with the reaction from the more refined chemistry of our own. Had *they* been better chemists, had *we* been worse, the mixed result, namely, that, dying for *them*, the flower should revive for *us*, could not have been effected. They did the thing proposed to them:

[1] The famous Sicilian fountain of Arethusa is said to be still visible, though in shrunken dimensions, in the ancient quarter of Syracuse called Ortygia. The English Mole is in Surrey, and has, or had, the trick of disappearing in summer, for a part of its course, into a subterranean channel: whence Milton's line in his poem *At a Vacation Exercise :*—

" Or sullen Mole, that runneth underneath."—M.

they did it effectually, for they founded upon it all
that was wanted : and yet ineffectually, since we
unravelled their work ; effacing all above which they
had superscribed ; restoring all below which they
had effaced.

Here, for instance, is a parchment which contained
some Grecian tragedy, the Agamemnon of Æschylus,
or the Phœnissæ of Euripides. This had possessed a
value almost inappreciable in the eyes of accomplished
scholars, continually growing rarer through generations. But four centuries are gone by since the
destruction of the Western Empire. Christianity,
with towering grandeurs of another class, has founded
a different empire ; and some bigoted, yet, perhaps,
holy monk, has washed away (as he persuades himself) the heathen's tragedy, replacing it with a monastic legend ; which legend is disfigured with fables
in its incidents, and yet in a higher sense is true,
because interwoven with Christian morals, and with
the sublimest of Christian revelations. Three, four,
five centuries more, find man still devout as ever ;
but the language has become obsolete, and even for
Christian devotion a new era has arisen, throwing it
into the channel of crusading zeal or of chivalrous
enthusiasm. The *membrana* is wanted now for a
knightly romance—for "My Cid," or Cœur de Lion ;
for Sir Tristrem, or Lybæus Disconus. In this way,
by means of the imperfect chemistry known to the
mediæval period, the same roll has served as a conservatory for three separate generations of flowers

and fruits, all perfectly different, and yet all specially adapted to the wants of the successive possessors. The Greek tragedy, the monkish legend, the knightly romance, each has ruled its own period. One harvest after another has been gathered into the garners of man through ages far apart. And the same hydraulic machinery has distributed, through the same marble fountains, water, milk, or wine, according to the habits and training of the generations that came to quench their thirst.

Such were the achievements of rude monastic chemistry. But the more elaborate chemistry of our own days has reversed all these motions of our simple ancestors, with results in every stage that to *them* would have realised the most fantastic amongst the promises of thaumaturgy. Insolent vaunt of Paracelsus, that he would restore the original rose or violet out of the ashes settling from its combustion—*that* is now rivalled in this modern achievement. The traces of each successive handwriting, regularly effaced, as had been imagined, have, in the inverse order, been regularly called back : the footsteps of the game pursued, wolf or stag, in each several chase, have been unlinked, and hunted back through all their doubles ; and as the chorus of the Athenian stage unwove through the antistrophe every step that had been mystically woven through the strophe, so, by our modern conjurations of science, secrets of ages remote from each other have been exorcised [1] from the accumulated shadows of cen-

[1] Some readers may be apt to suppose, from all English experi-

turies.   Chemistry, a witch as potent as the Erictho of Lucan (*Pharsalia*, lib. vi. or vii.),[1] has extorted by her torments, from the dust and ashes of forgotten centuries, the secrets of a life extinct for the general eye, but still glowing in the embers.   Even the fable of the Phœnix, that secular bird, who propagated his solitary existence, and his solitary births, along the line of centuries, through eternal relays of funeral mists,[2] is but a type of what we have done with Palimpsests.   We have backed upon each phœnix in the long *regressus*, and forced him to expose his ances-

ence, that the word *exorcise* means properly banishment to the shades.   Not so.   Citation *from* the shades, or sometimes the torturing coercion of mystic adjurations, is more truly the primary sense.

[1] The passage in Lucan referred to is in⁻ Book VI. of his *Pharsalia*, lines 507 *et seq.*; where the name, however, is spelt "Erichtho."—M.

[2] The fable respecting the Phœnix was that it was a marvellous Arabian bird, the sole bird of the sort alive, which went every 500 years to Egypt, to die there, and leave its own burnt ashes as relics out of which might spring its sole successor, the next Phœnix.   De Quincey had in his mind Milton's passage near the close of his *Samson Agonistes* :—

> "So Virtue, given for lost,
> Depressed and overthrown, as seemed,
> Like that self-begotten bird
> In the Arabian woods embost,
> That no second knows nor third,
> And lay erewhile a holocaust,
> From out her ashy womb now teemed,
> Revives, reflourishes, then vigorous most
> When most unactive deemed ;
> And, though her body die, her fame survives,
> A secular bird, ages of lives."—M.

tral phœnix, sleeping in the ashes below his own ashes. Our good old forefathers would have been aghast at our sorceries; and, if they speculated on the propriety of burning Dr. Faustus, *us* they would have burned by acclamation. Trial there would have been none; and they could not otherwise have satisfied their horror of the brazen profligacy marking our modern magic, than by ploughing up the houses of all who had been parties to it, and sowing the ground with salt.

Fancy not, reader, that this tumult of images, illustrative or allusive, moves under any impulse or purpose of mirth. It is but the coruscation of a restless understanding, often made ten times more so by irritation of the nerves, such as you will first learn to comprehend (its *how* and its *why*) some stage or two ahead. The image, the memorial, the record, which for me is derived from a palimpsest, as to one great fact in our human being, and which immediately I will show you, is but too repellent of laughter; or, even if laughter *had* been possible, it would have been such laughter as oftentimes is thrown off from the fields of ocean,[1] laughter that hides, or that seems to evade mustering tumult; foam-bells that weave gar-

---

[1] Many readers will recall, though, at the moment of writing, my own thoughts did *not* recall, the well-known passage in the Prometheus—

——ποντιων τε κυματων
Ανηριθμον γελασμα.

"O multitudinous laughter of the ocean billows!" It is not clear whether Æschylus contemplated the laughter as addressing the ear or the eye.

lands of phosphoric radiance for one moment round the eddies of gleaming abysses; mimicries of earth-born flowers that for the eye raise phantoms of gaiety, as oftentimes for the ear they raise the echoes of fugitive laughter, mixing with the ravings and choir-voices of an angry sea.

What else than a natural and mighty palimpsest is the human brain? Such a palimpsest is my brain; such a palimpsest, oh reader! is yours. Everlasting layers of ideas, images, feelings, have fallen upon your brain softly as light. Each succession has seemed to bury all that went before. And yet, in reality, not one has been extinguished. And if, in the vellum palimpsest, lying amongst the other *diplomata* of human archives or libraries, there is anything fantastic or which moves to laughter, as oftentimes there is in the grotesque collisions of those successive themes, having no natural connection, which by pure accident have consecutively occupied the roll, yet, in our own heaven-created palimpsest, the deep memorial palimpsest of the brain, there are not and cannot be such incoherencies. The fleeting accidents of a man's life, and its external shows, may indeed be irrelate and incongruous; but the organising principles which fuse into harmony, and gather about fixed predetermined centres, whatever heterogeneous elements life may have accumulated from without, will not permit the grandeur of human unity greatly to be violated, or its ultimate repose to be troubled, in the retrospect from dying moments, or from other great convulsions.

Such a convulsion is the struggle of gradual suffo-
cation, as in drowning; and, in the original Opium
Confessions, I mentioned a case of that nature communicated to me by a lady from her own childish
experience. The lady was then still living, though
of unusually great age; and I may mention that
amongst her faults never was numbered any levity of
principle, or carelessness of the most scrupulous
veracity; but, on the contrary, such faults as arise
from austerity, too harsh, perhaps, and gloomy, in-
dulgent neither to others nor herself. And, at the
time of relating this incident, when already very old,
she had become religious to asceticism.[1] According
to my present belief, she had completed her ninth
year, when, playing by the side of a solitary brook,
she fell into one of its deepest pools. Eventually,
but after what lapse of time nobody ever knew, she
was saved from death by a farmer, who, riding in
some distant lane, had seen her rise to the surface;
but not until she had descended within the abyss of
death and looked into its secrets, as far, perhaps, as
ever human eye *can* have looked that had permission
to return. At a certain stage of this descent, a blow
seemed to strike her, phosphoric radiance sprang
forth from her eyeballs; and immediately a mighty
theatre expanded within her brain. In a moment, in
the twinkling of an eye, every act, every design of
her past life, lived again, arraying themselves not as

---

[1] The description suits what we know of the character of De
Quincey's own mother; and perhaps it is she that is meant.—M.

a succession, but as parts of a coexistence. Such a light fell upon the whole path of her life backwards into the shades of infancy, as the light, perhaps, which wrapt the destined Apostle on his road to Damascus. Yet that light blinded for a season ; but hers poured celestial vision upon the brain, so that her consciousness became omnipresent at one moment to every feature in the infinite review.

This anecdote was treated sceptically at the time by some critics. But, besides that it has since been confirmed by other experience essentially the same, reported by other parties in the same circumstances, who had never heard of each other, the true point for astonishment is not the *simultaneity* of arrangement under which the past events of life, though in fact successive, had formed their dread line of revelation. This was but a secondary phenomenon ; the deeper lay in the resurrection itself, and the possibility of resurrection, for what had so long slept in the dust. A pall, deep as oblivion, had been thrown by life over every trace of these experiences ; and yet suddenly, at a silent command, at the signal of a blazing rocket sent up from the brain, the pall draws up, and the whole depths of the theatre are exposed. Here was the greater mystery : now this mystery is liable to no doubt ; for it is repeated, and ten thousand times repeated, by opium, for those who are its martyrs.

Yes, reader, countless are the mysterious handwritings of grief or joy which have inscribed themselves successively upon the palimpsest of your brain ; and, like the annual leaves of aboriginal forests, or the undissolving snows on the Himalaya, or light falling upon light, the endless strata have covered up each other in forgetfulness. But by the hour of death, but by fever, but by the searchings of opium, all these can revive in strength. They are not dead, but sleeping. In the illustration imagined by myself, from the case of some individual palimpsest, the Grecian tragedy had seemed to be displaced, but was *not* displaced, by the monkish legend ; and the monkish legend had seemed to be displaced, but was *not* displaced by the knightly romance. In some potent convulsion of the system, all wheels back into its earliest elementary stage. The bewildering romance, light tarnished with darkness, the semi-fabulous legend, truth celestial mixed with human falsehoods, these fade even of themselves, as life advances. The romance has perished that the young man adored ; the legend has gone that deluded the boy ; but the deep, deep tragedies of infancy, as when the child's hands were unlinked for ever from his mother's neck, or his lips for ever from his sister's kisses, these remain lurking below all, and these lurk to the last. Alchemy there is none of passion or disease that can scorch away these immortal impresses ; and the dream which closed the preceding section,[1] together

---

[1] These words, as used in *Blackwood* for June 1845, referred to a dream of his sister's funeral with an account of which the preceding section of the SUSPIRIA, in the April number of the

with the succeeding dreams of this (which may be viewed as in the nature of choruses winding up the overture contained in Part I.[1]), are but illustrations of this truth, such as every man probably will meet experimentally who passes through similar convulsions of dreaming or delirium from any similar or equal disturbance in his nature.[2]

magazine, had closed ; and, as the whole of that section, this dream included, is now removed from the context of the SUSPIRIA, having been converted into a chapter of the AUTOBIOGRAPHIC SKETCHES, the words are now irrelevant. They are retained, however, in order that *The Palimpsest* may end as De Quincey ended it, and that his final footnote may be saved. —M.

[1] The reader will remember that all the papers actually published in *Blackwood*, in March, April, and June 1845, with the title of SUSPIRIA DE PROFUNDIS, formed together only what was offered as Part I. of a projected series. —M.

[2] This, it may be said, requires a corresponding duration of experience ; but, as an argument for this mysterious power lurking in our nature, I may remind the reader of one phenomenon open to the notice of everybody, namely, the tendency of very aged persons to throw back and concentrate the light of their memory upon scenes of early childhood, as to which they recall many traces that had faded even to *themselves* in middle life, whilst they often forget altogether the whole intermediate stages of their experience. This shows that naturally, and without violent agencies, the human brain is by tendency a palimpsest.

UPON me, as upon others scattered thinly by tens and twenties over every thousand years, fell too powerfully and too early the vision of life. The horror of life mixed itself already in earliest youth with the heavenly sweetness of life; that grief, which one in a hundred has sensibility enough to gather from the sad retrospect of life in its closing stage, for me shed its dews as a prelibation upon the fountains of life whilst yet sparkling to the morning sun. I saw from afar and from before what I was to see from behind. Is this the description of an early youth passed in the shades of gloom? No; but of a youth passed in the divinest happiness. And if the reader has (which so few have) the passion, without which there is no reading of the legend and superscription upon man's brow, if he is not (as most are) deafer than the grave to every *deep* note that sighs upwards from the Delphic caves of human life, he will know that the rapture of life (or anything which by approach can merit that name) does not arise, unless as perfect music arises, music of Mozart or Beethoven, by the confluence of the mighty and terrific discords with the subtile concords. Not by contrast, or as reciprocal foils, do these elements act, which is the feeble conception of many, but by union. They are the sexual forces in music : "male and female created he them;" and these mighty antagonists do not put forth their hostilities by repulsion, but by deepest attraction.

As "in to-day already walks to-morrow," so in the past experience of a youthful life may be seen dimly the future. The collisions with alien interests or hostile views, of a child, boy, or very young man, so insulated as each of these is sure to be,—those aspects of opposition which such a person *can* occupy,—are limited by the exceedingly few and trivial lines of connection along which he is able to radiate any essential influence whatever upon the fortunes or happiness of others. Circumstances may magnify his importance for the moment; but, after all, any cable which he carries out upon other vessels is easily slipped upon a feud arising. Far otherwise is the state of relations connecting an adult or responsible man with the circles around him, as life advances. The network of these relations is a thousand times more intricate, the jarring of these intricate relations a thousand times more frequent, and the vibrations a thousand times harsher which these jarrings diffuse. This truth is felt beforehand misgivingly and in troubled vision, by a young man who stands upon the threshold of manhood. One earliest instinct of fear and horror would darken his spirit, if it could be revealed to itself and self-questioned at the moment

of birth : a second instinct of the same nature would
again pollute that tremulous mirror, if the moment
were as punctually marked as physical birth is marked,
which dismisses him finally upon the tides of absolute
self-control.   A dark ocean would seem the total
expanse of life from the first; but far darker and
more appalling would seem that inferior and second
chamber of the ocean which called him away for ever
from the direct accountability of others.   Dreadful
would be the morning which should say, "Be thou a
human child incarnate;" but more dreadful the
morning which should say, "Bear thou henceforth the
sceptre of thy self-dominion through life, and the
passion of life!"   Yes, dreadful would be both; but
without a basis of the dreadful there is no perfect
rapture.   It is in part through the sorrow of life,
growing out of dark events, that this basis of awe
and solemn darkness slowly accumulates.   *That* I
have illustrated.   But, as life expands, it is more
through the *strife* which besets us, strife from conflict-
ing opinions, positions, passions, interests, that the
funereal ground settles and deposits itself, which
sends upward the dark lustrous brilliancy through
the jewel of life, else revealing a pale and superficial
glitter.   Either the human being must suffer and
struggle as the price of a more searching vision, or
his gaze must be shallow, and without intellectual
revelation.

HEAVENS! when I look back to the sufferings which I have witnessed or heard of, I say, if life could throw open its long suites of chambers to our eyes from some station *beforehand*,—if, from some secret stand, we could look *by anticipation* along its vast corridors, and aside into the recesses opening upon them from either hand, halls of tragedy or chambers of retribution, simply in that small wing and no more of the great caravanserai which we ourselves shall haunt,—simply in that narrow tract of time, and no more, where we ourselves shall range, and confining our gaze to those and no others, for whom personally we shall be interested,—What a recoil we should suffer of horror in our estimate of life! What if those sudden catastrophes, or those inexpiable afflictions, which *have* already descended upon the people within my own knowledge, and almost below my own eyes, all of them now gone past, and some long past, had been thrown open before me as a secret exhibition when first I and they stood within the vestibule of morning hopes,— when the calamities themselves had hardly begun to gather in their elements of possibility and when some of the parties to them were as yet no more than infants! The past viewed not *as* the past, but by a spectator who steps back ten years deeper into the rear, in order that he may regard it as a future; the calamity of 1840 contemplated from the station of 1830,—the doom that rang the knell of happiness viewed from a point of time when as yet it was neither feared nor would even have been intelligible,—the name that killed in 1843, which in 1835 would have struck no vibration upon the heart,—the portrait that on the day of her Majesty's coronation would have been admired by you with a pure disinterested admiration, but which, if seen to-day, would draw forth an involuntary groan,—cases such as these are strangely moving for all who add deep thoughtfulness to deep sensibility. As the hastiest of improvisations, accept, fair reader (for such reader it is that will chiefly feel such an invocation of the past), three or four illustrations from my own experience :—

Who is this distinguished-looking young woman, with her eyes drooping, and the shadow of a dreadful shock yet fresh upon every feature? Who is the elderly lady, with her eyes flashing fire? Who is the downcast child of sixteen? What is that torn paper lying at their feet? Who is the writer? Whom does the paper concern? Ah! if she, if the central figure in the group—twenty-two at the moment when she is revealed to us—could, on her happy birthday at sweet seventeen, have seen the image of herself five years onwards, just as *we* see it now, would she have prayed for life as for an absolute blessing? or would she not have prayed to be taken from the evil to come—to be taken away one evening, at least, before this day's sun arose? It is true, she still wears a look of gentle pride, and a relic of that noble smile which belongs to *her* that suffers an injury which many times over she would have died sooner than inflict. Womanly pride refuses itself before witnesses to the total prostration of the blow; but, for all *that*, you may see that she longs to be left alone, and that her tears will flow without restraint when she is so. This room is her pretty boudoir, in which, till to-night —poor thing!—she has been glad and happy. There stands her miniature conservatory, and there expands her miniature library; as we circumnavigators of literature are apt (you know) to regard all female libraries in the light of miniatures. None of these will ever rekindle a smile on *her* face; and there, beyond, is her music, which only of all that she possesses will now become dearer to her than ever; but, not, as once, to feed a self-mocked pensiveness, or to cheat a half visionary sadness. She will be sad, indeed. But she is one of those that will suffer in silence. Nobody will ever detect *her* failing in any point of duty, or querulously seeking the support in others which she can find for herself in this solitary room. Droop she will not in the sight of men; and, for all beyond, nobody has any concern with *that*, except God. You shall hear what becomes of her, before we take our departure ; but now let me tell you what has happened. In the main outline I am sure you guess already, without aid of mine, for we leaden-eyed men, in such cases, see nothing by comparison with you our quick-witted sisters. That haughty looking lady, with the Roman cast of features, who must once have been strikingly handsome,—an Agrippina, even yet, in a favourable presentation,—is the younger lady's aunt. She, it is rumoured, once sustained, in her younger days, some injury of that same cruel nature which has this day assailed her niece, and ever since she has worn an air of disdain, not altogether unsupported by real dignity, towards men. This aunt it was that tore the letter which lies upon the floor. It deserved to be torn ; and yet she that had the best right to do so would *not* have torn it. That letter was an elaborate attempt on the part of an accomplished young man to release himself from sacred engagements. What need was there to argue the case of *such* engagements. Could it have been requisite with pure female dignity to plead anything, or do more than *look* an indisposition to fulfil them ? The aunt is now moving towards the door, which I am glad to see ; and she is followed by that pale, timid girl of sixteen, a cousin, who feels the case profoundly, but is too young and shy to offer an intellectual sympathy.

One only person in this world there is who *could* to-night have been a supporting friend to our young sufferer, and *that* is her dear, loving twin-sister, that for eighteen years read and wrote, thought and sang, slept and breathed, with the dividing-door open for ever between their bed-rooms, and never once a separation between their hearts; but she is in a far distant land. Who else is there at her call? Except God, nobody. Her aunt had somewhat sternly admonished her, though still with a relenting in her eye as she glanced aside at the expression in her niece's face, that she must "call pride to her assistance." Ay, true; but pride, though a strong ally in public, is apt in private to turn as treacherous as the worst of those against whom she is invoked. How could it be dreamed, by a person of sense, that a brilliant young man, of merits various and eminent, in spite of his baseness, to whom, for nearly two years, this young woman had given her whole confiding love, might be dismissed from a heart like hers on the earliest summons of pride, simply because she herself had been dismissed from *his*, or seemed to have been dismissed, on a summons of mercenary calculation? Look! now that she is relieved from the weight of an unconfidential presence, she has sat for two hours with her head buried in her hands. At last she rises to look for something. A thought has struck her; and, taking a little golden key which hangs by a chain within her bosom, she searches for something locked up amongst her few jewels. What is it? It is a Bible exquisitely illuminated, with a letter attached by some pretty silken artifice to the blank leaves at the end. This letter is a beautiful record, wisely and pathetically composed, of maternal anxiety still burning strong in death, and yearning, when all objects beside were fast fading from *her* eyes, after one parting act of communion with the twin darlings of her heart. Both were thirteen years old, within a week or two, as on the night before her death they sat weeping by the bedside of their mother, and hanging on her lips, now for farewell whispers and now for farewell kisses. They both knew that, as her strength had permitted during the latter month of her life, she had thrown the last anguish of love in her beseeching heart into a letter of counsel to themselves. Through this, of which each sister had a copy, she trusted long to converse with her orphans. And the last promise which she had entreated on this evening from both was, that in either of two contingencies they would review her counsels, and the passages to which she pointed their attention in the Scriptures; namely, first, in the event of any calamity, that, for one sister or for both, should overspread their paths with total darkness; and, secondly, in the event of life flowing in too profound a stream of prosperity, so as to threaten them with an alienation of interest from all spiritual objects. She had not concealed that, of these two extreme cases, she would prefer for her own children the first. And now had that case arrived, indeed, which she in spirit had desired to meet. Nine years ago, just as the silvery voice of a dial in the dying lady's bed-room was striking nine, upon a summer evening, had the last visual ray streamed from her seeking eyes upon her orphan twins, after which, throughout the night, she had slept away into heaven. Now again had come a summer evening memorable for unhappiness; now again the daughter thought of those dying lights of love which streamed at sunset from the closing eyes of her mother; again, and just as she went back in thought to this image, the same silvery voice of the dial sounded nine o'clock. Again she remembered her mother's dying request; again her own tear-hallowed promise,—and with her heart in her mother's grave she now rose to fulfil it. Here, then, when this solemn recurrence to a testamentary counsel has ceased to be a mere office of duty towards the departed, having taken the shape of a consolation for herself, let us pause.

*   *   *   *   *

Now, fair companion in this exploring voyage of inquest into hidden scenes, or forgotten scenes of human life, perhaps it might be instructive to direct our glasses upon the false, perfidious lover. It might. But do not let us do so. We might like him better, or pity him more, than either of us would desire. His name and memory have long since dropped out of everybody's thoughts. Of prosperity, and (what is more important) of internal peace, he is reputed to have had no gleam from the moment when he betrayed his faith, and in one day threw away the jewel of good conscience, and "a pearl richer than all his tribe." But, however that may be, it is certain that, finally, he became a wreck; and of any *hopeless* wreck it is painful to talk,—much more so, when through him others also became wrecks.

Shall we, then, after an interval of nearly two years has passed over the young lady in the boudoir, look in again upon *her?* You hesitate, fair friend; and I myself hesitate. For, in fact, she also has become a wreck; and it would grieve us both to see · her altered. At the end of twenty-one months she retains hardly a vestige of resemblance to the fine young woman we saw on that unhappy evening, with her aunt and cousin. On consideration, therefore, let us do this.—We will direct our glasses to her room at a point of time about six weeks further on. Suppose this time gone; suppose her now dressed for her grave, and placed in her coffin. The advantage of that is, that though no change can restore the ravages of the past, yet (as often is found to happen with young persons) the expression has revived from her girlish years. The child-like aspect has revolved, and settled back upon her features.˙ The wasting away of the flesh is less apparent in the face; and one might imagine that in this sweet marble countenance was seen the very same upon which, eleven years ago, her mother's darkening eyes had lingered to the last, until clouds had swallowed up the vision of her beloved *twins.* Yet, if that were in part a fancy, this, at least, is no fancy,—that not only much of a child-like truth and simplicity has reinstated itself in the temple of her now reposing features, but also that tranquillity and perfect peace, such as are appropriate to eternity, but which from the *living* countenance had taken their flight for ever, on that memorable evening when we looked in upon the impassioned group,—upon the towering and denouncing aunt, the sympathising but silent cousin, the poor, blighted niece, and the wicked letter lying in fragments at their feet.

Cloud, that hast revealed to us this young creature and her blighted hopes, close up again. And now, a few years later,—not more than four or five,—give back to us the latest arrears of the changes which thou concealest within thy draperies. Once more, "open sesame!" and show us a third generation. Behold a lawn islanded with thickets. How perfect is the verdure; how rich the blossoming shrubberies that screen with verdurous walls from the possibility of intrusion, whilst by their own wandering line of distribution they shape, and umbrageously embay, what one might call lawny saloons and vestibules, sylvan galleries and closets? Some of these recesses, which unlink themselves as fluently as snakes, and unexpectedly as the shyest nooks, watery cells, and crypts, amongst the shores of a forest-lake, being formed by the mere caprices and ramblings of the luxuriant shrubs, are so small and so quiet that one might fancy them meant for *boudoirs*. Here is one that in a less fickle climate would make the loveliest of studies for a writer of breathings from some solitary heart, or of *suspiria* from some impassioned memory! And, opening from one angle of this embowered study, issues a little narrow corridor, that, after almost wheeling back upon itself, in its playful mazes, finally widens into a little circular chamber; out of which there is no exit (except back again by the entrance), small or great; so that, adjacent to his study, the writer would command how sweet a bed-room, permitting him to lie the summer through, gazing all night long at the burning host of heaven. How silent *that* would be at the noon of summer nights,—how grave-like in its quiet! And yet, need there be asked a stillness or a silence more profound than is felt at this present noon of day? One reason for such peculiar repose, over and above the tranquil character of the day, and the distance of the place from the high-roads, is the outer zone of woods, which almost on every quarter invests the shrubberies, swathing them (as one may express it), belting them and overlooking them, from a varying distance of two and three furlongs, so as oftentimes to keep the winds at a distance. But, however caused and supported, the silence of these fanciful lawns and lawny chambers is oftentimes oppressive in the depths of summer to people unfamiliar with solitudes, either mountainous or sylvan; and many would be apt to suppose that the villa, to which these pretty shrubberies form the chief dependencies, must be untenanted. But that is not the case. The house is inhabited, and by its own legal mistress, the proprietress of the whole domain; and not at all a silent

mistress, but as noisy as most little ladies of five
years old, for that is her age.   Now, and just as we
are speaking, you may hear her little joyous clamour,
as she issues from the house.   This way she comes,
bounding like a fawn ; and soon she rushes into the
little recess which I pointed out as a proper study for
any man who should be weaving the deep harmonies
of memorial *suspiria*.   But I fancy that she will soon
dispossess it of that character, for her *suspiria* are
not many at this stage of her life.   Now she comes
dancing into sight ; and you see that, if she keeps
the promise of her infancy, she will be an interesting
creature to the eye in after life.   In other respects,
also, she is an engaging child,—loving, natural, and
wild as any one of her neighbours for some miles
round, namely, leverets, squirrels, and ring-doves.
But what will surprise you most is, that, although a
child of pure English blood, she speaks very little
English ; but more Bengalee than perhaps you will
find it convenient to construe.   That is her ayah,
who comes up from behind, at a pace so different
from her youthful mistress's.   But, if their paces are
different, in other things they agree most cordially ;
and dearly they love each other.   In reality, the child
has passed her whole life in the arms of this ayah.
She remembers nothing elder than *her ;* eldest of
things is the ayah in her eyes ; and, if the ayah
should insist on her worshipping herself as the goddess
Railroadina or Steamboatina, that made England, and
the sea, and Bengal, it is certain that the little thing

would do so, asking no question but this,—whether kissing would do for worshipping.

Every evening at nine o'clock, as the ayah sits by the little creature lying awake in bed, the silvery tongue of a dial tolls the hour. Reader, you know who she is. She is the grand-daughter of her that faded away about sunset in gazing at her twin orphans. Her name is Grace. And she is the niece of that elder and once happy Grace, who spent so much of her happiness in this very room, but whom, in her utter desolation, we saw in the boudoir, with the torn letter at her feet. She is the daughter of that other sister, wife to a military officer who died abroad. Little Grace never saw her grandmamma, nor her lovely aunt, that was her namesake, nor consciously her mamma. She was born six months after the death of the elder Grace ; and her mother saw her only through the mists of mortal suffering, which carried her off three weeks after the birth of her daughter.

This view was taken several years ago ; and since then the younger Grace, in her turn, is under a cloud of affliction. But she is still under eighteen ; and of her there may be hopes. Seeing such things in so short a space of years, for the grandmother died at thirty-two, we say,—Death we can face : but knowing, as some of us do, what is human life, which of us is it that without shuddering could (if consciously we were summoned) face the hour of birth ?

GOD smote Savannah-la-mar, and in one night, by earthquake, removed her, with all her towers standing and population sleeping, from the steadfast foundations of the shore to the coral floors of ocean. And God said,—"Pompeii did I bury and conceal from men through seventeen centuries : this city I will bury, but not conceal. She shall be a monument to men of my mysterious anger, set in azure light through generations to come ; for I will enshrine her in a crystal dome of my tropic seas." This city, therefore, like a mighty galleon with all her apparel mounted, streamers flying, and tackling perfect, seems floating along the noiseless depths of ocean ; and oftentimes in glassy calms, through the translucid atmosphere of water that now stretches like an air-woven awning above the silent encampment, mariners from every clime look down into her courts and terraces, count her gates, and number the spires of her churches. She is one ample cemetery, and *has* been for many a year ; but in the mighty calms that brood for weeks over tropic latitudes, she fascinates the eye with a *Fata-Morgana* revelation, as of human life still subsisting in submarine asylums sacred from the storms that torment our upper air.

Thither, lured by the loveliness of cerulean depths, by the peace of human dwellings privileged from molestation, by the gleam of marble altars sleeping in everlasting sanctity, oftentimes in dreams did I and the Dark Interpreter cleave the watery veil that divided us from her streets. We looked into the belfries, where the pendulous bells were waiting in vain for the summons which should awaken their marriage peals; together we touched the mighty organ-keys, that sang no *jubilates* for the ear of heaven, that sang no requiems for the ear of human sorrow; together we searched the silent nurseries, where the children were all asleep, and *had* been asleep through five generations. "They are waiting for the heavenly dawn," whispered the Interpreter to himself: "and, when *that* comes, the bells and the organs will utter a *jubilate* repeated by the echoes of Paradise." Then, turning to me, he said,—"This is sad, this is piteous; but less would not have sufficed for the purpose of God. Look here. Put into a Roman clepsydra one hundred drops of water; let these run out as the sands in an hour-glass; every drop measuring the hundredth part of a second, so that each shall represent but the three-hundred-and-sixty-thousandth part of an hour. Now, count the drops as they race along; and, when the fiftieth of the hundred is passing, behold! forty-nine are not, because already they have perished; and fifty are not, because they are yet to come. You see, therefore, how narrow, how incalculably narrow, is the true and actual present. Of that time which we call the present, hardly a hundredth part but belongs either to a past which has fled, or to a future which is still on the wing. It has perished, or it is not born. It was, or it is not. Yet even this approximation to the truth is *infinitely* false. For again subdivide that solitary drop, which only was found to represent the present, into a lower series of similar fractions, and the actual present which you arrest measures now but the thirty-sixth-millionth of an hour ; and so by infinite declensions the true and very present, in which only we live and enjoy, will vanish into a mote of a mote, distinguishable only by a heavenly vision. Therefore the present, which only man possesses, offers less capacity for his footing than the slenderest film that ever spider twisted from her womb. Therefore, also, even this incalculable shadow from the narrowest pencil of moonlight is more transitory than geometry can measure, or thought of angel can overtake. The time which *is* contracts into a mathematic point ; and even that point perishes a thousand times before we can utter its birth. All is finite in the present ; and even that finite is infinite in its velocity of flight towards death. But in God there is nothing finite ; but in God there is nothing transitory ; but in God there *can* be nothing that tends to death. Therefore, it follows, that for God there can be no present. The future is the present of God, and to the future it is that he sacrifices the human present. Therefore it is that he works by earthquake. Therefore it is that he works by grief. O, deep is the ploughing of earthquake! O, deep "—(and his voice swelled like a *sanctus* rising from the choir of a cathedral)—" O, deep is the ploughing of grief! But oftentimes less would not suffice for the agriculture of God. Upon a night of earthquake he builds a thousand years of pleasant habitations for man. Upon the sorrow of an infant he raises oftentimes from human intellects glorious vintages that could not else have been. Less than these fierce ploughshares would not have stirred the stubborn soil. The one is needed for earth, our planet,—for earth itself as the dwelling-place of man; but the other is needed yet oftener for God's mightiest instrument,—yes" (and he looked solemnly at myself), "is needed for the mysterious children of the earth!"

DAMASCUS, first-born of cities, *Om el Denia*,[1] mother of generations, that wast before Abraham, that wast before the Pyramids! what sounds are those that, from a postern gate, looking eastwards over secret paths that wind away to the far distant desert, break the solemn silence of an oriental night? Whose voice is that which calls upon the spearmen, keeping watch for ever in the turret surmounting the gate, to receive him back into his Syrian home? Thou knowest him, Damascus, and hast known him in seasons of trouble as one learned in the afflictions of man; wise alike to take counsel for the suffering spirit or for the suffering body. The voice that breaks upon the night is the voice of a great evangelist—one of the four; and he is also a great physician. This do the watchmen at the gate thankfully acknowledge, and joyfully they

---

[1] "*Om el Denia:*"—Mother of the World is the Arabic title of Damascus. That it was before Abraham—*i.e.*, already an old establishment much more than a thousand years before the siege of Troy, and than two thousand years before our Christian era—may be inferred from Gen. xv. 2; and by the general consent of all eastern races, Damascus is accredited as taking precedency in age of all cities to the west of the Indus.

give him entrance. His sandals are white with dust; for he has been roaming for weeks beyond the desert, under the guidance of Arabs, on missions of hopeful benignity to Palmyra;[1] and in spirit he is weary of all things, except faithfulness to God, and burning love to man.

Eastern cities are asleep betimes; and sounds few or none fretted the quiet of all around him, as the evangelist paced onward to the market-place; but there another scene awaited him. On the right hand, in an upper chamber, with lattices widely expanded, sat a festal company of youths, revelling under a noonday blaze of light, from cressets and from bright tripods that burned fragrant woods—all joining in choral songs, all crowned with odorous wreaths from Daphne and the banks of the Orontes. Them the evangelist heeded not; but far away upon the left, close upon a sheltered nook, lighted up by a solitary vase of iron fretwork filled with cedar boughs, and hoisted high upon a spear, behold there sat a woman of loveliness so transcendent, that, when suddenly revealed, as now, out of deepest darkness, she appalled men as a mockery, or a birth of the air. Was she born of woman? Was it perhaps the angel—so the evangelist argued with himself—that met him in the desert after sunset, and strengthened him by secret talk? The evangelist went up, and touched her fore-

---

[1] Palmyra had not yet reached its meridian splendour of Grecian development, as afterwards near the age of Aurelian, but it was already a noble city.

head ; and when he found that she was indeed human, and guessed, from the station which she had chosen, that she waited for some one amongst this dissolute crew as her companion, he groaned heavily in spirit, and said, half to himself, but half to her, " Wert thou, poor ruined flower, adorned so divinely at thy birth —glorified in such excess, that not Solomon in all his pomp—no, nor even the lilies of the field—can approach thy gifts—only that thou shouldest grieve the Holy Spirit of God ?" The woman trembled exceedingly, and said, "Rabbi, what should I do ? For behold ! all men forsake me." The evangelist mused a little, and then secretly to himself he said, " Now will I search this woman's heart—whether in very truth it inclineth itself to God, and hath strayed only before fiery compulsion." Turning therefore to the woman, the Prophet[1] said, " Listen : I am the messenger of Him whom thou hast not known ; of Him that made Lebanon and the cedars of Lebanon ; that made the sea, and the heavens, and the host of the

---

[1] " *The Prophet :* "—Though a Prophet was not *therefore* and in virtue of that character an Evangelist, yet every Evangelist was necessarily in the scriptural sense a Prophet. For let it be remembered that a Prophet did not mean a *P*redicter, or *Fore*shower of events, except derivatively and inferentially. What *was* a Prophet in the uniform scriptural sense ? He was a man, who drew aside the curtain from the secret counsels of Heaven. He declared, or made public, the previously hidden truths of God : and because future events might chance to involve divine truth, therefore a revealer of future events might happen so far to be a Prophet. Yet still small was that part of a Prophet's functions which concerned the foreshowing of events ; and not necessarily *any* part.

stars; that made the light; that made the darkness; that blew the spirit of life into the nostrils of man. His messenger I am : and from Him all power is given me to bind and to loose, to build and to pull down. Ask, therefore, whatsoever thou wilt—great or small —and through me thou shalt receive it from God. But, my child, ask not amiss. For God is able out of thy own evil asking to weave snares for thy footing. And oftentimes to the lambs whom He loves, he gives by seeming to refuse; gives in some better sense, or " (and his voice swelled into the power of anthems) " in some far happier world. Now, therefore, my daughter, be wise on thy own behalf; and say what it is that I shall ask for thee from God." But the Daughter of Lebanon needed not his caution; for immediately dropping on one knee to God's ambassador, whilst the full radiance from the cedar torch fell upon the glory of a penitential eye, she raised her clasped hands in supplication, and said, in answer to the evangelist asking for a second time what gift he should call down upon her from Heaven, "Lord, that thou wouldest put me back into my father's house." And the evangelist, because he was human, dropped a tear as he stooped to kiss her forehead, saying, "Daughter, thy prayer is heard in heaven; and I tell thee that the daylight shall not come and go for thirty times, not for the thirtieth time shall the sun drop behind Lebanon, before I will put thee back into thy father's house."

Thus the lovely lady came into the guardianship of the evangelist. She sought not to varnish her

history, or to palliate her own transgressions.   In so
far as she had offended at all, her case was that of
millions in every generation.   Her father was a prince
in Lebanon, proud, unforgiving, austere.   The wrongs
done to his daughter by her dishonourable lover,
because done under favour of opportunities created
by her confidence in his integrity, her father persisted
in resenting as wrongs done by this injured daughter
herself ; and, refusing to her all protection, drove her,
whilst yet confessedly innocent, into criminal com-
pliances under sudden necessities of seeking daily
bread from her own uninstructed efforts.   Great was
the wrong she suffered both from father and lover ;
great was the retribution.   She lost a churlish father
and a wicked lover ; she gained an apostolic guardian.
She lost a princely station in Lebanon ; she gained
an early heritage in heaven.   For this heritage is
hers within thirty days, if she will not defeat it herself.   And, whilst the stealthy motion of time travelled
towards this thirtieth day, behold ! a burning fever
desolated Damascus, which also laid its arrest upon
the Daughter of Lebanon, yet gently, and so that
hardly for an hour did it withdraw her from the
heavenly teachings of the evangelist.   And thus daily
the doubt was strengthened—would the holy apostle
suddenly touch her with his hand, and say, " Woman,
be thou whole !" or would he present her on the
thirtieth day as a pure bride to Christ ?   But perfect
freedom belongs to Christian service, and she only
must make the election.

Up rose the sun on the thirtieth morning in all his
pomp, but suddenly was darkened by driving storms.
Not until noon was the heavenly orb again revealed ;
then the glorious light was again unmasked, and
again the Syrian valleys rejoiced.   This was the hour
already appointed for the baptism of the new Christian
daughter.   Heaven and earth shed gratulation on the
happy festival ; and, when all was finished, under an
awning raised above the level roof of her dwelling-
house, the regenerate daughter of Lebanon, looking
over the rose-gardens of Damascus, with amplest
prospect of her native hills, lay in blissful trance,
making proclamation, by her white baptismal robes,
of recovered innocence and of reconciliation with
God.   And, when the sun was declining to the west,
the evangelist, who had sat from noon by the bedside
of his spiritual daughter, rose solemnly, and said,
"Lady of Lebanon, the day is already come, and the
hour is coming, in which my covenant must be fulfilled
with thee.   Wilt thou, therefore, being now wiser in
thy thoughts, suffer God thy new Father to give by
seeming to refuse ; to give in some better sense, or
in some far happier world?"   But the Daughter of
Lebanon sorrowed at these words ; she yearned after
her native hills ; not for themselves, but because there
it was that she had left that sweet twin-born sister,
with whom from infant days hand-in-hand she had
wandered amongst the everlasting cedars.   And again
the evangelist sat down by her bedside ; whilst she
by intervals communed with him, and by intervals

slept gently under the oppression of her fever. But as evening drew nearer, and it wanted now but a brief space to the going down of the sun, once again, and with deeper solemnity, the evangelist rose to his feet, and said, "O daughter! this is the thirtieth day, and the sun is drawing near to his rest; brief, therefore, is the time within which I must fulfil the word that God spoke to thee by me." Then, because light clouds of delirium were playing about her brain, he raised his pastoral staff, and pointing it to her temples, rebuked the clouds, and bade that no more they should trouble her vision, or stand between her and the forests of Lebanon. And the delirious clouds parted asunder, breaking away to the right and to the left. But upon the forests of Lebanon there hung a mighty mass of overshadowing vapours, bequeathed by the morning's storm. And a second time the evangelist raised his pastoral staff, and, pointing it to the gloomy vapours, rebuked them, and bade that no more they should stand between his daughter and her father's house. And immediately the dark vapours broke away from Lebanon to the right and to the left; and the farewell radiance of the sun lighted up all the paths that ran between the everlasting cedars and her father's palace. But vainly the lady of Lebanon searched every path with her eyes for memorials of her sister. And the evangelist, pitying her sorrow, turned away her eyes to the clear blue sky, which the departing vapours had exposed. And he showed her the peace which was there. And then he said, "O daughter! this also is but a mask." And immediately for the third time he raised his pastoral staff, and, pointing it to the fair blue sky, he rebuked it, and bade that no more it should stand between her and the vision of God. Immediately the blue sky parted to the right and to the left, laying bare the infinite revelations that can be made visible only to dying eyes. And the Daughter of Lebanon said to the evangelist, "O father! what armies are these that I see mustering within the infinite chasm?" And the evangelist replied, "These are the armies of Christ, and they are mustering to receive some dear human blossom, some first-fruits of Christian faith, that shall rise this night to Christ from Damascus." Suddenly, as thus the child of Lebanon gazed upon the mighty vision, she saw bending forward from the heavenly host, as if in gratulation to herself, the one countenance for which she hungered and thirsted. The twin-sister, that should have waited for her in Lebanon, had died of grief, and was waiting for her in Paradise. Immediately in rapture she soared upwards from her couch; immediately in weakness she fell back; and being caught by the evangelist, she flung her arms around his neck; whilst he breathed into her ear his final whisper, "Wilt thou now suffer that God should give by seeming to refuse?"—"Oh yes—yes—yes," was the fervent answer from the Daughter of Lebanon. Immediately the evangelist gave the signal to the heavens, and the heavens gave the signal to

the sun; and in one minute after the Daughter of
Lebanon had fallen back a marble corpse amongst
her white baptismal robes; the solar orb dropped
behind Lebanon; and the evangelist, with eyes
glorified by mortal and immortal tears, rendered
thanks to God that had thus accomplished the word
which he spoke through himself to the Magdalen of
Lebanon—that not for the thirtieth time should the
sun go down behind her native hills, before he had
put her back into her Father's house.

OFTENTIMES at Oxford I saw Levana in my dreams. I knew her by her Roman symbols. Who is Levana? Reader, that do not pretend to have leisure for very much scholarship, you will not be angry with me for telling you. Levana was the Roman goddess that performed for the new-born infant the earliest office of ennobling kindness,—typical, by its mode, of that grandeur which belongs to man everywhere, and of that benignity in powers invisible which even in Pagan worlds sometimes descends to sustain it. At the very moment of birth, just as the infant tasted for the first time the atmosphere of our troubled planet, it was laid on the ground. *That* might bear different interpretations. But immediately, lest so grand a creature should grovel there for more than one instant, either the paternal hand, as proxy for the goddess Levana, or some near kinsman, as proxy for the father, raised it upright, bade it look erect as the king of all this world, and presented its forehead to the stars, saying, perhaps, in his heart, "Behold what is greater than yourselves!" This symbolic act represented the function of Levana. And that mysterious lady, who never revealed her face (except to me in dreams), but always acted by delegation, had her name from the Latin verb (as still it is the Italian verb) *levare*, to raise aloft.

This is the explanation of Levana. And hence it has arisen that some people have understood by Levana the tutelary power that controls the education of the nursery. She, that would not suffer at his birth even a prefigurative or mimic degradation for her awful ward, far less could be supposed to suffer the real degradation attaching to the non-development of his powers. She therefore watches over human education. Now, the word *edŭco*, with the penultimate short, was derived (by a process often exemplified in the crystallisation of languages) from the word *edūco*, with the penultimate long. Whatsoever *educes*, or develops, *educates*. By the education of Levana, therefore, is meant,— not the poor machinery that moves by spelling-books and grammars, but by that mighty system of central forces hidden in the deep bosom of human life, which by passion, by strife, by temptation, by the energies of resistance, works for ever upon children,—resting not day or night, any more than the mighty wheel of day and night themselves, whose moments, like restless spokes, are glimmering[1] for ever as they revolve.

[1] As I have never allowed myself to covet any man's ox nor his ass, nor anything that is his, still less would it become a philosopher to covet other people's images, or metaphors. Here, therefore, I restore to Mr. Wordsworth this fine image of the revolving wheel, and the glimmering spokes, as applied by him

If, then, *these* are the ministries by which Levana works, how profoundly must she reverence the agencies of grief! But you, reader! think, —that children generally are not liable to grief such as mine. There are two senses in the word *generally*,—the sense of Euclid, where it means *universally* (or in the whole extent of the *genus*), and a foolish sense of this world, where it means *usually*. Now, I am far from saying that children universally are capable of grief like mine. But there are more than you ever heard of who die of grief in this island of ours. I will tell you a common case. The rules of Eton require that a boy on the *foundation* should be there twelve years: he is superannuated at eighteen, consequently he must come at six. Children torn away from mothers and sisters at that age not unfrequently die. I speak of what I know. The complaint is not entered by the registrar as grief; but *that* it is. Grief of that sort, and at that age, has killed more than ever have been counted amongst its martyrs.

Therefore it is that Levana often communes with the powers that shake man's heart: therefore it is that

to the flying successions of day and night. I borrowed it for one moment in order to point my own sentence; which being done, the reader is witness that I now pay it back instantly by a note made for that sole purpose. On the same principle I often borrow their seals from young ladies, when closing my letters. Because there is sure to be some tender sentiment upon them about "memory," or "hope," or "roses," or "reunion;" and my correspondent must be a sad brute who is not touched by the eloquence of the seal, even if his taste is so bad that he remains deaf to mine.

she dotes upon grief.   " These ladies," said I softly to myself, on seeing the ministers with whom Levana was conversing, "these are the Sorrows ; and they are three in number, as the *Graces* are three, who dress man's life with beauty : the *Parcæ* are three, who weave the dark arras of man's life in their mysterious loom always with colours sad in part, sometimes angry with tragic crimson and black ; the *Furies* are three, who visit with retributions called from the other side of the grave offences that walk upon this ; and once even the *Muses* were but three, who fit the harp, the trumpet, or the lute, to the great burdens of man's impassioned creations.   These are the Sorrows, all three of whom I know."   The last words I say *now ;* but in Oxford I said, " one of whom I know, and the others too surely I *shall* know."   For already, in my fervent youth, I saw (dimly relieved upon the dark background of my dreams) the imperfect lineaments of the awful sisters. These sisters—by what name shall we call them ?

If I say simply, " The Sorrows," there will be a chance of mistaking the term ; it might be understood of individual sorrow,—separate cases of sorrow,—whereas I want a term expressing the mighty abstractions that incarnate themselves in all individual sufferings of man's heart ; and I wish to have these abstractions presented as impersonations, that is, as clothed with human attributes of life, and with functions pointing to flesh.   Let us call them, therefore, *Our Ladies of Sorrow.*   I know them thoroughly, and have walked in all their kingdoms.   Three sisters they are, of one mysterious household ; and their paths are wide apart; but of their dominion there is no end. Them I saw often conversing with Levana, and sometimes about myself. Do they talk, then? O, no! Mighty phantoms like these disdain the infirmities of language. They may utter voices through the organs of man when they dwell in human hearts, but amongst themselves is no voice nor sound; eternal silence reigns in *their* kingdoms. *They* spoke not, as they talked with Levana; *they* whispered not; *they* sang not; though oftentimes methought they *might* have sung : for I upon earth had heard their mysteries oftentimes deciphered by harp and timbrel, by dulcimer and organ. Like God, whose servants they are, they utter their pleasure, not by sounds that perish, or by words that go astray, but by signs in heaven, by changes on earth, by pulses in secret rivers, heraldries painted on darkness, and hieroglyphics written on the tablets of the brain. *They* wheeled in mazes ; *I* spelled the steps. *They* telegraphed from afar ; *I* read the signals. *They* conspired together; and on the mirrors of darkness *my* eye traced the plots. *Theirs* were the symbols ; *mine* are the words.

What is it the sisters are? What is it that they do? Let me describe their form, and their presence; if form it were that still fluctuated in its outline ; or presence it were that for ever advanced to the front, or for ever receded amongst shades.

The eldest of the three is named *Mater Lachrymarum*, Our Lady of Tears. She it is that night and day raves and moans, calling for vanished faces. She stood in Rama, where a voice was heard of lamentation,—Rachel weeping for her children, and refusing to be comforted. She it was that stood in Bethlehem on the night when Herod's sword swept its nurseries of Innocents, and the little feet were stiffened for ever, which, heard at times as they trotted along floors overhead, woke pulses of love in household hearts that were not unmarked in heaven.

Her eyes are sweet and subtle, wild and sleepy, by turns; oftentimes rising to the clouds, oftentimes challenging the heavens. She wears a diadem round her head. And I knew by childish memories that she could go abroad upon the winds, when she heard the sobbing of litanies, or the thundering of organs, and when she beheld the mustering of summer clouds. This sister, the elder, it is that carries keys more than papal at her girdle, which open every cottage and every palace. She, to my knowledge, sate all last summer by the bedside of the blind beggar, him that so often and so gladly I talked with, whose pious daughter, eight years old, with the sunny countenance, resisted the temptations of play and village mirth to travel all day long on dusty roads with her afflicted father. For this did God send her a great reward. In the spring time of the year, and whilst yet her own spring was budding, he recalled her to himself. But her blind father mourns for ever over *her;* still he dreams at midnight that the little guiding hand is locked within his own; and still he wakens to a darkness that is *now* within a second and a deeper darkness. This *Mater Lachrymarum* also has been sitting all this winter of 1844-5 within the bedchamber of the Czar, bringing before his eyes a daughter (not less pious) that vanished to God not less suddenly, and left behind her a darkness not less profound. By the power of the keys it is that Our Lady of Tears glides a ghostly intruder into the chambers of sleep-less men, sleepless women, sleepless children, from Ganges to the Nile, from Nile to Mississippi. And her, because she is the first-born of her house, and has the widest empire, let us honour with the title of " Madonna."

The second sister is called *Mater Suspiriorum*, Our Lady of Sighs. She never scales the clouds, nor walks abroad upon the winds. She wears no diadem. And her eyes, if they were ever seen, would be neither sweet nor subtle; no man could read their story; they would be found filled with perishing dreams, and with wrecks of forgotten delirium. But she raises not her eyes; her head, on which sits a dilapidated turban, droops for ever, for ever fastens on the dust. She weeps not. She groans not. But she sighs inaudibly at intervals. Her sister, Madonna, is often-times stormy and frantic, raging in the highest against heaven, and demanding back her darlings. But Our Lady of Sighs never clamours, never defies, dreams not of rebellious aspirations. She is humble to abject-ness. Hers is the meekness that belongs to the hope-less. Murmur she may, but it is in her sleep.

Whisper she may, but it is to herself in the twilight.   Mutter she does at times, but it is in
solitary places that are desolate as she is desolate, in
ruined cities, and when the sun has gone down to
his rest.   This sister is the visitor of the Pariah, of
the Jew, of the bondsman to the oar in the Mediter-
ranean galleys; of the English criminal in Norfolk
Island, blotted out from the books of remembrance in
sweet far-off England ; of the baffled penitent reverting
his eyes for ever upon a solitary grave, which to him
seems the altar overthrown of some past and bloody
sacrifice, on which altar no oblations can now be avail-
ing, whether towards pardon that he might implore,
or towards reparation that he might attempt.   Every
slave that at noonday looks up to the tropical sun
with timid reproach, as he points with one hand to
the earth, our general mother, but for *him* a step-
mother,—as he points with the other hand to the
Bible, our general teacher, but against *him* sealed and
sequestered ; [1]—every woman sitting in darkness,
without love to shelter her head, or hope to illumine
her solitude, because the heaven-born instincts
kindling in her nature germs of holy affections, which
God implanted in her womanly bosom, having been
stifled by social necessities, now burn sullenly to waste,
like sepulchral lamps amongst the ancients ; every nun

[1] This, the reader will be aware, applies chiefly to the cotton
and tobacco States of North America ; but not to them only : on
which account I have not scrupled to figure the sun, which looks
down upon slavery, as *tropical ;* no matter if strictly within the
tropics, or simply so near to them as to produce a similar climate.

defrauded of her unreturning May-time by wicked kinsman, whom God will judge; every captive in every dungeon; all that are betrayed, and all that are rejected; outcasts by traditionary law, and children of *hereditary* disgrace,—all these walk with Our Lady of Sighs. She also carries a key; but she needs it little. For her kingdom is chiefly amongst the tents of Shem, and the houseless vagrant of every clime Yet in the very highest ranks of man she finds chapels of her own; and even in glorious England there are some that, to the world, carry their heads as proudly as the reindeer, who yet secretly have received her mark upon their foreheads.

But the third sister, who is also the youngest——! Hush! whisper whilst we talk of *her!* Her kingdom is not large, or else no flesh should live; but within that kingdom all power is hers. Her head, turreted like that of Cybele, rises almost beyond the reach of sight. She droops not; and her eyes rising so high *might* be hidden by distance. But, being what they are, they cannot be hidden; through the treble veil of crape which she wears, the fierce light of a blazing misery, that rests not for matins or for vespers, for noon of day or noon of night, for ebbing or for flowing tide, may be read from the very ground. She is the defier of God. She also is the mother of lunacies, and the suggestress of suicides. Deep lie the roots of her power; but narrow is the nation that she rules. For she can approach only those in whom a profound nature has been upheaved by central convulsions; in whom the heart trembles and the brain rocks under conspiracies of tempest from without and tempest from within. Madonna moves with uncertain steps, fast or slow, but still with tragic grace. Our Lady of Sighs creeps timidly and stealthily. But this youngest sister moves with incalculable motions, bounding, and with a tiger's leaps. She carries no key; for, though coming rarely amongst men, she storms all doors at which she is permitted to enter at all. And *her* name is *Mater Tenebrarum*,—Our Lady of Darkness.

These were the *Semnai Theai*, or Sublime Goddesses,[1] these were the *Eumenides*, or Gracious Ladies (so called by antiquity in shuddering propitiation), of my Oxford dreams. Madonna spoke. She spoke by her mysterious hand. Touching my head, she beckoned to Our Lady of Sighs; and *what* she spoke, translated out of the signs which (except in dreams) no man reads, was this :—

"Lo ! here is he, whom in childhood I dedicated to my altars. This is he that once I made my darling. Him I led astray, him I beguiled, and from heaven I stole away his young heart to mine. Through me did he become idolatrous ; and through me it was, by languishing desires, that he worshipped the worm, and prayed to the wormy grave. Holy was the grave to

---

[1] "*Sublime Goddesses.*"—The word σεμνος is usually rendered *venerable* in dictionaries ; not a very flattering epithet for females. But I am disposed to think that it comes nearest to our idea of the *sublime*, as near as a Greek word *could* come.

him; lovely was its darkness; saintly its corruption. Him, this young idolater, I have seasoned for thee, dear gentle Sister of Sighs! Do thou take him now to *thy* heart, and season him for our dreadful sister. And thou,"—turning to the *Mater Tenebrarum*, she said,—"wicked sister, that temptest and hatest, do thou take him from *her*. See that thy sceptre lie heavy on his head. Suffer not woman and her tenderness to sit near him in his darkness. Banish the frailties of hope, wither the relenting of love, scorch the fountains of tears, curse him as only thou canst curse. So shall he be accomplished in the furnace, so shall he see the things that ought *not* to be seen, sights that are abominable, and secrets that are unutterable. So shall he read elder truths, sad truths, grand truths, fearful truths. So shall he rise again *before* he dies. And so shall our commission be accomplished which from God we had,—to plague his heart until we had unfolded the capacities of his spirit."[1]

[1] See Appended Note, *De Quincey's Superseded Note to his* "*Levana and Our Ladies of Sorrow.*"—M.

APPENDED NOTE

De Quincey's Superseded Note to his "Levana and Our Ladies of Sorrow"

To Levana and Our Ladies of Sorrow as originally printed in *Blackwood* of June 1845 De Quincey subjoined this important note :—"The reader, who wishes at all to understand the " course of these Confessions, ought not to pass over this dream-" legend.   There is no great wonder that a vision, which occu-" pied my waking thoughts in those years, should reappear in " my dreams.   It was, in fact, a legend recurring in sleep, " most of which I had myself silently written or sculptured in " my daylight reveries.   But its importance to the present " Confessions is this, that it rehearses or prefigures their course. " This first part belongs to Madonna.   The third belongs to " the 'Mater Suspiriorum,' and will be entitled *The Pariah* " *Worlds*.   The fourth, which terminates the work, belongs " to the 'Mater Tenebrarum,' and will be entitled *The Kingdom* " *of Darkness*.   As to the second, it is an interpolation requi-" site to the effect of the others, and will be explained in its " proper place."—Such was De Quincey's prefiguration in 1845 of the course of those Suspiria de Profundis papers, then only begun, which, when completed, were to be offered by him in his old age as a second, and more profoundly conceived, set of his Confessions of an English Opium-Eater.   I detect signs in the footnote of a mere momentary attempt to forecast the probable nature and range of a series of papers yet unborn for the most part, and to bespeak a plausible principle for their classification when they should all be in existence. It was a mere extempore scheme, very hazy in the gap between the finished Part I., which the *Mater Lachrymarum* was supposed already to own, and the projected Parts III. and IV., which were to belong to the *Mater Suspiriorum* and the *Mater Tenebrarum* respectively ; and I doubt whether the scheme could, in any circumstances, have been consistently and acceptably carried out. In fact, as has been explained in our Introduction to the SUSPIRIA, it broke down ; and perhaps it is as well that it did so, and that a few fine fragments, each readable independently, are all that we have of De Quincey under the title he meant to be so significant. What is most interesting in the above footnote now is the evidence it affords of the value which De Quincey himself attached, and partly for autobiographic reasons, to his mythological conception of "The Three Ladies of Sorrow" and of the diverse realms and functions of those three sister-goddesses in the world of mankind. —D. M.

THE END

Printed by R. & R. CLARK, *Edinburgh*